PENGUIN BOOKS

TAKING SHELTER

Jessica Anderson was born in Queensland, Austra-
lia, and now lives in Sydney. Her first novel, *An
Ordinary Lunacy*, was published in Australia in
1963. Two of her later novels, *Tirra Lirra by the
River* and *The Only Daughter*, won the Miles
Franklin Award, Australia's most prestigious liter-
ary prize, in 1978 and 1981 respectively. Jessica
Anderson is also the author of *Stories from the
Warm Zone and Sydney Stories* (1987).

TAKING SHELTER •

JESSICA ANDERSON

PENGUIN BOOKS

PENGUIN BOOKS
Published by the Penguin Group
Viking Penguin, a division of Penguin Books USA Inc.,
375 Hudson Street, New York, New York 10014, U.S.A.
Penguin Books Ltd, 27 Wrights Lane, London W8 5TZ, England
Penguin Books Australia Ltd, Ringwood, Victoria, Australia
Penguin Books Canada Ltd, 2801 John Street,
Markham, Ontario, Canada L3R 1B4
Penguin Books (N.Z.) Ltd, 182–190 Wairau Road,
Auckland 10, New Zealand

Penguin Books Ltd, Registered Offices:
Harmondsworth, Middlesex, England

First published in the United States of America by
Viking Penguin, a division of Penguin Books USA Inc., 1990
Published in Penguin Books 1991

10 9 8 7 6 5 4 3 2 1

LIBRARY OF CONGRESS CATALOGING IN PUBLICATION DATA
Anderson, Jessica.
Taking shelter/Jessica Anderson.
p.   cm.
ISBN 0 14 01.2593 0
I. Title.
PR9619.3.A57T35   1991
823—dc20   90–44956

Printed in the United States of America

TAKING SHELTER •

ONE •

'Scraps,' said Juliet McCracken. 'Debris from the day before.'

'Oh, I don't know,' said Miles, lazy on one of Juliet's sofas, stretched out straight from his propped head to his propped heels.

Beth said, 'Mine just melt away.'

'You have to be quick-quick,' said Juliet, 'and capture them.'

'Capture debris?' asked Miles, his top lip curling from his teeth, as it did when poised for laughter.

'To show it up for what it is,' said Juliet. 'I wrote all mine down for a while. In an old notebook. At Cable House. Before they fixed the reception.'

'Some research supports Juliet,' said Beth. In one of her little spasms, she twisted an ankle round the leg of her chair. Miles glanced at it. She untwisted it and said, 'According to these people, while we sleep, our brain processes the experiences of the day. It stores some, maybe for future use, and dumps the rest.'

'Dumps,' said Juliet. 'See? Like rubbish. That's what I said. And how did the clever things find this out, Beth?'

'REM sleep came into it,' said Beth.

Miles had been watching Beth as she spoke, sending his usual encouragement. 'And computers, no doubt?'

'Computers,' agreed Beth, laughing. 'Setting one

computer to catch another. They think the brain is a kind of computer.'

'In any case,' said Juliet, 'it's only another way of proving what I proved with my notebook.'

'Proving?' murmured Beth.

'Inferring,' said Miles.

'Proving,' insisted Juliet. 'What I proved with my notebook.'

A coffee jug sat on a hot plate before Juliet's chair. She laid a hand on its side and turned up the thermostat. 'It was when I had those two young men planting the garden at Cable House. Expecting all you stinkers to come down and join me at weekends. And not one of you did. Yes, one, Clem, he did, once. My ideal community. Pooh.'

'But think of the wonderful profit when you sold it,' said Miles, teasing, his lip curling.

'I wish I had seen it, Cable House,' said Beth.

'Razed to the ground,' said Juliet. 'And all the land, the whole beautiful headland, subdivided for retirement villages. No doubt I should be in one myself, but I'm not, am I?'

Miles and Beth agreed that she certainly was not.

'No, I'm not,' said Juliet, caressing the jug. 'It was so damn lonely down there, I kept that damn dream book faithfully, wrote down every dream I had. And I had them, I had them.'

'The absence of TV,' suggested Miles.

'Making your own images?' said Beth.

'Or,' said Miles, 'the withdrawal. In one of the ancient cults, devotees went into sanctuary and prepared themselves for instructive dreams.'

'Asclepius?' whispered Beth, while Juliet hooted and said, 'Instructive my eye. If I drove into the township one day and saw, say, boots in a shop window, there they would be in my dream that night. Boots. Debris.' She picked up the cream jug and proffered it to Beth. 'Darling, do you mind?'

As Beth left the room, Juliet said loudly, 'They say you shouldn't. But I never put on an ounce.' But Beth going out of earshot, she leaned out of her chair and said, 'It's a miracle. Hardly a trace of that silly shyness, that fidgeting and hand-waving.'

'Oh, come on,' said Miles. 'It wasn't as bad as that.'

'It was. After an absence the change strikes one afresh.' Juliet had just returned from two months in London. 'You can't see it,' she told Miles, 'because of the way you took to her, right from the start.'

'Juliet, I should hope so.'

'Yes, yes, it couldn't be a cold-blooded thing. We agreed on that. All the more credit to you for seeing what I didn't, what none of us did. The change in her simply shows the degree of your concentration on her.'

'It simply shows her quality,' said Miles, frowning; but Juliet shook her head and said, 'And to do it without breaking up our little group, to draw her in.'

'You drew her in, too, Juliet.'

'For your sake, at first. I'm fond of her now, I admit. Have you asked her yet?'

'Not in so many words.'

'Two years, Miles. More.'

'Words,' drawled Miles.

'I suspect you're being too damn refined.'

Beth came back with the cream. 'Beth,' said Juliet, 'don't you think Miles is too damn refined?'

'Sometimes,' said Beth, laughing as she gave Juliet the jug. She sat down, twisted her ankle round a leg of her chair, untwisted it, and said, still laughing, 'Debbie Youdall, my best friend in Melbourne, and I, we kept dream books. We were eleven. We accused each other of making them up, and had a fight, and I threw mine out.'

'I kept mine,' said Juliet.

'Did you dream about the footie, Beth?' asked Miles.

'Now that's curious,' said Juliet, half to herself, and for a little while, she did not fully attend to the football story Beth was telling; but since Miles appeared so charmed, and curled his top lip back, and shook with silent laughter, Juliet began to smile, as she drank her coffee, and to murmur, though rather absently, 'Hilarious.'

Beth came from a Melbourne family dedicated to Australian Rules football, and since coming to Sydney, and especially since meeting Miles and his friends, she rather traded in her football stories. Now, as she continued to invent a football dream for Miles, and did not wave her hands about, Juliet joined Miles in his laughter, his fond assessing watchfulness.

When Juliet finished her coffee, Beth and Miles got up to leave, Beth saying that working girls had their chores on Saturday afternoons, and besides, she had to do something to her hair before she and Miles and Clem and Conrad went to see that play Juliet refused to come to.

'Because only Americans can do Sam Shephard,' said Juliet, saying goodbye at her door. 'Your hair, though,' she added, putting out a hand and stroking Beth's straight buoyant reddish hair. 'It looks as if you need only run a comb through it. Though we know that's the art, of course.'

A lemon tree grew compactly beside Juliet's front door. It was the winter of 1986. The shadows on the white wall were of distorted fruit and wildly outstretching leaves, though there was a softness, a blurriness, on both. Juliet stroked Beth's hair and looked at the pale subtle wools she wore, chosen or approved by Miles. Miles, tall, solid, excellently dressed, his body columnar, his skin pocked, stood at Beth's side. He was twenty-nine, Beth twenty. Juliet, sixty-eight, tallish and thin, with a long white scooped face, wore her usual black-and-something, today black and dark blue.

Miles also put a hand to Beth's hair, but then dropped it to her shoulders, and turned her towards the street.

Juliet closed her door slowly enough to watch them walk up her straight path, between her rows of young standardised camellias, each in its pool of pink or white petals, and observed that Beth did not stop to give her ohs and ahs, nor to make that tiddelly wave from the gate, nor that salute from the car. Her reform in the matter of protracted farewells did seem complete.

'Was Juliet really so offended about Cable House?' asked Beth in the car.

'N-ho,' said Miles, breathing it out, amiably scoffing.

'I had only just met her then.'

'She bought it with absolutely no consultation, because it reminded her of the old family homestead. It was a monster. *Incurably cavernous.*'

'Oh,' said Beth, hunching her shoulders against the imaginary coldness of those rooms.

'So you see, we had to save her, and it was best to be firm from the start.'

'Would the others have gone if you had?'

'N-ho.'

When Juliet climbed stairs, her legs and ankles hurt. She liked to tell people lately, in a loud voice and a confidential tone, 'You know, I do believe I am going in the pasterns and the hocks.'

The bedrooms were on the upper floor. She was still

5

using the sunless one as a storeroom. As soon as she found the notebook, in a trunk she had not unpacked since moving it from Cable House, she sank to the floor, unsupported, her forelegs flung like two fish to one side. It was still easy to imagine Juliet as she had been in the uniform of her boarding school, sitting on the lawn, secure in the ring of her dark-dressed friends, her long narrow face extended, her thick brown hair falling on shoulders hunched as she pressed into the centre to listen, to talk, to suddenly fling away hacking with laughter.

The notebook was in fact an old ledger she had found in the basement of Cable House. Her loneliness and offendedness in that house having put her in a mood of nostalgia, she had caught her breath at the linen-bound spine, the marbled covers. On the first page she read:

Any child scribbling in this book will be whipped. Signed, W. Cable.

The handwriting was flowing, firm, and masculine. Juliet gave a sharp nod.

On the next page, in the same hand, she found entries of stock and feed purchases, wages (from wages book), agistment fees and stock sales. Juliet had once watched her father's station manager, then her father himself, make similar entries.

W. Cable's entries stopped, unresolved, half way down the third page. *Dead*, decided Juliet in the dank cellar, seeing how the entries were followed by a painful attempt to write *stock*, which, failing on the k, ended in a wild zig-zag across the page, the pencil pressed so hard that its channels were visible on the next few pages, across drawings of motor cars (as if formed in dough) and games of noughts and crosses. Juliet put a forefinger to her tongue, touched the centre of a cross, and saw the blurred purple star appear.

Indelible pencil. The brutal young.

All the other pages were unused. Holding the ledger clasped to her breast, Juliet mounted the two flights of stairs from the cellar to her bedroom. Here she set the ledger down on the little writing table which overlooked the lawn, and beyond that, far below, the sea. On the lawn were the cedar benches and tables which she had expected would be used at weekends by Miles and Conrad and Clem, by Victoria and Bryan and Kate, by – possibly – Gilda and Phillip.

From her bedside table she brought the loose pages on which she had scribbled the dreams. Liz Ballard, an old school friend, had come to Cable House for two days, and she and Juliet had argued, indeed almost quarrelled, about dreams. 'Debris,' Juliet had insisted. 'Debris from the day before.'

In the city the dispute would have been forgotten by the next day; here, it rankled. On these scribbled pages was her proof, her further case against Liz. She had ceremoniously chosen a pen, then had turned to the first page of the ledger free of the colourless channels. She had run a hand over the paper in appreciation of its quality, and had begun, with reproving care, to transcribe the dreams.

Now, in her sunless storeroom, she slowly turned the pages, whispering, 'Boots, boots, boots,' until she came to the dream she wanted.

DREAM 6 = Not much colour, though still quite positive of colour in others. Greyish series of rooms. I don't live here. Am being shown over by Thai couple. They say they are refugees. 2 of those adorable little dolly children with them. Strange no colour. Keep saying it is boots I want, but they ignore. Blank here, even though I am writing this down <u>straight away</u>. Then mother and I standing at the door of big sunken room. Still greyish. Thais gone. Mother wears horrid tizzy specs. Says, There are your boots. Refrigerators round wall of sunken room. Like showroom. Fridges all open, strong light from each, yes, <u>yellow</u>. In each light standing man boy yes big boy wearing football <u>boots</u>. Then all in full football rigout. And yes <u>primary colour</u>. All big boys unmoving heads down one knee bent looking into fridges. 4-5-6? They grow bigger. Huge. I am amazed. I say, Mother, they're papier mâché models. I put arm round mother. She feels slender and young. I say, Mother, they're meditating on the food. She says, That's not funny. I feel snubbed. Something else here. A hand? No, all gone, though I am putting this down <u>straight away</u>. Haven't even had a pee. Trace origins later.

The bones in Juliet's legs were hurting in spite of that supple-seeming casing of flesh. Too engrossed to move far, she shifted until her back rested against the trunk. She stretched her legs out straight, turned the page, pressed the foot of the ledger into her waist, and bent her head to read.

<u>ORIGINS DREAM 6</u> = Once again, debris from the day before. Series of rooms = well, one lives in rooms, after all. Thais = Those two young men planting the garden say they are <u>Thai</u> buddhists. Went on about it till to shut them up said I disliked all Asians except the adorable <u>little dolly children</u>. Boots = In township saw rubber <u>boots</u> suitable for gardening but thought, What's the use? Mother = everyone dreams about mothers, even Liz would

admit. Tizzy specs = Certainly not Mother's, she wouldn't have been seen dead in them. Liz's? Not quite. Now wait, that sandyhaired girl with the pale lashes Miles has taken a fancy to, her father an optometrist. Yes. Has 4 shops in Melbourne. Ruth. Never knew mother. Stepmother and 6 stepbrothers and yes whole family mad about Australian Rules football. Nice girl, do like her. Miles saying, Tell one of your football stories, Beth. Yes Beth not Ruth. Told about going into kitchen one night and seeing stepbrothers at refrigerators. Amusing story, must admit. Actually quite like mine, only must say mine better. Love those papier mâché models. Meditation = Those two young gardeners meditate, as they will tell you, if you let them, till the cows come home.

NOTES DREAM 6 = Not all from the day before. Though, to be meticulous, I could have been thinking about Miles and Beth the day before. Thinking it may well be a damn good thing. We have often agreed that for a man with his ambitions marriage and children will be necessary one of these days. Am sure Conrad and Clem accept that too. No judge on the High Court, which is where everybody says he is heading, can admit to his preference, especially lately. It is just that I didn't imagine a girl quite like that. Not that she is common, exactly. Must be fair. If only he would come, we could talk it over.
If accurate about these origins, must admit that thoughts of the day must also be taken into account. However, it is all debris.
Colour = Quite definite, Liz notwithstanding.
Voices = Perfectly distinct, espec. Mother saying, That's not funny.

Spooky. Quite thrilling really. Will keep on.

'Debbie Youdall,' said Miles to Beth. They were waiting at a pedestrian crossing. 'You still feel that compulsion to say the name?'

'If something reminds me I do. And to add the rest to myself, especially the two sets of footprints.'

'Well,' said Miles, 'if it works.'

'Doctor Gelthartz said not to keep it right down there.'

'If it works,' said Miles again. The light had turned green, but in spite of hooting behind him, he waited for a slow old woman to cross. 'They should give them more time here,' he murmured.

'The only part I don't add to myself,' said Beth, 'is overhearing Judy say to dad, when they heard the news, "Thank God we have only sons," and dad just nodding and hugging her.'

'Beth! Really?'

'Oh yes,' said Beth, pleased to have startled him. 'Really.'

'But how utterly crass.'

'Mmmmm.'

'And how strange, dearest, that you've never told me.'

'I haven't thought of it so much since meeting you.'

'That's pleasant news, at least.'

'And besides, we're not alone so very much, are we? Even when you're not in London.'

'Don't let's complain if the firm selects me to go to London.'

'I know I mustn't. I know it's an honour. But I keep thinking of things I want to tell you. I think, When Miles comes back, I'll tell him that. And when you do come back, I think, I'll tell Miles that today. Or tonight.

And when today or tonight comes, there isn't room for all I've saved up, because somehow or other, one or all of the group is always there.'

'Not always, Beth.'

'Often.'

'So they ought to be. They're our chosen tribe. Our little community. We need them.'

'I guess so.'

'Guess?'

'Suppose. But there are other things, like the Debbie thing, any part of it. I don't want to tell the others.'

'Better not to, I agree.'

'It doesn't go with the communal mood.'

'Not if we make a misery of it.'

'The communal mood is stoical.'

'Not grimly so, I hope,' said Miles, laughing.

'No,' said Beth, in puzzled consideration.

Again they were waiting at a pedestrian crossing. 'Look at them,' said Miles. 'They have almost to run. It's too bad. And listen to that hoon behind me.'

'She had pierced ears, Debbie,' said Beth, 'and breasts.'

'Good for her,' said Miles, still ruffled by the hoon. But when the car was moving again, he asked, with his usual concern, 'What did Doctor Gelthartz say about the conversation you overheard?'

'He thought I made it up.'

He gave her a quick look. 'Not possible?'

'No. I know what I heard. But Judy and dad utterly denied it. So shocked, I think they honestly had forgotten it. So Doctor Gelthartz told me it was my way of expressing my resentment of Judy, and said he admired my creativity. And of course I agreed. I was in love with him. One day I fell to the floor and embraced his knees. Grey pin-stripes, knife-edge creases, *very* good shoes. I kissed his kneecaps through the pin-stripes.'

She watched Miles's profile for the sign of his amusement. Beth liked talking to Miles while he was driving, and his hands and eyes were of less influence on her. At these times she had begun to try to disturb the surfaces, to fill in the blanks. She saw Miles's upper lip curl. He laughed and said, 'I suppose all little girls of eleven fall in love with their psychiatrists.'

'He bent down and lifted me up, so nicely.'

'Not a bit put out,' offered Miles.

'Not a bit. Then I fell on his neck and hugged him, and he just put his two hands on my ribs – '

'On your dear little rib cage.'

'Yes,' said Beth, her two hands extended, 'and put me away from him. Saying nice things. Smiling.'

But Miles had stopped smiling.

'Gently but firmly,' said Beth, 'just like you do.'

'Beth – '

'Just *as* you do.'

'Beth dearest. Sweet Reason –' He often called her this, as if to induce by naming. ' – not now. Please.'

'Miles, I've decided to leave my job and go to Europe.'

'You mentioned that last Sunday, after Matins.'

'My cousin says I could easily get a job in London.'

'I don't doubt it, Beth. But you know you won't. Juliet said today that I ought to be more specific about our plans. But surely it's been taken for granted, at least since our last talk with mother and father, that we'll marry in March and you'll come over with me in April.'

'Somehow I can't imagine it, this marriage.'

'You don't have to. Just do it. You know how I look forward to showing you London.'

'I've seen London.'

He flicked her a glance. 'Are you quite happy with yourself when you sulk?'

She shrugged. He said, 'You've seen London from your

child's-eye-view. When you were seven. Tagging about after Bill and Judy and – which one was it?'

She wanted to continue to sulk, but could not resist saying, 'Would the king really have killed Scheherazade if she had failed to tell him a story?'

His lip curled. He said with delight, 'N-ho. It was a lover's game.'

His appreciation was so flattering. 'All right,' she said. 'It was Gerard.'

'And?'

'Ho-hum. And James in utero.'

His smile increased. 'And where were all the others?'

'Back in Melbourne, being looked after by Judy's mother.'

Miles laughed. Himself the only late-born child of an Anglican clergyman, now retired, and his small shy English wife, he could always be amused by 'the awful prodigality' of Beth's father and stepmother. When in Melbourne representing a client, he had insisted on visiting them, and had been as impressed by them as they were by him. He had returned saying that he adored them all, and Judy had rung Beth to congratulate her on an amazing good fortune.

Miles said, 'I long for you to see London from your adult's-eye-view, Beth. And we could go to Paris. And yes, poor old Rome too, if you like.'

'Not Rome,' said Beth.

'I suspect you want to keep Rome to yourself.'

Beth hoped it was not too late to keep her childish little Roman adventure to herself, and that it had not been too much distorted by its presentation, first to Doctor Gelthartz, then, selectively, for the amusement of Miles and Clem and Conrad. She shut her eyes and conjured up the rhino's head, clearly delineated against the blue sky, glossy ivy spilling out of its

13

mouth. It seemed intact. Miles said, 'I think you ought to drive this last bit, Beth.'

She opened her eyes. 'My instructor says not yet.'

'Oh, come along.' Miles stopped the car and opened the door on his side. 'I want to see you park.'

Beth took her lower lip in her teeth as she drove slowly down the street and stopped outside the block of flats.

'Perfect,' said Miles.

Beth looked down at the kerb, the neatly aligned wheels. 'How on earth did I fluke that?'

'We'll have to get you another instructor.' Miles got in beside her, turned in the seat, and lifted a strand of her hair. His eyes, their shining browns and blacks and flecks of amber, so deep and soft and childishly eager, seemed to Beth to contradict his unrelenting critical spirit. He smiled, lifting her hair. 'Will you have to fight for the bathroom?'

'No. Nicole and Angela are both out, threshing around with their fellers in hot beds.'

'I happen to know that Angela is playing ten-nis.'

'Yes, well – ' confessed Beth, on a sudden laugh.

Miles laughed too. With the tip of a finger, he traced the curve of her eyebrows. 'How I love these. The lovely moderate golden curve of these.'

'Oh, my.' Beth shut her eyes again. 'Nobody else has ever noticed them.'

'All the better.' He kissed each eyelid. She gave a little moan, half-comedy, all she dared. 'Darling,' he said, 'my sweet, do you believe I'm the only man in this city who believes in celibacy before marriage?'

She opened her eyes. 'Just about. Besides, you didn't at first.'

'We made a mistake.'

'Two mistakes. More than two years ago. That's what makes it so hard.'

'Forgive me, so that I may forgive myself. And Beth, if we must go into all this again, let's remember that people in former ages believed as I do. They suffered, perhaps, but not intolerably.'

'Everybody about them wasn't doing it. Not so openly. Aids might have made people more careful, but it's also made them more frank.'

He said coldly, 'Aids need concern only unbridled goats, needle sharers, and certain homosexuals. Have you been seeing much of Kyrie?'

'I think you're saying my cousin's an unbridled goat.'

He put a hand to her cheek and turned her to face him. 'I'm sorry. That was harsh and bad-tempered. Let me say only that Kyrie lacks all discrimination.'

Beth knew that once again, having made an opportunity, she had let it pass, and that once again, she was relieved. She took his hands in both of hers, and collected his fingers into her grip. 'Is it true that you told Angela I am a connoisseur's piece?'

His eyes smiled. 'Do you object to that?'

'I don't want to be shoved away in a glass case.'

'Shoved?'

'Put.'

'All I meant is that your beauty isn't immediately noticeable. Do you mind that? Do you want to be noticed by everyone?'

Beth's silently mouthed *no* was sincere. She had no craving to be noticed, and did not think it strange that Miles himself seemed to feed on his noticeability. Miles, entering a crowded room, pausing to dip two fingers into a waistcoat pocket to pull out a small piece of paper, which he then absently returned, would cause everyone there, for that moment, to pause. When he came first to Beth to kiss her, though she might mutter, 'Arise, Sir Beth,' she could not help her suffusion of pride in him.

15

Now she drew his clustered fingers up to her mouth. She bit them lightly. She kissed them. 'Is Juliet right? Can only Americans do Sam Shephard?'

'N-ho. Juliet's jet-lagged, but it's not her way to say so.'

'I do admire that,' sighed Beth.

'At any time, Juliet's likely to revive herself with a dose of solitude. That's why she won't have anyone living in.'

'Angela thinks it's hilarious that an awful racist like Juliet employs a Chinese woman. Have you ever seen the legendary Mrs Ho?'

'Beth! It was I who found her for Juliet.'

'Oh. I suppose so.'

'A Chinese from Vietnam.'

'Juliet and you are always doing things for people. You found Nicole and Angela for me. Juliet found me my job – '

'Nothing legendary about your job. Shall I pick you up at seven-thirty?'

' – you found a house for Gilda and Phillip – '

'Naturally, we all like to help our friends. Seven-thirty?'

Juliet sat at her kitchen table. Her unfinished dinner was pushed aside; her wineglass was still half full; the knuckles of her fists raised the flesh of her cheeks. Between her elbows, on the table, the ledger lay open.

DREAM 20 = Series of rooms. No colour. With shadowy man again. Suddenly no roof. Earth floor, stone walls, no doors. Me in that strawberry silk dress saying, I hate this dress. Man laughs. Scorn. Says, hem dips too. I look down. My feet bare covered thickly with black blisters even on insteps. Heavy sadness. That feeling, rooted to spot. Blank then looking at fallen tree. Same man still shadowy. Roots of tree like claw holding earth. I say trying to please man, Like king's sceptre. He laughs scornfully. Then I am climbing tower – Meccano? – with Mrs Ho and same man still shadowy. He tells me to hold on to babies. Mrs Ho puts a baby on a sort of ledge and kisses it hard on lips. I say, But that's a white baby. Baby swaddled tightly. Too neat. Not real. Then tower is toppling. Man calls out, No need to worry. Then babies spinning through air, still neat, like cocoons – bullets – Man calls out, Hold on fast. Tower falling. Wake up with big start, as if my insides had risen above my body and were dropping back into place, as in Dreams 10 & 14.

ORIGINS DREAM 20 = The clearest proof yet of debris theory. No roof, earth floor etc. = Said to those young gardeners when they gave me their account, Well, you two might be spiritual, but it doesn't stop you charging the earth. They talked about usual rates, and one said, Look, you will live in that garden. And I said, How fortunate, since people like you are taking the roof from over my head. Strawberry dress = My first silk dress Daddy brought back from Paris. But I didn't hate it, I doted on it. No, concentrate on yesterday. Here we are = Strawberries Clem brought me, which I told him were unripe and perfectly insipid. Showed him white area near stalk while he was telling me about Miles and Beth, saying, Not quite inseparable. Black blisters = Markham brothers testing tv. One clear image. Doctor pointing to photograph, saying, This girl had smallpox. Utter horror. Couldn't look. Clustered like black pearls. Also possibly connected with Clem saying later, You know we are all at your feet. Tower = Liz with her theories! Quite clearly tv aerial and Markham brothers climbing up to adjust. Once more! Falling = I asked Markham brothers to show me evidence of their accident insurance, and after they did, one of them said that now they could fall and break their necks at their own expense. Mrs Ho & kiss = I told Clem there was no household help here half as good as Mrs Ho and that if she walked in that door now I would kiss her. Fallen tree = I'm always driving past them, but not yesterday, I admit. Rather melancholy really. Nothing on babies either. It is possible that I dream so often of babies, as in 3 & 5 & 7 & 9, because I've never had any. It must be remembered, however, that Clem and I were talking of the children Miles would have, which of course is the reason for his interest in this girl. Miles and I often say that I am his spare godmother, even though he has that other dowdy old thing tucked away somewhere. Therefore, Miles's children would be like my grandchildren, and it would be natural for me to think of them as swaddled up and precious.

I told Clem there was nothing I hoped for Miles more than marriage. Wanted to ask if it could be satisfactory. But so delicate. Not that kind of intimacy. And having to be so damn careful about words. Can't say bi any more. They hate it. And as for versatile! Only Aunt Bob would dare. They have really become quite intimidating about things like that. In the end, while sorting the strawberries and opening the champagne etc. decided that Miles must be bi, and that the marriage would be satisfactory, and told Clem quite sincerely that the girl has a lovely body, as they all do, and quite a nice face, and that there was no getting away from the fact that Miles must have a wife and family. Clem and I got rather tipsy and I said, Though the way we go on about Miles, you would think he was a prince of the realm instead of a very ambitious young lawyer. And Clem said, Well, admit it, whatever he has, he has it. And we sort of ruminated about that, as we always do, saying he wasn't even good-looking, and Clem telling me about Phillip and Gilda leaving the group at last, and Miles calling it <u>defecting</u>. And going into fits of laughter, as we always do. It was lovely sitting out there with Clemmie in the sun at the back, though at one stage he really annoyed me by saying that Cable House looked like a house of correction. I said, Don't go too far. And he said, That's exactly what we all think you have done, about one hundred miles too far. I got really annoyed, and asked him if he was the king's messenger. There – <u>sceptre</u> – I got that one without even trying.

<u>NOTES ON DREAM 20</u> = Everything originated in events or actual speech, nothing in thoughts. That's because it was an eventful day, as days in this place go. See also <u>falling</u> in dreams 10 & 12 & 13, when leak in roof being fixed. The Markham brothers again tomorrow. Will it never end? However, must persist. tv reception good selling point, and I'll be here a good bit, I expect, while I'm selling, or else I'll be jinked by that agent. Country people are not what they used to be.

<u>COLOUR</u> = Only in strawberry dress and strawberries? Yet, if there was no colour elsewhere, how did I know photo of girl with smallpox was in

black and white? The answer is = I dream in full colour, as I told Liz, but happen to remember only bits of it.

VOICES = Just before I woke up, I certainly heard the words, Hold on tight, but could have said them myself, talking in my sleep. Shouting in my sleep. I don't like it. To be candid, I feel so melancholy writing this. Something unhealthy about it. Also much too time-consuming. No more.

Juliet, her fists still pushing up her cheeks, stared out of the kitchen window at the first flower on the magnolia bush, lit by the light over the sink, the purple stain rising from the calyx. She unclenched her hands, rubbed her cheeks, then turned a page of the ledger and ran a hand over the paper, appreciating the quality.

In Miles's car, stationary near the theatre in Hickson Road, Miles put his splendid head on Beth's shoulder, his forehead on the shawl collar of her dress, and said in a low voice, 'No more talk. Please. Please. I love you. I need you. I need you.'

Beth laid a hand on the back of his head, while the familiar need burned in her body, and her eyes asked questions of the distance.

TWO •

From Rome, when she was seven, Beth had started a letter to Debbie Youdall.

Dear Debbie, Today when they were having one of their siestas I sneaked out and met a boy . . .

She never finished the letter, but when back in Melbourne, she showed Debbie a photograph Judy had taken.

Beneath an arch of roses in pink bud, a boy sat on a stone bench holding a clip board. Beth sat beside him with her hands under her buttocks. Her father stood nearby, holding Gerard, asleep, against one shoulder. On the back, Judy had asked Beth to write, lightly in pencil, *With Australian boy.*

'Look, Deb, one day during one of their siestas, I sneaked out and met this boy outside a museum.'

But Debbie was climbing over the backs of upholstered chairs, and had some kind of green sweet in her mouth, and said indistinctly, 'Who cares?'

When Beth was eleven, she found her unfinished letter to Debbie and took it to Doctor Gelthartz. After coaxing the story out of her, detail by detail, he smiled at its harmlessness.

'But what about after the boy's mother came and got him,' protested Beth, 'and I was going back to the hotel?'

'When you pretended to be lost?'

'And stared into people's faces.'

'And asked the way in your best Italian? I've told you why, Beth. You were feeling neglected, and wanted attention.'

'Did Debbie want attention? When she went with him?'

'It is not certain that Debbie went of her own accord,' said Doctor Gelthartz, in a light conversational voice.

But there had been her footsteps, side by side with the big footsteps, leading across the damp ground of the park.

'Nothing is proved,' said Doctor Gelthartz. 'Also, please remember that you are not Debbie. You are *Beth Jeams*.'

'But the way I stared into people's faces.'

'Attention, attention,' Doctor Gelthartz almost sang.

'But staring so hard.'

Whatever advice Doctor Gelthartz gave her father and Judy, it made them treat her with a care which added to the distance already established. The six boys, obviously instructed, also tried to treat her with care, but were defeated by their own high spirits. They teased. They called her Snail, or Snailey. Even a loud noise, they said, made her draw back into her shell. She would retort that she wished she *had* a shell. It rather summed up what she longed for, but as she grew older, she knew that she did not want to inhabit that shell alone.

She was eighteen, working as a draftsman and going to Tech. three nights a week, when her cousin Kyrie suggested that she leave Melbourne for Sydney. She agreed with Kyrie that she needed to break away, to come out of herself, but when confronted with the fast robust jeering style of Kyrie's world, and perceiving it as a style predominant in the youth of Sydney, it was a matter of curling up, of retreating, all over again. It was also a matter of keeping her sexual longings curled up. The two needs, for the shell, and the emergence from the shell, seemed strangely one.

22

In those first weeks in Sydney, homesick for Melbourne, she began to see that if an enclave was what she needed, she could more easily have found it there, where the courtesies were less often jettisoned. But she did not want to lose the distance she had put between herself and her father's household. She did not want even to visit them until she had learned to bear the faint, dissatisfied, yet clinging love she felt for her father, and to find some ordinary everyday reason for her dislike of Judy. Judy had been so good to her, so conscientious in such matters as health, orthodonty, hair-styling, shoe-fitting, and attention to grades. And though Beth's halfbrothers and their host of football friends created in the house a rushing tide of activity that threatened to lift Beth's feet off the ground, she knew that not one was malicious, not one brutal. In fact, she had a general fondness for them, liking all of them sometimes, and some of them most of the time.

In her disillusionment with Sydney, Beth began a plan to go to London. Her mother had been English; her grandmother sent her money for birthdays and Christmas; she had nearly enough for the fare. Kyrie agreed that London would suit Beth, though this was hardly a compliment, Kyrie herself preferring New York or Tokyo.

'But you're a patrial in England, Beth, so that's the place you can work.'

'I'll live in a Georgian house,' said Beth, 'on a green square.'

'Gee gosh golly,' said Kyrie, with lazy sarcasm. She was five years older than Beth, and had been on all the continents but Africa.

Beth saved more money, consulted by mail with her grandmother (unfortunately in Yorkshire), scanned air fares, and dreamed over Palladio, Nash, and Inigo Jones. When attacked by torpor or feelings of futility, she shielded herself with her plan. But sometimes the plan itself threatened to fail her, to become abstract, and then she would enliven it with a stack of new brochures, with details of alternate routes and maps of the London underground. She had saved her fare, and a bit over, when Miles walked into the architectural studio where she worked, paused at her drafting table, looked at her briefly but intently, and paused again on his way out to ask if he may drive her home.

'I'm not suggesting that you leave early,' he said. 'I'll be downstairs at five o'clock.'

Weeks later, he said to her, 'It has happened to me before. I've simply known at once that the person was one of us.'

Kyrie said, when Beth told her this, 'Sounds like he's into soulmates.'

'I feel like I am,' said Beth. 'As if I am,' she amended.

'Is he into star signs, too?'

'N-ho,' said Beth, with Miles's exact lilt.

Juliet McCracken found Beth a more profitable job with her nephew, Andrew McCracken, an entrepreneur who had recently descended on the bathroom renovation business, and she met Conrad and Clem, Victoria, Bryan, Kate, and the others. Beth had never imagined that the generations could mix so naturally. From herself and Conrad and Clem, still in their teens, they rose in their decades to Juliet, who claimed 'years immeasurable to man'. Beth was happy with them. She liked their surfaces, their artifice, the places where they lived; she liked their games and ceremonies; she liked (at first) their acceptance of her as one of those who could pick up knowledge from the air, and did not need everything explained in dreary words. After Miles had taken her twice to his bed, she spent her airfare on clothes that brought him nearer to her heart's desire, and avidly studied Greek myths because he quoted from them. Juliet gave her a cameo. Kate and Bryan gave her a teddy bear. Conrad and Clem gave her an Afghan prayer rug.

She moved into the flat with Angela and Nicole. On a wall of her room she painted, in *tromp-l'oeil*, another room, and learned to refrain, when Nicole and Angela showed it to people, from running up and saying anxiously, 'But it's only a copy of a David Hockney.' She continued to see Kyrie, but only when her cousin was alone, and Beth was in no danger of having, *Zilch!* or *What shit!* shouted at her in response to her opinions. They were becoming estranged. Slowly, as Beth absorbed Miles's contempt for blabbermouths, and his injunctions to keep their private affairs private, Beth became reticent with her cousin.

Beth may never have lost her reticence with Kyrie if, on the Sunday morning after seeing the Sam Shephard play, she had not spilled a punnet of black olives on the floor of Kyrie's kitchen. She did not know, as she knocked on the door of Kyrie's flat, that her questions had grown too urgent to contain. She had been shopping, and was carrying a bag of provisions. Kyrie led her into the kitchen and offered coffee, and when Beth sat down and put her bag beside her, the sides of the bag contracted on impact with the floor, and the punnet of olives fell off the top. Beth, as she crawled about gathering them up, suddenly cried out that she couldn't stand swinging between belief and doubt, sure one minute and unsure the next; she couldn't bear it any longer.

Kyrie, tall and very beautiful, with restless eyes and a fast loping walk, sold and installed sound equipment. She was not a good listener, herself admitting to a limited attention span for human malfunction, but curiosity, and a light affection for Beth, made her compact herself into a listening position, to smoke and to frown and to watch Beth's face until, impatient at last, she interrupted to say that there was no real problem.

'You suspect the guy's gay. You think that matters. Right then, ask him.'

'But if I'm wrong! It could just as easily be his idealism. He believes in people committing themselves to groups, you see, chosen tribes, and to a chosen pairing-off *within* the group.'

'Not bad stuff. A hippie hangover.'

'No, he believes in chastity before pairing-off, which would be marriage.'

'That's more the impression I got of him.'

'Then there's his religion. Oh, I'm sure that's genuine.'

'He could still be gay. What about those other two I met?'

'Clem and Conrad. Yes, they are, quite openly. But everyone knows someone who is.'

'Right,' said Kyrie. 'So here we go again. Ask him.'

'I almost have.'

'So what stopped you?'

'Somehow, he made me feel so crass.'

'Oh, *riiiight*,' said Kyrie, stubbing out her cigarette. 'I know those people who make you feel crass. It's a technique. I send an account. Then another. I send it three times. Then I ring. And they try to wither me.'

'What do you do?'

'I go right ahead and *be* crass. Usually, though, I end up writing them off, those. Usually, they get out of paying, those.'

'But that's business. That's different.'

'Sure it is. Look, Beth, I don't like Miles. I hate the guy. I mean, how can anyone that young be that conservative? But you don't think – I mean, he's obnoxious, but he would pride himself on being a pretty responsible kind of character. And from what you just told me, you two stopped fucking just about the time aids came to be news.'

Beth, who had been craning forward, brought her neck into line with her spine and said quietly, 'Kyrie, you've only met Miles twice. If you knew him better, you couldn't possibly associate him with a scene like that.'

Kyrie jumped up and opened a cupboard. 'I'm not into bondage myself, but there's no doubt it suits some people. I promised myself I would vacuum this place out before midday.'

Beth slid off her stool and grasped her bag. 'One thing,' she said urgently.

'What? Shit, I've got to empty the bag first.'

'You won't mention this to anyone, will you, Kyrie? Though I know that doesn't need to be said.'

'Then why the fuck did you say it?' demanded Kyrie, with real anger.

'You're right. I'm sorry.'

'That Miles person has changed you, Bethie. He's made you *real* feeble. And anyway, who the hell would I want to mention it to? Who's interested? Who is this little lawyer guy? *We've* never heard of him.'

Beth rang Miles. Determined not to be feeble, prepared to feel crass, she was disarmed by his quiet agreement.

'You're right. It's time some things were said.'

She almost, in her gratitude, babbled out that she was just being silly, and that she was sure it wasn't important at all. But he was saying, 'And now that we've come to it, dearest, the sooner the better. This afternoon?'

'All right,' gasped Beth.

'Binyon's for coffee?'

'Not Binyon's!'

'Certainly not, if it causes you such anguish, as it does me, quite often, I'm sure. Will Angela and Nicole be at home?'

'I don't know. Probably. Yes.'

'And father and mother are using my place to change. They've come down for Juliet's dinner, you know. Now there's an idea. I'll ask Juliet to lend us the webbed glade.'

It was Beth who had given this name to a part of Juliet's garden, slightly more depressed than the rest, its grass greener, circular, which was dappled in summer and webbed in winter. Afraid of its enfeebling effect on her, she said, 'But if Juliet's having a dinner tonight – '

'She won't mind a bit. She can tuck us away out there while she and Mrs Ho get on with the doings. It's a perfect day. Suppose I pick you up at three-thirty?'

'No, no. It *is* a perfect day. I'll walk from the bus.'

Outside Juliet's house, behind Miles's Volvo, stood a shining Holden. The old Chinese woman in the passenger seat smiled at Beth, and Beth, who was in that inwardly distraught state which always intensified her visual perception, took away with her, down Juliet's path, a pattern of furrows in flesh so sparse that they appeared to reach the bone. She calculated that this complex but logical pattern, if lifted off, would be the perfect grinning mask of comedy.

The front door opened to disclose a younger Chinese woman who called and waved to the woman in the car. Beth walked down the path under the exchange of their glottal cries. Juliet appeared in the doorway, behind the younger Chinese woman, who waved again and disappeared indoors. After Juliet and Beth had touched cheeks, Beth said, 'So that's the legendary Mrs Ho?'

'Yes indeed. And that's her mother, out there in the car. Mrs Ho often brings her. I was disturbed by it at first, all that damn sitting, and Mrs Ho's English wasn't up to an explanation. You look hot, Beth dear. It suits you, that pretty flush. Miles has mineral water out there.'

'Please,' said Beth, 'a glass of water from the tap.'

'So I kept asking Mrs Ho why,' continued Juliet, at the kitchen tap, 'and that poor old thing kept sitting, and Mrs Ho kept going yabber-yabber, until one fine day Mrs Ho gives me a bit of paper, and on it is written, *Mother likes sitting in cars.*'

Beth took the glass of water. 'But if she could write it – '

'I expect it was one of her children. Their children,' confided Juliet, 'are always so damn smart. So I stopped wondering how the poor old thing gets on for the basic human needs. It's very mysterious. I need Mrs Ho today because of this dinner for my Aunt Bobbie. Eighty-six today, if you please. Just a little family thing.'

Beth was drinking very slowly. 'But Miles's parents aren't family.'

'Miles's grandfather married Aunt Bob. Officiated. The first time. So I thought it would be nice.'

Juliet's head was wrapped in a beautiful black and magenta scarf. The many fine lines covering the waxy flesh of her face, if lifted off, would have made only an irresolute attempt at a mask. When Beth finished drinking, Juliet put the fingertips of one hand lightly on her back, and conducted her through the house towards the garden.

'I gather from what Miles said, or rather from what he didn't say, that there is to be a *big talk* today. I hope I am wrong. Talk should be kept small, in my opinion. It says just as much in the end. When it tries to get big, cut it down, head it off. Aunt Bob knew Noel Coward.

Lots of people say they did, now that he's dead, but Aunt Bob *did*. In her young days, the twenties, girls were often called Bobbie and Bunty and Billy and Jackie. And the young men, my dear, would you believe? were often called, quite simply, Boy.'

They were crossing the grass towards – in the green circle – the cedar table and benches Juliet had brought from Cable House. Miles got to his feet, rather awkwardly, for him, his shoulders uneven and the fingertips of one hand pressing on the table.

'Dearest.'

Beth saw him step forward, his hands curled ready to grip her shoulders. As she felt their familiar grasp, and obediently raised her face, she heard Juliet say, 'You wouldn't be old enough to remember that, Miles. The sons called Boy.'

Miles kissed Beth, and with an arm remaining round her shoulders, said to Juliet, 'In fact, father once had a visit from a dear friend, as grey and sere and shaky as possible, and father said to me, "Miles, this is Boy Hallard."'

Beth said, 'I won't let you do this to me. I won't keep it small.'

Taking Miles's hands from her shoulders, stepping apart, she saw their faces politely waiting for her to explain. 'I must know – ' she said; then, angry at the tremor in her voice, her fear of crassness, she blurted out: ' – if Miles is a homosexual.'

'Goodness gracious me,' whispered Juliet. She broke into soft laughter and took a few long backward strides on the grass before turning to walk quickly to the house. Miles, pouring mineral water into a glass, also laughed.

'If the article is necessary at all, shouldn't it be *an*? You had better sit down and drink this, Beth.'

No mask had yet formed on Miles's face. Across his forehead, one light continuous line repeated the curve of his mobile eyebrows. One feathery line tried to rise from the septum of his nose. A mask maker would have been baffled by the irregular circle of pocked skin on his right cheek, clearly visible in this webbed sunlight, which had so often aroused in Beth a tender sympathy for the suffering of his pride as a boy. None of the group ever mentioned it. A moonscape in sunlight, thought Beth, as she listened to him saying that it had only very recently occurred to him that all this needed to be stated.

'You mean,' she said, insistent to halt her threatened slide into feebleness, 'your sexual preference.'

'Yes,' he said, 'since you force me to repeat it. For men. At this time of my life it is a preference, which doesn't mean that it will remain one. It's known to quite a number of discreet and decent people, including my parents, who have always been simply splendid about it. As I took it for granted you would be, too, Beth. Took it for granted you *were* being. I'm sorry. It's my fault. Loving you so much, I made you into something you were not. I overestimated your empathy. I knew you had some little – ' He wiggled the fingers of one hand. ' – doubts. But I didn't dream you supposed me to be one hundred percent straight, or that we would ever have to be so solemn and earnest and explicit about it.'

'So crass,' said Beth.

'It's you who say so.' He leaned across the table and took both her hands. 'Dearest, this needn't affect our marriage. You have proof of that. Oh, look – ' He broke off to laugh, to squeeze her hands ' – I still can't believe we're sitting in Juliet's garden gloomily *discussing* it.'

'I don't believe you,' said Beth.

He looked at her with sympathy. 'I'm sorry you said that, Beth.'

'Just tell me, with men, are you so celibate?'

'*So* celibate? Can celibacy be qualified?'

'You know what I mean.'

'Oh, that phrase! That cry of the slovenly!' Smiling, he tightened his grip on the hands she tried to tug from his. 'But yes, I do know what you mean.'

'Well?'

'Well, I don't propose to marry a man, do I?'

'Just tell me – '

He abruptly released her hands. 'You do have a taste for these dreary discussions, don't you?'

Beth's face twisted out of control. Her voice trembled. 'We're not discussing anything. We're doing what we always do. I'm asking questions, and you're putting me off.'

'You never used to ask all these questions. You were so lovely before, so gentle and clever and funny. It's only in the last six months – '

'It's only in the last six months that I've really suspected.'

'Suspected?' he said, laughing. 'Suspected me of this crime?'

'Did I use the word crime? You're trying to put me in the wrong.'

'You are in the wrong. At least, I *suspect* you are. I suspect that like everyone else, you take it for granted that homosexual love must be physically expressed.'

Beth stared. She sat back in her seat and said weakly, 'Everyone seems to believe – '

'Exactly. They do. They imagine no variation. I've just said so. You're agreeing with me. Now, ask your question. Do I express my homosexual love physically? Put it however you like. Speak of penetration. I'm waiting. Please.'

But Beth, looking at her hands clasped in her lap, said nothing.

'I'll answer you in any case. No, I don't. You're entitled to ask, and entitled to a reply. Aids has given you that entitlement. I don't express it in any way that could be injurious to you.'

Beth's head was slowly tilting to one side, though she did not look up. 'And how would our love be expressed,' she asked, 'in our marriage?'

'That's different,' he said, with his first show of bluster. 'There would be children.'

'Yes, but apart from that?'

He was rarely slow to answer. The silence made her raise her head. Meeting her eyes, he said slowly, 'I don't know.'

She was amazed to see him raise his hands and strike them together, at the base of the palms, as he spoke. 'I love you. I believed in my . . . reversal . . . for a while. I did. And when I fell back into . . . doubt - not about loving you, never about that - but about the . . . sexual aspect, I kept hoping, you see, hoping.'

She had never before seen him defenceless. The swift suspicion that it might be calculated scarcely touched her. She said, 'That's what you ought to have told me before.'

'But everybody knows, don't they? that there are doubts - imponderables - in any marriage?'

'Yes, but there are reasonable hopes, too.'

'Hope,' he said. 'But hope is exactly my explanation. Haven't you understood? My hope - ' As if inspired by the word, he leaned forward and said seriously, 'and my faith. My faith in our union.'

She saw that he was no longer defenceless. 'Speaking of faith,' she said, 'you let me believe that your scruples were religious.'

33

'But they were, they are,' he said, laughing. 'They are that, too. I can't shred myself, like a – a *cabbage*, and say this bit is this, and that is that. Impossible. A denial of faith.'

'Yes, but I would need faith too. And I have none. Not in you. You're as evasive now as you've always been. I think,' she said slowly, while observing how the moonscape on his face resisted the flush from his cheeks, 'that what hurts most is that I didn't see it before. Your deceit. When I asked you why you stopped – with me – you had all those reasonable arguments, never quite the same each time. They didn't convince me. They confused me. It was you who convinced me. Somehow. Your presence. You are one of those convincing people. I could even let it happen again now.'

'Then do,' he said. 'Do that. You won't regret it.'

'I see it too clearly now.'

'You see it too crudely now.'

'Clearly. Clearly. Your use of me. You needed to appear conventional, because of your ambition. So you used me as a shield.'

'I've served you as a shield.'

In Juliet's lovely garden, on this hot winter day, the birds were silent in the trees. Miles reached out, and, as he often did, encircled one of Beth's wrists with a thumb and forefinger. 'Sweet. Sweet Reason. You *wanted* a shield. And I'll keep on shielding you. Marriage is a shield. Look back. Look back on these last years. You can't doubt that I love you.'

She was silent. He gently shook her wrist. 'Well?'

'You love so many things. You love your teddy bear.'

'I don't need my teddy bear. Though heaven forbid that he should hear me say so. I do need you. You spoke of my ambition. I've always been frank about it, and frank about my doubt of achieving it without marriage and children.

And Juliet and the others, I've been frank about needing them too. Especially, in my case, and I think in yours too, Juliet, Clem, and Conrad. Perhaps I've been less frank about my need for money. I've never told you how Juliet, who calls herself my spare godmother, and has lent me this house so often, and entertained for me so often, how Juliet herself points out that she can't last for ever. It was she who raised the subject. You see how frank I am about what I need. Ask yourself what you need.'

'More than that.'

'Is it such a bad deal? Even if you are disappointed in what you call your reasonable hope, is it such a bad deal?'

She looked aside and said stiffly, 'It's a terrible deal.'

'Take some time, Beth. Think about it.' He set her hand on the table, palm downward, and looked at his watch. 'And so will I, if you don't mind. I find I can't quite get over your having told bloody plastic Kyrie.'

Beth was dismayed to hear the apologetic note in her voice. 'I had to talk to somebody.'

'What about Juliet, who has been so good to you?'

'Juliet? Well, I am so fond . . . she makes me laugh . . . but somehow we are never intimate enough . . .'

'Dearest, please excuse me. I hate to go, but mother and father need me. So come along. Ups-a-daisy.'

Beth, at the last moment, resisted her impulse to obey. She settled into the seat. Her hand lay where he had put it. She did not turn her head. 'I'll walk to the bus,' she said, 'thank you.'

Juliet's head was still wrapped in the silk black and magenta scarf, but she now wore an apron, with many pockets, over her dress, and rubber gloves on her hands, in one of which she held a small paring knife.

'Of course you may sit here as long as you please, my dear. But it seems to unsettle Mrs Ho. One at the front and one at the back. It's too much. Come and let's drive to the bus in my dear old Jaggy.'

Beth rose stiffly and stamped her feet, as if they had pins and needles, before setting out at Juliet's side towards the garage.

'I've no idea what all that was about,' said Juliet, slipping the knife into a long pocket on the tab of her apron. 'About sex, I assume. It so often is. It's very mysterious. As you know, I am one of those rare creatures born absolutely without sexual feelings.'

So Juliet often proclaimed, in her high and carrying voice, at dinner tables, in clusters of drinkers, on chairs overlooking beaches or bush valleys. Beth, who did not believe it, did not reply, but looked dully down at her obedient feet.

'Which makes me able to be impartial,' said Juliet. 'And I want to say to you, my dear girl, that before you act hastily, do give some thought to all the time and trouble that Miles has put into you.'

'I don't believe this is happening,' said Beth.

'I don't see why not,' said Juliet, on a note of surprise.

Beth came suddenly to a halt. 'No,' she said loudly.

'No what?' said Juliet, on a startled half-turn.

'I don't want you to drive me. I'll walk.'

'She will run, evidently,' muttered Juliet, as she quickly crossed the grass, looking at her watch, after Beth had run along the side of the house towards the street.

Only the Holden stood in the street now. As Beth ran past it, she saw the smiling mask dissolved and sparkling through her tears.

THREE •

The writing table which, at Cable House, had overlooked the lawn and the ocean, was now within touching distance of a maple tree. The light from the lamp moulded its bare branches. Juliet, still shrugging into place her dressing gown, wrote swiftly, in a big sprawling hand. She had not had time to find her spectacles.

DREAM 21 = Outside cinema like Village Double Bay. Liz Ballard saying, Don't go in. Won't answer turn away take money from purse. Then Liz+Mother one person shadowy say they know they are possessive but can't help it. I run into cinema laughing. Liz+Mother call out after me, It isn't done. Young in school uniform I run. Long tables lengthwise with buckets of flowers, flowers galore. Price tickets men in butcher's aprons selling. Man in apron like mine red rose in knife pocket gives it to me. John's face. I smell rose I say Where is the meat? I laugh. Blank them am in seat looking at screen horses galloping. The cinema has small low windows trees outside though screen still flashing. Suddenly see Miles's mother flinging one

little leg over sill climbing in and oh her face so
grim and old and sad. Want to run to help but hear
HO-HO-HO kind of laughing on screen. Red Indian
on screen very fat waddles hands on belly saying
Me Old Stupid Chief Big Talk. I laugh not alone
now everyone in cinema laughing. Wake up
laughing shaking trembly laughter all through me.

The room was light when she sat down to write again.
She was dressed, and had eaten breakfast. As she put
on her spectacles, pain crossed her skull, behind her
eyeballs, but she soon became amused, as she called it,
and forgot it.

ORIGINS DREAM 21 = Debris as usual.
Cinema = Liz Ballard ringing yesterday asking me
to go to cinema Double Bay. Said sorry too busy, my
dinner for Aunt Bob etc.
Possessive = Liz possessive in school and Mother
always. Nice of them to admit it, even if only in
dream, as they always claimed I was.
School uniform = Liz I suppose, though John is in
this dream too, and he knew me then, and later
used to like me to put it on. Thought it would help.
Well it might have helped him.
Flowers = Doing flowers for Aunt Bob's dinner.
Also connection with John? So many flowers he
used to bring me when still in school and always
when married. Red rose certainly John. But wait,
outsize bunch of red roses Andrew brought for Aunt
Bob last night. Too many, as usual. The money that
young man is making in the bathroom renovation
business. Mentions figures all the time. Aunt Bob
remarked that it never used to be done. Said she
didn't mind vulgarity in the right place, but! Miles's

father said million-dollar has become an accepted adjective. We all made up money adjectives.

Aprons = Preparing dinner in apron.

Neat = Mrs Ho and me chopping meat for dinner.

Screen = Liz's suggestion again.

Miles's mother climbing in window = Realise I've been putting off coming to this part but here goes. She took me aside, very upset, and said Miles came home, very upset, and said Beth talks of breaking with him. And me so busy! I said to her, Lorna, one good rule, never intrude (climbing in window) into the affairs of the young. I said the break might be a good thing, and asked if she had ever looked at it from the point of view of the girl. Poor old Lorna, though not as old as I am really, but her little bony head and that greenish-grey hair. Tears in her eyes and saying that marriage is often the cure. Asked me to speak to the girl. I said, Lorna dear, please! Aunt Bobbie's birthday! And walked firmly away. I most certainly will not speak to Beth unless Miles himself asks me to. It would be damn intrusive. It is between the two of them. She will find some more suitable chap and no doubt Miles will turn up one day with another lass.

HO-HO-HO = Andrew laughing at our money adjectives and saying But you can't beat million-dollar bathrooms. Ho ho ho. Aunt Bob suddenly admiring laughing too.

Red Indian and Old Stupid Chief Big Talk = Miles's father and Uncle Walter talking about abo land rights vs. mining etc. Miles's father pro-abo but Uncle Walter saying there was too much stupid talk about the abos and it was once the same story with the American Indian etc. I got that name wrong. It must have been Old Big Chief Stupid Talk.

Galloping horses = Connection with Western
movies via Red Indians.

NOTES DREAM 21 = All debris from the day
before except John's face, and that possibly from
thought-debris. Possible that he is always there,
deep down in my thoughts, too deep for me to know.
Colour = Single rose certainly red. Flowers in
buckets rich clustered thick the way I love them.
But colour? Don't quite know.
Voices = I hear with my brain but not with my
ears??? Am inclined to think that's about the size of
it. Certainly heard laughter at the end, but that was
my own. Well, how nice to have hilarious dreams
for a change. But to be meticulous, not really. That
trembly feeling, weak, sad. Dribbling too, and I hate
that.
I wonder if this is good for me. That night in
kitchen after I read Cable House dreams was quite
thrilled and thought maybe not just debris after all.
Even wondered if they were telling me something.
Not the nonsense Liz goes on with, but something.
So thought it would be amusing to keep on and
discover what, if anything. But until last night
couldn't catch them. Little scraps of things that
melted away before I could sit up. And now trouble
seems to be that as I write down one Origin, I miss
others i.e. Didn't I put my knife in my apron pocket
when Beth got up to leave? And i.e. (from mental
debris section) John used to call his member the
meat. J standing shaving, me in bath, J singing that
song about Mrs Murphy which is too vulgar to put
in writing. Rolled round in water laughing. J's
puzzled face. Beats me how a frigid woman can see
the humour. Rolling in water together laughing.

Bubbles. Aunt Bob would call it vulgarity in the right place. Not that it was the cure. No cure. But if J hadn't been killed in that ridiculous war by those loathsome little Japanese, would it have changed? It will come right. He used to say that. And I would never have married Fergie and become a McCracken again. I used to call him Cousin Fergus because he was nearly as old as Daddy, and quite often afterwards used to call him Daddy and so did most of his young men. But not Miles. Mr McCracken, Miles used to call Fergie. Miles was only a boy when Fergie introduced us, and from the first he was like my son. Miles is our Galahad, Fergie used to say. Well, all this is very time-consuming, not to say rather pointless. Those two books I bought on the subject are damn rubbish. The green one I can't understand and the other one just superstitious shopgirl nonsense.

FOUR •

Beth was living in a turmoil of unexpressed anger. She was angry with Miles for his successful deceit, with his parents for their complicity, with her father and Judy for their doting approval of his person and prospects. And, most of all, with herself, for her meekness and stupidity. About the group she wavered, sometimes seeing them as Miles's cabal, but more often as her fellow victims.

Yet when Miles wrote to her, saying he trusted that by now her good sense had prevailed, and that he loved and needed her so much that he would forgive her foolish confidences in Kyrie, her hands holding the letter weakened, as Miles proximity had so often weakened her body, and she was flooded with a sickly gratitude. This frightened her. She seized a pen and wrote on the back of the letter: *To see you would make me sick. I would die rather than touch you*.

She ran to post it, then fell into dull misery. The loss of hope disclosed its former stupid persistence. She felt sweaty and ugly, her face always red. She said to Nicole and Angela, 'Don't talk to me for a while. Pretend I'm an apparition.'

'Are you taking calls?'

'Well . . .' said Beth dubiously.

Her absorption by the group having left her with no

friend but Kyrie, who had gone to check one of her installations in a western city, Beth did await a reply to the cry for help she had left on Kyrie's answering machine. She knew better than to unburden herself to Nicole and Angela, who clearly intended to maintain the distance they had insisted, at the start, was necessary to success in sharing a flat. Angela was a lawyer, and Nicole a design co-ordinator. They had lived together for five years. Nicole controlled her natural volubility, and Angela, less successfully, her fits of weeping. Both admired Miles, but not Juliet. Both tired quickly of the lovers their beauty and refinement attracted. Both detested such things as pink soap and plastic rain hoods; their unassertive humour issued from these aversions.

'Well . . .' said Beth, 'I'll take calls. Except, please, from Miles.'

'That's not on, Beth,' said Nicole.

'No, Beth,' said Angela, 'it is not.'

Miles rang. Angela summoned Beth, saying simply, 'Miles.' Beth went to the phone, and stealthily, guiltily, broke the connection.

Conrad and Clem rang, each on an extension, talking singly or together, saying, 'Come back, little Bethie.' And she wept as she said she was sorry, and rang off, because she liked them so much, those two especially. When Miles was in London, they would go to restaurants and clubs, just the three of them, and would play games and jokes much sillier than when Miles was present. They had been her comrades; she knew she would miss them, but she was dulled by humiliation, and could not rise to the unshadowed occasions they offered.

Juliet McCracken rang. 'My dear Beth, that was a brutal letter you wrote to Miles.'

Her tone, reproachful yet throbbing with secrecy, disarmed Beth. 'Oh, Juliet, I had to be brutal, to get away.'

There was a silence before Juliet asked, with simply curiosity, 'And *have* you got away?'

'If I haven't, I will, no matter what it takes.'

There was another silence before Juliet said, in her usual manner, lively and humorously hectoring, 'Beth, you and I have no quarrel. Do one thing for me.'

'What?' Beth was conscious of her dullness and sullenness, her failure to match Juliet.

'Be honest. Think back to the time before you met Miles. Cast your mind back to what you were.'

'Ah!' cried Beth, with vehement grief, 'I would cast *myself* back, if I could.'

Juliet's silence disbelieved, and against her concurrence in that disbelief, Beth raised her barrier of anger.

'You are obeying Miles, Juliet, as usual. He told you to ring.'

'I think you must mean he suggested it. Yes, he did. He asked me to tell you he still trusts in your reason.'

'Sweet Reason,' said Beth with bitterness.

'So valuable,' said Juliet, rather languidly. 'Am I to tell him it's turned sour?'

'Tell him nothing, from me.'

'Very well,' Juliet said briskly. 'I have done my best.'

At work, Beth kept her head down and spoke only when spoken to. Sitting at her drafting table, tormented by her recollection of this occasion or that – her importunity, Miles's masterly calm – she would blush deeply, and lower her head still more. Andrew McCracken, paying one of his visits, paused at her drafting table, as Miles had once done, and she looked up in a panic, with a plea, but he only gripped the edge of the table and said jovially, to the room at large, 'These will soon be a thing of the past.'

Beth heard an argument break out. No computers, voices said, could do what they were doing. But Andrew

McCracken sagely said, 'Wait. They're on their way.' He was a muscular, fleshy caricature of Juliet. In the scooped planes of his face, the neat nose dipped over an ever-smiling mouth, the uncleft chin jutted.

As Beth came out of work one rainy night, her head down, Juliet appeared before her, seeming to rise from the pavement. In response to Beth's recoil, she said lightly, 'You weren't looking where you were going, my dear. I thought you and I might have a little drink and some dinner together.'

'But here comes my cousin,' said Beth, blundering past Juliet. Kyrie was crossing the street. 'I am having dinner with Kyrie,' Beth called back weakly to Juliet.

Kyrie had been back in Sydney for a week. Her lover having been detained in that western city, loneliness made her more than usually patient with Beth's repetitive anguish, with Beth's cry, as they cooked for themselves in Kyrie's big kitchen, of, 'Oh, Kyrie, I can't help remembering . . .'

'Right,' said Kyrie. 'Like those mornings you wake up remembering the night before. And you say to yourself, Oh, shit, no, I couldn't have, not with him. But you have, and in a few days, few weeks at most, what does it matter?'

'But when it's only one night – '

'Getting to be one too many. I'm through with it. Not only because of aids. Sick of it. From now on it's just this one guy.'

But Beth was selfish in her obsession. 'Kyrie, I'm talking about two and a half years. I was eighteen, and now, in October, I'll be twenty-one. And oh, Kyrie, I keep remembering – '

'Beth, the steak, turn it. That's enough of him.'

Beth tried to repress her cry that she kept remembering, but Miles's name always did make its way into their conversation, and on that rainy night, as they finished their dinner at the round table in Kyrie's kitchen, it was Kyrie herself who introduced it.

'I guess I've got to tell you Miles rang me. He advised me – his word – advised – fascinating – advised me not to broadcast any of the exaggerated nonsense you confided in me. By the way,' said Kyrie, lowering her eyes to light a cigarette, '*was* it exaggerated?'

'*No!*'

'Right, don't take off, I believe you. Anyway, I said I wouldn't, meek as a lamb. And I won't, either. I wonder how he does that.'

'I don't know,' said Beth, 'but he does.'

'Authority?' mused Kyrie.

'I don't know,' said Beth again.

'He only had to take that bit of trouble with me, and there I was, simpering into the phone, half-hoping he would ask me for a date. Anyway, he said to tell you he's still hoping you'll regain your sense of proportion.'

'What sense of proportion?' said Beth with her bitterness.

'It does happen. We do lose it.'

'He has taken some trouble with you, yes.'

Kyrie, smoking, shrugged. Beth said abruptly, 'Kyrie, I'm going to London.'

'What, again?'

'I will. I'll go. I've got to get away. I can't help remembering – '

'Oh Jesus, Beth, then remember this. There are other men.'

Beth flung back her head and shut her eyes.

'Why not?' argued Kyrie. 'There's nothing sexually wrong with you.'

'There must be,' whispered Beth.

'Why? Didn't you say you did it twice?' But Kyrie

suddenly found this funny, and burst into laughter, shouting, 'Twice! Twice!'

'I suppose it is funny,' said Beth.

'It's not. It is not.' Remorseful, Kyrie became as serious as Beth. She reached across the table and wiped Beth's tears away with a red paper napkin. Beth began to shake with tearful laughter, while Kyrie said crooningly, 'No, no, not funny. Not a bit funny. Now let's both be sensible and think what to do.'

Beth put her head on her arms on the table, while Kyrie smoked in silence for a while, then said, 'The trouble is, you wouldn't like the people I know.' Almost in a whisper, Beth said, 'I might,' and Kyrie suddenly put out her cigarette and suggested that Beth should come with her to a party in a disused warehouse about to be demolished, but that first, Beth should get out of those Laura Ashley clothes and buy some decent gear.

Beth raised her head in shocked protest against this simplistic description of clothes approved by Miles, but at this demonstration – they kept coming – of her deep submission to Miles's opinions, she looked thoughtfully aside, and said slowly, 'What you once said to me about bondage, Kyrie, that's true.'

'Sure. Now about this party?'

'All right. Thank you. And I'll buy a dress.'

'I'll come and help you choose.'

'I think you had better.'

'Right. Lunch hour tomorrow.'

'Right,' said Beth.

Miles would have gently echoed her. Right? And she would have changed it to *All right* or *Yes*.

'That one,' said Kyrie in the fitting room.

It was black, low-cut, made of a polyester version of

satin-backed crêpe. Beth could hear Miles's comment. 'A cartoon vamp,' she said.

'Sure, why not?'

'It's so obvious it's silly,' said Beth, and began to take it off. But standing with her arms upraised, carefully tugging, she felt the satin pressing like hands on the undersides of her breasts. Anger and excitement surged through her. She took it off and said, 'All right. This one.'

She dressed at Kyrie's flat. 'It needs something,' said Kyrie, and slid twenty silver bangles on to Beth's arm. 'There. Nice to shake. Now – what else?'

She jumped up to a high shelf, came down holding a black bowler hat, and set it on Beth's head. 'That's it.'

Beth stood with both hands covering her mouth, her eyes above them fixed on her reflection. She said, 'I can't.'

'You can. I'll put a rubber in your purse.'

Engrossed in the mirror, Beth said, 'A what?'

'A condom.'

'I have really no intention of just rushing off – '

'Don't dodge, Beth. Yes or no?'

'Oh, all right.' But then Beth, suddenly solemn, pointed at the mirror. 'I can't do this, you know.'

'It's supposed to be *fun*.'

Beth, still pointing, heard Miles saying in disparagement, *The fun society*. But now Kyrie also pointed, fervently, at the mirror. 'Do you want to despise yourself?'

Both stood there pointing, Beth limply, Kyrie with energy. 'No?' said Kyrie. 'Then try it. For one night. Don't tell me you're going to wear that coat.'

'It's cold out.'

'We'll be in my car.

The warehouse smelled of tar and lanoline. Dust in the shafts of light from the softly blackened walls was stirred by the band and the movement of bodies below.

There were other bowler hats; there were caps; there were silver wigs and bow ties on bare necks and striped braces on bare torsos. Kyrie immediately pushed Beth off to fend for herself. Miles would have called the music barbaric, but for Beth it acted as a sort of shelter. Because she could not be heard, she fancied she could not be seen, and slithered through the crowd in this fancied invisibility until, in less than a minute, her body began to respond to the beat of the music. It invigorated her; it gave her back her first fury with Miles. She stood against a wall, drinking wine, extending and twisting her left arm to keep the bangles jingling, and looked about for an enemy. Men halted before her. She quickly estimated them and said, 'Go away. I'm waiting.' The music prevented them from hearing her, but they understood. Her eyes looked beyond them to search the room. The satin underside of her black dress slithered in secret over her skin. In the heat of the room, her face was so flushed that her hair and eyebrows looked flaxen.

Shifting about was a group of five or six men, led by a thickset man in black waiter's pants supported by braces crossing his bare chest and shoulders. Beth, seeing this group, losing sight of them, seeing them again, guessed they were playing some sort of a game. The leader would halt before a girl, lower his head, pull in his chin, and hook the girl's eyes into his own with a long stare. If he unnerved the girl into speaking – Beth saw their lips move – the man would turn sideways, with military smartness, and send another stare along his shoulder before moving on with his impassive cohort.

Beth, interpreting this game according to the pranks of her halfbrothers, made a guess that the first look would be called *the significant look*, and the second *the enigmatic look*. She could imagine no other aim but the solidarity of the group, but knew that no other would be needed.

Miles – if he had bothered to comment at all – would have called it unbelievably juvenile. Beth observed that though the cohort was allowed to speak, the leader was not, and that he responded to shouted greetings of *Marco!* and *Marcus!* by raising one arm high while laying the forefinger of the other hand across compressed lips.

A flickering forward glance, above that finger across his lips, warned Beth that she had been chosen. She waited, willing at last to jeer with the jeering society, fiercely ready to enjoy it. It made her no less angry to remember that Miles, in public, had always been composed, always protective. When the bare-chested man stopped before her, and the cohort shifted to a halt behind him, she gave him no time to send his significant look, but stretched forth an arm and shook her bangles in his face, while thrusting forward her own face and laughing to show both her top and bottom teeth.

He pulled back his head and opened very wide his blue eyes. The cohort gave a soft concerted *Whoo-hoo!* Beth followed the retraction of the man's head with her angry fist and jingling bangles. He kept the rule of silence, but grinned, his mouth squaring in a tense and peculiar way, and caught her forearm at the wrist, holding it hard, silencing the bangles.

The rousing spirit left Beth's body. She let her lips cover her teeth and stared unguardedly into his face. The peculiar tension of his smiling mouth, and the protuberant glossy eyes, combined with the name, Marcus, to bring forward in her recollection the stone seat in the Roman cloister, herself edging along her buttocks towards the boy, reaching out for his folder and saying in an affected voice, 'Show me!' while he grinned and held it at arm's length. She said uncertainly, 'I've seen you before.'

But there was the music. He cocked an ear. She repeated it in a shout. He shouted back, 'Where?'

The others, hissing between their teeth, turned their thumbs down and moved away.

Beth shouted, uncertain again, 'Rome?'

He brought his mouth close to her ear. 'Rome?'

She nodded.

'Could be. When?'

His breath smelled of mushrooms and red wine. She said, 'When I was seven.'

He drew back in disbelief. Now it was she who pursued him with her lips. 'In a cloister.' Her tone strangely echoed the childish affectation, the cheekiness, of that other encounter. 'In a museum. You were making a list of the animals.'

'Aaaaah.' He breathed it out in wonder and agreement. His eyes became intensely bright. He cupped her head with a hand, drew it towards his own, and spoke with his lips at her ear. She gave little nods as she said, 'Horse, bull, lion, tiger, sheep – '

'And the rhinoceros.'

He gave another long *Aaaaah!* and drew back his head. He put a cluster of fingers to his lips, and, watching her face, drew out the ivy.

She nodded and laughed. He came close again and said, 'Dusty.'

'What?' she said, her eyes flickering everywhere. She had always seen the ivy as so green and shining. 'Dusty ivy. No.'

He said, as if it were a matter of great importance, '*Yes.*' He cupped her head in a hand again and drew it towards his own. Her eyes, downcast in listening, took in the line of hair travelling up his trunk to branch across his chest in two delicate dark feathers disturbed by the braces. 'I remember the cloister, and the list, but not much more. It's pretty amazing. Tell me about it someplace we can hear. Come and we'll go someplace and eat.'

He went ahead to clear a path, not an easy matter now that the wine and sweet smoke were taking hold. Beth caught a glimpse of Kyrie's astonished face. She looked quickly away.

She told him about it while they were descending in the big scarred warehouse lift and crossing the two roads and the broken macadam of the carpark to his car. She was glad to have it to tell, grateful for the surprise and excitement of reviving it, now that she had lost the music, and her enmity, and had goosepimples beneath her audacious dress.

'I was there with my father and stepmother and one of their children, a little boy. When they took him to the loo, I tried to make you show me your list. I hadn't even noticed all those animals. You told me to look on the sarcophagi. You held the list away and smiled. I noticed your smile.'

'Fair enough,' he said. 'People do.'

'And when you did show me, I had time to read only one bit. "And the rhino has ivy growing out of his mouth." That's the bit I read. And then Judy and dad called out that the museum was closing. You went out into the statuary garden, and Judy was worried that your mother hadn't come to get you, and went and spoke to you. A tall woman? Pregnant?'

He shook his head.

'Well, at our hotel, they all went to sleep, and I crept out and ran back to the museum. It was all locked up? And you were standing outside the gates?'

'Sure. That part. Clear as day. Being turfed out. Standing outside the gates. And the cloister. Ma and Gavin usually dumped me in some shitty old cinema, so the cloister was different. And the list. Distinctly. Because

I went on with that list all over Rome. Ran out of real animals, and started on the fabulous ones. Griffin and satyr and so on. Lord, what an assiduous kid.'

They were walking close together, but he did not touch her, and as she began to feel his physical magnetism, she turned suppliantly towards him as she spoke (already behaving as she had done with Miles). 'But what about when they came to get you? Your mother and – was Gavin your stepfather?'

'Yeah, poor bastard.'

'They had been out watching Burt Lancaster making a film.'

'Oh, right, they did that. They couldn't get a taxi, and there I was, turfed out of the museum, and bloody starving. Ma,' he added, in an indulgent, almost admiring tone, 'was always forgetting the siesta.'

It was exactly the way he had spoken of his mother then. 'And then they came,' Beth said. 'They came running through the traffic. And that's when I heard your name. Marcus. And I remembered that. And your smile.'

'To say nothing of all the rest.' And how she heard an hostility, a truculence, in his voice. He said, 'How come you remember it all so well?'

She felt a strong resistence to telling him of her letter to Debbie, and of how her own examination in the Roman incident, step by step, by Doctor Gelthartz, had fixed it in her memory. With relief, she remembered the photograph. She said, 'Judy took a photograph. You and me on the stone bench, and my father holding Gerard. And she got me to write on the back of it – With Australian boy.'

They laughed. She walked more freely. He said, 'Wait – there *was* a woman. Asking if I used to be a hippie.'

'That was me. I asked that. Because you said you and your mother used to live on a commune.'

He shook his head. 'Don't see a girl. Not a trace of a girl.'

'Oh, it's well-known that I'm unnoticeable.'

He gave her a sidelong glance. 'I wouldn't have said so.' He put a hand lightly on her bare back. 'You're cold, aren't you, Beth? Why didn't you wear a coat?'

He wore a coat. He put the hand back in its pocket and looked at her sidelong again, rather derisively. 'It's all pretty remarkable. Any particular place you want to eat?'

'Yes, it is. No, I'll leave it to you.'

'Ma took me to Rome in, let's see, spring of seventy.'

'Seventy-one. You used to call her mummy.'

'Oh, I was a mummy's boy, all right. You and I must be the same age.'

'October sixty-five.'

'December sixty-five. Great, I like older women.'

'Mummy must have set a pattern.'

He looked at the sky. 'Ho-hum, she talks psychology.'

She said instantly, 'I don't.'

'I've got patterns all through me. So have you. A cross-section might be useful. Visually presented, examined by God. Otherwise, let's do without the psychological potshots. Stick to what we can know.'

They were crossing the second road, running through the splay of lights from an oncoming car. When they reached the other side, she said angrily, 'And what can we know?'

'Sensation and hard fact.'

'And how to play games. What were you doing, Marcus, playing that juvenile game with your cohort back there?'

'Aaaah, just one of those things that comes out of a store of common reference. I like cohort, though.' Again he looked at her with that sidelong movement of the eyes. 'And what were you doing, Beth, coming out without a coat? Didn't it go with your dress?'

Beth could think of no better response than to hunch her shoulders and make the cartoon noise. 'Brrr-rr.'

'This is me here. Your dress won't go with this, either.'

Her svelte dress did look out of place in his old red Nissan, the front littered with newspapers and the back full of angular pieces of Styrofoam. As he was getting in beside her he said, 'Hey, I do remember a girl.'

'No doubt someone else.'

'No wait, this kid did come back, running, after they turfed me out.'

'Me, after all.'

'You wanted my list.'

'Only to see it. But before I could, your mother arrived.'

He was nodding. 'See? I do remember.'

'What I looked like?'

'No, only this – pushy little kid.'

'Pushy?'

'Sure.'

She laughed and shrugged. Her fear as she left the hotel in the silence of the siesta, her hard staring into the faces of strangers on the way back, were not to be shared with this grinning man whose presence beside her so painfully animated her need. Quickly opening and shutting her purse to check that the condom was there, she arrived at the definition of her course: she was curing herself of Miles by outraging the sensibilities he had helped her to cultivate. She said curtly, 'Where's the rest of this seat belt?'

He reached across her and searched in the back. She looked down at the thick dry hair barbered exactly across the nape of his neck. 'Where is your mother now?' she asked.

He pulled the buckle of the belt forward. 'West Australia. She married a character over there named

Ralfe. They've opened a fish restaurant. She reckons he's an old sea-dog.' He clipped her into the belt. 'As in Ralfe-Ralfe,' he said, making two barks of the name. He watched her, his face inches from hers, while she laughed, then briefly kissed her. 'Pushy little kid, trying to pinch my list.'

She said, as she had once said to Doctor Gelthartz, 'I think I only wanted someone of my own age to play with.'

'Do you still?'

She shut her eyes while she said it. 'Oh, yes.'

She liked his voice when he said, 'Open your eyes, Beth.' She was pleased to find something about him she could like in merely a friendly way. When she opened her eyes, he said, 'After all, we know each other from way back. Do you live alone?'

'I share.'

'With Kyrie?'

'No. She's my cousin. But I had a friend who doesn't – didn't like her.'

'A guy?'

She set her lips and nodded.

'And now you don't have him?'

'I most definitely do not.'

'I don't share,' he said. 'I did, but it broke up, like it always does, so I've just moved into my own place. It's a bit of a dump, and I had to go away, see? just after I took it, so I'm only half unpacked. But I got in tucker and wine today. Or we could eat out. You choose.'

'Your place,' she said, and irrepressibly smiled at having taken part in that dialogue she had read, and heard repeated by others, so often. Looking triumphant, he mimed a punch at her leg before turning forward to the wheel. Her smile became vague; the mimed punch made her slightly homesick for Miles, who would not have done it.

His flat was in an old building on the Darlinghurst side of the Cross. There was no lift. The mimed punch made her suspect that he would walk behind her on the stairs, slapping her bottom, as a man had done to her when she first came to Sydney. But he walked at her side, and said he happened to have some good wine. He named it, as Miles might have done, and added, running his tongue over his upper lip, that he was building up a bit of resistance to the cask stuff.

'Not for long, though,' he said, as he opened his door. 'The cask stuff's a financial imperative.'

The only room was not big. It had been freshly and badly painted in an apricot colour. Doors to the tiny kitchen and bathroom were set in the wall facing the street. The only window was crossed by the upper branches of a street tree. A red knitted sleeve hung from a carton. In an open suitcase, clothes rose in a rummaged heap. A telephone, wrapped in its cord, sat on a television.

'Oh, I like this,' said Beth, turning round and round and laughing.

'I always like this temporary phase myself,' said Marcus. 'So did Ma.'

'I love it.' Beth, hearing her own voice, too high, hoped the wine would make her less nervous. She laughed and said, 'It's like a little cabin in a tree.'

At the last moment, she did not want to take off her dress, She had leapt with candid eagerness from the sofa, which Marcus was now extending into a bed, but as she stood with her head concealed by the black tent of her dress, and her arms raised to lift it free of her head, she wanted only to let it drop and to feel again its neutral yet sensuous folds slithering on her skin. And when she did lift it, and saw him standing there, watching her, his penis springing straight from the nest of hair in his crotch, she gave a startled laugh and looked distractedly around the room, saying that she must hang up her dress.

'Have you done this often?' he asked, as startled as she.

'I am not very experienced,' she said, and burst into tears.

Weeping women are led easily to bed. The fondlings of comfort merge unnoticed into the erotic, and the fluids seem compatible. In the incidents with Miles, she had reached a muffled satisfaction but had never imagined that ecstasy could arrive so easily, nor leave behind it such deferential joy. He lay heavily upon her. She felt the pressure of his inhalations. With her lips against his sweating skin, he began to murmur and hum. It was like a low song, with a little anguish in it. He had given into her plea for darkness, but now he reached up an arm, turned on the lamp, and looked with transfixed curiosity into her face. Her gaze moved from his eyes to his raised arm, lit down by its underside by the lamp. She lifted a hand, stroked the soft damp hair in his armpit, and whispered, 'That is so beautiful.'

'That is?' he said.

'Yes.'

'*You* are,' he said accusingly. Then, 'I'm sorry. No condom.'

'Oh,' she said, with peaceful amusement, 'I had one, too.'

He rolled off her and lay on his back. She instantly turned on her side and laid a hand on his belly. She watched his face, saw him frowning thoughtfully at the ceiling. He said, 'She doesn't seem very inexperienced to me.'

Perhaps it was a wish to bring him back to her, away from this third person he seemed to address, that made her fling herself on to her back, turn her head away on the pillow, and begin to tell him about Miles. She meant to give him only the barest outline, but once she had started, she could not stop. He lay propped on an elbow at her side, listening with sympathy at first, then, sighing with boredom or anger, caressing her breasts and nipples as she spoke. She pushed his hands away; her rising desire impeded the flow of her lamentations on Miles, which now came tumbling out, brokenly but irresistibly, in a detail that would have been impossible with Kyrie. Marcus did not let her finish, but with a long groan, pulled her on top of him, holding her gripped by the buttocks.

Hating his shining blue eyes, the rictus of his grin, she surlily resisted his mechanical ferocity, but even as she did, her body responded, so that her protest, when she could put it into words, lacked conviction, and Marcus scarcely bothered to laugh it off. He went immediately to sleep. She sat up in bed, staring ahead of her, thankful at least that she had not, even then, used Miles's name. She scrambled off the mattress, went to the bathroom, washed herself, and put on her briefs, but when she returned to the room, and saw the black dress draped over a carton, and envisaged herself walking alone in the cold fluorescent lit street, and the face of some taxi driver as she bent to his window, she had reminded herself that she had expected nothing more, after all, from this man. He lay fast asleep in the full light of the lamp, his head lolling to one side, his mouth hanging open, and one hand resting with delicacy and grace on his bare chest.

FIVE •

'Right, no questions, no condom, and then she tells me, then, that she's been running around for two years with this gay guy.'

Followed by steam, he had come in talking from the shower, waking her up, and was now moving about dressing. The sofa bed was merely a rumpled mattress on the floor. She lay upon it, under a sheet and a blanket, and he, to avoid cartons and suitcase, trod on the foot of it as he moved about. She wanted to defend herself from his remarks, though they sounded casual and humorous rather than accusing. In fact, she could imagine him standing somewhere, delivering a monologue such as he was now rehearsing, to amuse the cohort.

'Acquired immune deficiency syndrome, in case we've got so used to the initials we've forgotten the words. Right, she says they haven't done it for two years, in which case I suppose it's okay. But she was angry, and angry people don't bother to be accurate.'

She sat up. Her back was stiff, and her voice issued weakly, with none of the hostility she felt. 'It was actually two and a half.'

He came and stood at the foot of the mattress. 'Well, Beth, here we are. Be careful in the shower cubicle, Beth. Just where you step in, there's a broken tile.'

'And he never expressed it physically.'

'Is that what he told you?'

'You don't understand.' Beth put both her hands to her head. 'I think I have a cold.'

He turned away. 'So have I. They're going round. Aspirin in the bathroom.'

Beth lay back on the mattress and cautiously shifted her body. Her head, her limbs, even her hands, were weak, dry, and aching. Only her genital area was alive, with a fleshy soreness, like a flower blossoming on bones. Marcus, his back turned, was saying that anyway, he couldn't stand girls with hang-ups about their pasts.

'She reckoned the guy was only using her. So she wanted to find out if there was anything sexually wrong with her. So, great, happy to be of use.'

He came again to the foot of the mattress, putting on his shirt. 'And did you ask me the questions? Not one. In future, always ask the guy the questions.'

She found herself offended by his assumption, so soon, that there would be others. And when he dropped to one knee on the mattress, and said rapidly, 'But you're sweet, Beth, all the same. You are so sweet,' she turned her head away and said, 'Don't call me that. I don't like it. And please, I would like to get up.'

He had not touched her, though his hands were poised above her shoulders. He stood up at once. 'Your voice, Beth. You've got quite a cold. It was that dress you had on. You certainly can't go to work in that dress. I'll drive you home to change. Come on, I'll make us coffee and orange juice while you shower.'

Aspirin and a shower made her feel better, but in the black dress she looked so shrunken and ghastly that she stood, arrested, in front of the narrow mirror, her mind resisting what Miles might have said.

Marcus, wearing Kyrie's bowler hat, came in with the coffee. 'Jesus,' he said, 'you look like something by Munch.'

He put down the coffee and fetched a raincoat. 'Known in my class at Brigden High,' he said soothingly, 'as the mad munk.' He helped her into the gabardine raincoat, and turned back the cuffs. 'Duty free in Amsterdam when I was a courier,' he told her.

He turned her by the shoulders to face the mirror. He stood behind her, his mouth hidden by her hair. Their reflected eyes met. 'You all like that coat,' he said, and transferred the hat from his head to hers, hiding his face.

In the hard gritty light of the street, her hostility to him waned, overwhelmed by her longing to be in her own surroundings. She made conversation, such as saying that parking must be hard to get around here, but was indifferent to his easy voluble answers.

He maintained his volubility in his car. He said it was really pretty remarkable, their meeting again. She said she supposed so. He said he thought he remembered her father in the cloister now. She made a polite show of interest. It seemed that her whole body, down to the pores of her skin, was craving the salve of her daytime clothes, now so nearly attainable. He remembered a group of gypsies outside the museum gates. She shook her head while meditating on the fresh underclothes, the silk shirt, the heliotrope pullover, the soft chequered skirt.

He was talking, again with that effect of addressing nobody in particular, about his job. He was a computer operator, but was going to turn it in.

'How did I get to be one of those? A good school record in maths, for Christ's sake. It's bloody boring, except when they send me on demos, but I don't want to turn it in yet, not till I've built up a bit of a bank.'

'I suppose not,' said Beth, drawing the thin stockings over her white legs, slipping her feet into soft low-heeled shoes. She would not ring Miles, but would ring Juliet. She would test the water.

They had almost reached her building before Marcus said, 'Look, Beth, if harm's been done, it's been done, and anyway the odds are thousands to one against, so we've nothing to lose, and might as well enjoy it. I'm not putting this well, but you know what I mean. What's his name, anyway?'

She held the collar of his coat round her aching throat. Kyrie's twenty silver bangles jingled in one pocket. 'His name doesn't matter,' she said. 'You can let me out here.'

'What's the big secret? Most of them have come out and proud of it. Good God, I nearly had a bit of a run-in with a guy myself when I was fourteen-fifteen. You don't want me to drive up the side there?'

'No.'

She had already released the catch of the door. He leaned across her and opened it. He handed her the bowler hat. 'See you, Beth.'

'I'll send back your coat.'

He called something after her while she ran up the path. She heard his car move away as, on the single step, she trod on the hem of his coat, and barely saved herself from falling.

On the most celebrated and quoted of Andrew McCracken's visits, he had addressed the staff, saying he wanted to make it quite clear that this was no place for wimps, that he paid well, and in return expected a full and flat-out effort, and no staying away for hangovers, minor bereavements, or the lesser maladies.

'You've got a cold, Beth,' said the senior draftsman.

'A lesser malady,' Beth hoarsely agreed.

'Maria, go out and get Beth some Codral and a carton of orange juice.'

'It's not that virus, is it?' asked Maria.

'Which particular virus?' asked another, sardonic voice.

There were hisses and mild boos; this man, Jack Best, was always talking about it. Maria said coldly, 'I mean the winter one that's going round.'

Beth worked on, light-headed and aching, slow and precise, while sexual feeling rose in her body like the pressure of a mass of water. At lunch time she went out to buy coffee, and in the crowded lift, the shop and the street, had the sense of herself barging weakly and softly about. Bumping into others, brushing against a woman's breast or a man's arm warm through the sleeve, she wanted to stop and lay her head there. She avoided Jack Best, who had always attracted her. Every now and again, she put a hand over her mouth to keep back laughter or shock. In the afternoon, when her membranes began to release mucous, Maria found her in the washroom, leaning against the wall, blowing her nose and shaking with laughter.

'Beth, you do have that virus.'

'I certainly have something,' said Beth, with clotted consonants.

'I'm going to tell them. It's not fair. We'll all get it. You've got to go home. See a doctor on the way. Get antibiotics.'

In the doctor's chair, Beth sat slumped, her hands hanging between her knees, weakly laughing. 'Every bone aches,' she told him.

'It's doing the rounds,' he said. 'An influenza virus. Unfortunately, we don't know what strain it is. I wish it made everybody laugh.'

'I've got the giggles.'

Although she had not listened to Marcus's voice as he called after her from his car, she was now certain of what he had said. In her shared flat, the phone was on the wall near the door. It was ringing when she came in.

'Rang you at work,' he said. 'Got your number. Got your wog, too.'

'It's doing the rounds,' she said.

'A week off work. Bed for three or four days.'

She was shaking with laughter again. She leaned against the wall, weak with her sickness and this silent laughter.

'They don't know what strain it is.' He was hoarsely shouting. 'So – no antibiotics. Aspirin. Fluids. Light diet. Bed.'

Now her laughter made her slide down the wall and sit on the floor. He did not understand when she said, 'Vitamin C', and she had to repeat it.

'Right!' he shouted then. '*Vidabin C*. Me too. Pack a bag, leave a note, and I'll come and get you.'

She was impressed by his ability to halt himself and be practical. She would not have remembered to leave a note for Angela and Nicole. Afraid that the birth control pills prescribed for her years ago would have lost their efficacy, she took a card of twenty-one from Angela's bedside drawer.

She waited with her bag on the footpath. When he ran round the car to let her in, their smiles burst out at once. Inside the back of the car, instead of the Styrofoam shapes, she saw cartons of food, local champagne, boxes of tissues, chemist's packages, and two pink light globes.

On the way, after he had explained that he had stayed only an hour at work, and had fixed his place up a bit, they hardly spoke. Beth felt that her fears and discriminations had been lifted like a weight into the air, leaving her light and bold and free and able to sit straight-backed beside Marcus in his car. She recalled her childhood self loitering on the Roman pavement, after Marcus had been taken away, and those feelings of freedom and expectancy, and of having nothing to expend them on. She turned her head and said, smiling, 'It's fate that we met again.'

'I said so this morning.'

'Oh, you did not.'

'Driving you home. I did. More or less.'

Juliet McCracken, sitting behind the wheel of her old Jaguar, saw Marcus throw Beth's bag into his car. She saw Beth get in, then she watched the red car draw away. She was about to drive away herself when she saw the two girls coming home, on foot, and she got out of the car, rather flustered, calling, 'Oh, Nicole! Angela dear!'

SIX •

From inside the building, they were reached by the ringing of telephones, faint music, voices at the pitch of anger or advertising, and the thuds and gurgles of plumbing. From outside, from the silky continuous tumult of the city, the rush of trains sprang at intervals and receded to leave dominant again the slurring of cars through the underpass. Single cars moved softly in the square below. At night headlamps fanned on to the ceiling distorted shadows of the tree and the window frame.

Marcus's telephone still sat in its coils on the TV. The ringing telephones were signals of their exemption, their isolation on their pink raft of pleasure and sickness, some delirium, and talk that often ended when one or the other fell asleep as if some gentle hungry force had reached up and pulled them down.

Entwined, or breast to breast, they whispered with satisfaction that they were very sick people, but thought it a joke at first. The course of the malady varied in each. On the third day, delirium put Beth briefly out of Marcus's reach. He laughed and said, 'What?' at her garbled husky talk, but held her upright and made her take aspirin dissolved in water. He helped her to the lavatory, and when she sat slumped and said she couldn't get up, they were both attacked again by their laughter. He leaned his forehead against the cracked tiles and howled, while Beth, bent double, shaking, hung heavily on his arm. As he led her back to bed, she said querulously, 'It isn't as if I even remember her,' but looked at him blankly when he asked who she meant.

After he put her into bed, he said softly, 'We've been doing it too much.'

'Oh, no,' she said, throwing weak arms round his neck, their weakness drawing him down.

She was better next day. 'But I am still very sick,' she assured him. They ate over-ripe pears after cutting out the bruises, and toast which they ate standing up while the coffee was brewing. Marcus was boisterous as they stripped the bed and opened the window to let air through the room, but when they shut themselves in the steaming heated bathroom to wash and dry each other's body and hair, he was slow and quiet. He sat on the toilet seat while Beth, with conscientious busyness, passed the blow-dryer over his hair, but when she put his head back to dry the hair over his forehead, she saw that his wide-open eyes were pale and remote. 'Marcus. Marcus,' she said. 'Okay, okay,' he mumbled, but his eyes did not change.

Speaking rapidly and soothingly as she made sure his hair was dry, she recalled how she had run up to the boy standing outside the locked gates of the museum. There, too, his eyes had been dry and pale, and had looked beyond her. They had anxiously searched the street, while there, too, she had spoken to him in the tone she was using now, assuring him, then, that his mother would soon come. When his hair was dry, she wrapped him in towels, and in the same reassuring tone, told him to stay there, just like that, while she got the bed ready.

She led him in, his weight making them both stagger – as she said, laughing – like two drunks. With pettish vehemence, he rejected the shirt she tried to put on him, pushed her aside, fell to the mattress, and was asleep before she could draw up the covers.

Beth, cross-legged on the end of the mattress, watched Marcus while he slept. She had put ice cubes and water into a dish, and had brought a washcloth from the bathroom, and occasionally leaned forward to sponge his hot forehead. Such services she had sometimes done for her halfbrothers.

In this room, Marcus had not once reverted to the jeering style she had braced herself to meet in the warehouse. Yet she must have been slightly bracing herself to meet it, or she would not now be feeling his defencelessness as a respite.

Marcus's casual questions about Miles had been easily diverted. It had been a triumph for Beth that Miles could be made to retreat, but now, in this respite, she let herself summon him, and immediately found herself wanting to tell him about her reunion with the boy who had written, *And the rhino has ivy growing out of his mouth.*

She was so accustomed to storing incidents to tell Miles. She still had an expectation of, a hankering after, his attentive listening, his anticipatory smile. But this was her only sorrow for the loss of a man over whom, less than a week ago, she had wept all those tears, and taken all those postures. As this reversal settled in her mind, was tested and found true, she wondered if she were not capable of a frivolity more devastating than the social kind Miles had helped her to cultivate. Marcus threw one arm out of the covers. She picked up the hand and rested it on her open palm, then, making a wry mouth, she arranged it on the mattress like the plaster cast of a man's hand that had hung on the wall of the art room at school, or like those others in Rome, where, at her eye level, as she walked behind her father and Judy, marble fingers had curled against buttocks and thighs.

Marcus broke into brief incoherent speech and flung out his other arm, exposing his naked torso. She got up and fetched the shirt he had flung aside. He was heavy and inert, and as she patiently worked to put it on him, she was moved by a flooding of tenderness to babble endearments she knew he could not hear.

She buttoned the shirt, sponged his forehead and hands, and returned to her cross-legged vigil. She knew that there was a maternal element in her feeling for him, and that she was demonstrating it now, watching so contentedly while he slept. But she was disturbed by an occasional fusion of his presence with her own dreams of the maternal. At some time during those days and nights, she had told him she had no memory at all of her mother, unless she could count the sensation, when half-awake or half-asleep, of being held, of being utterly safe and at peace. Her father's household had been so busy; she had felt that a tide was continuously rushing past her, threatening to lift her feet from the bottom, so that when, just before waking, she had fallen into that state while conscious of the activity beginning, she had tried to stay within its confines, to delay waking up.

She had told Marcus of that dream embrace, but had suppressed her fancy that it did not issue from a memory of her mother, but was a prefiguration of Marcus himself. Miles had called her Sweet Reason; Marcus believed in sensation and hard fact: Beth was rather alarmed that sexual release should have awakened in her a store of lush superstition. She could not repress it, and in fact enjoyed it. But she kept it to herself, releasing only as the lightest of jokes her fancy that their meeting under the strobe lights on the blackened walls of the warehouse was not a coincidence, but had been ordained by their first meeting in the cloister.

Their conversations in this room, whether broken or sustained, in daylight or beneath the wheeling reflections of the window frame and tree, had often returned to that childhood meeting. Beth now knew Marcus's mother's name to be Nita. He spoke of her both as Nita and ma. Either could bring a look of reserve to Beth's face. She rather luxuriated in pity for the child Marcus, whose mother had left his father on the commune, had married Gavin, and after only a few years had left him too, all the while dragging her adoring and neglected child in her erratic wake. But when Beth hinted at this, Marcus said, with his amused indulgence, 'Oh, ma's all right. She just gets carried away.'

Even in Rome, Nita had looked the kind that got carried away. Beth's recall of her was more altered by Marcus's description of how, on leaving the commune at Toomba, she had instantly discarded her hand-made sandals for the grotesque shoes fashionable at that time. The thin heels of winkle-pickers had damaged the floors of Gavin's house. Dirty winkle-pickers lay kicked off in every room. Beth could no longer see so clearly the feet set together on the Roman pavement, the short skirt riding up silken thighs as Nita squatted to console her son, while Beth, loitering, watched. Beth had been a watcher of real mothers, her eyes always clinging, wondering.

Marcus's memory of the incident in Rome was fragmentary, and he submitted it to Beth's more sequential recall. Yesterday, stroking her hair back from her face, he asked if she had pierced ears then. She said no, but she had talked in the cloister about her best friend, Debbie Youdall, who had pierced ears. When she told him what had become of Debbie, he said it was a pity those guys couldn't just be killed. He agreed with her humanitarian objections, but said that all the same, it was a pity. Miles had come and sat on Beth's shoulder; an argument had broken out, diverting her from going on to tell Marcus about Doctor Gelthartz.

She leaned forward and felt Marcus's forehead. Not all the heat had gone from his skin. Drowsy herself now, she was becoming impatient with his fever. She got up and wandered about the room, picking up soiled clothes and linen and stuffing them on top of the rest in the big plastic laundry bag. Then she examined the apricot walls and tried to devise a mural, but they were so cluttered that she could think only of painting more cartons – of painting cartons, at differing angles to each other, right up to the ceiling, and restoring to one the red knitted sleeve she had seen dangling on that first night. She put her hands behind her head and laughed aloud, then yawned again and again, and on the last yawn thought suddenly of Angela coming away from the phone and saying, 'Yes, very attractive, but not my type.'

She knelt again to the mattress, judged Marcus's temperature to be normal, and slipped under the covers beside him. Luxuriating in the relief from the weakness left by her illness, she curled her body to conform to his, and put her lips against the back of his neck.

The saltiness, and the smell natural to him, eliminated by the shower, had returned. She breathed deliberately, drawing it in. Jack Best, who worked with her, had come one day to her drafting table. He was a middle-aged man, clever, jocular, and morose. He had recently stopped smoking. 'My wife says I smell better,' he said. 'Do I? Encourage me.' She was sitting, he standing. Humoring him, she advanced her face to his belly, and the smell his skin released, pungent yet with the sweetness of some unknown edible substance, had immediately weakened and embarrassed her. He understood – they always understood – but he was gentle, and did not tease her. Her devotion to Miles was known.

Kissing Marcus's neck, it occurred to Beth that he had released in her something better than superstition. He had released in her the ability to adventure. It would not be with Jack Best, who, apart from the disqualification of marriage, was not her type either, but with someone still unknown. Shutting her eyes on this dim desirable figure, she put her forehead into the back of Marcus's neck and went to sleep.

Juliet opened her eyes and looked at the glowing hands of her bedside clock. It was 3 a.m. Having failed to capture one the night before, she had put paper and pencil on her bedside table. She sat up and turned on the light.

DREAM 22 = Lovely at first. Putting flowers on table smiling busy happy. People round table shadowy talking laughing. Me moving chair suddenly anxious pushing hard grinding teeth chair won't budge. Then in dry paddock running still anxious. Sticks in way. Fallen trees. Scabs on legs scratches. Shadowy figure calling out Get him. Horse very big standing profile. Me tired tired panting running holding bridle almost touch him off he trots. Tired lie on ground but voice still saying Get him. Blank then running up hill no bridle. Child or woman? Then hill grassy short rippling soft green grass beautiful. Touch grass see hooped silver back moving. Snake touch back wet not snake fish. Not earth water. Rippling apple green water. Put hands in but fish gone. Slide into water cleave through it arms outstretched straight white silent.

Cool cool all through me. So happy. No voice. Silent.

Late that morning, Juliet transcribed Dream 22, adding a little punctuation, into the ledger. Then, slowly – until impetuosity took over – she went on to the origins.

ORIGINS DREAM 22 = Debris. Memory (thought debris). Message? Command??? Get him = Miles saying yesterday he can't find Beth. Saying, Help me to find her. Voice in dream saying, Get him, but suspect gender unimportant to the Lord of our dreams. I see it now. The Lord of our Dreams uses any old scraps of material, ancient or new, and cobbles them together to wear once. Oh yes, that horse we used to call the Jew or Solly, the one I learned to ride on. Daddy made me catch him myself. Inches away, and off that damn old Solly would trot, and Daddy calling out Get him.
Falling over = Always falling over when child. Scabs and scratches all too real too, let alone broken legs I am paying for now.
Water = Me saying, Miles, next week she will be back at Andrew's water works and you can catch her there. And poor Miles, I have never seen him like it before, saying that the note she left for Nicole and Angela said she was going to have flu at a friend's place, and who else could that be but Kyrie? And if she's not there, Miles said in that terribly un-Milesish doggy way, Kyrie must know where she is, but won't say, not to me. But she might to you, he said, and asked me if I would ring Kyrie, if I would just test the water. Well I must say I looked at him open-mouthed. I said, Miles darling, I've done everything you've asked. 1, I said, 1 – I lent you my garden for your discussion, 2 – I waited for Beth

outside Andrew's in the rain. 3 – I tried to talk sense into her on the phone. 4 – When you asked me to ring her the other day at Andrew's, I did, and when they told me she had gone home sick, I – and this is 5, I said – I drove to her flat, exactly as you wished, and was perfectly prepared to take her in here and care for her, as I did when she had that sprained wrist. But the bird had flown, and Angela and Nicole didn't know where, and more I cannot do. I said, I happen to be <u>tired, tired</u>. He said, It is not like you to say so. And I said, Well, I am saying it now, and moreover I happen to have an appointment with my masseur in half an hour. You know how my poor old pasterns and hocks – oh, this is an easy one – have been lately. And I must say, Miles, I said, that you of all people, with your right-to-privacy committees and so on, and even going on to tv about it, ought to be the first person to grant that poor little thing her own privacy. He sat down and said, Don't say I have lost my sweet girl. And I sat down and took his hands and said, I didn't know you felt quite so strongly, and he said, Neither did I. I wanted to ask about the other thing, I mean, <u>les boys</u>, but didn't dare, even then. I said, Well, you still have your old spare godmother, and he clung on to my hands, and in the end I'm sure it brought us closer together.

More water = After my massage I had a spa bath, and lying back and letting the water run over me, how contented I felt. I confess not the bliss of the dream, but a nice ordinary everyday contentment. At the time, I couldn't think what stopped me from telling Angela and Nicole that I had just seen Beth go off in that fat man's car, when I had jumped out of my Jaggy and was toddling up to them for that very purpose. But now I see that even then I was worried about intruding into her privacy. And that could also be why in the dream I dropped or threw down the bridle and refused to catch Solly-Beth.

If, however, Beth comes back, I shall, naturally, be the first to welcome her. It is simply that I happen to remember the fat man's smile, as he ran round and threw her bag into the car. And her back, as she got in, her animal back. No, that was no abduction. Beth has gone.

Fat is unfair. Thickset is nearer the mark. Must be meticulous. Face rather like one of those cupids you see in paintings, in pairs. Not the sweet one, the wicked one.

NOTES DREAM 22 = Not certain whether child or woman except at the end when swimming. Woman then. Water flowing over breasts arms thighs between legs. Beautiful. Legs not a bit sore.

COLOUR = Begin to wonder if like the voices. Colour = I know but do not see??

Must confess that all the time I've been writing this, and talking about being meticulous and so on, I've been thinking, just like in that book, not the green one the shopgirl one, that Dream 22 is an important dream, and remembering that numerologist ages ago who said 4 was my dominant number. Well 2+2 undeniably = 4. So, if I'm going to be absurd, I might as well be utterly absurd, and amuse myself by saying that as I failed to "obey" the command to catch Solly-Beth in the middle part of the dream, I might as well "obey" one of the other parts, and much as I would like to be young, and swimming in apple-green water and so on, it does seem more practical to "obey" the very first part, and give a little impromptu dinner party, just for the group, as it used to be. I'll get someone to take Mrs Ho's place. What a time for her to get sick. Some damn Ho relative rang, a son I think, and on he went, yabber-yabber, and it turned out she has the flu. I didn't think they got it.

Beth said she couldn't stand the noise of the train. She lay prone, her face in her folded arms, and when the train rushed by, shook her head as if to jolt the noise out. She shook her head again when Marcus leaned over her to question and coax.

'I don't know why. I'm just down.'

'It's your period coming?'

'It's not due. And I never get like this anyway.'

'Then it's post-coital tristesse. There you are, very distinguished and French. It comes from doing it too much.'

'You got that from one of your manuals.'

'Sure. It's physiological. It's to be disregarded. Turn over, Bethie.'

She rolled on her side, but lay turned away from him, her head propped on one hand, the other stifling the dry hollow cough left by her flu. Marcus ran a hand down the curve of her hip. 'That's a great shape,' he said. 'I always like that shape.'

She said thoughtfully, 'You all like that coat.'

He gave a whoop of laughter and turned her forcibly on to her back. She put the inside of a wrist to her mouth, but when he lifted it away, her smile appeared. He said,

'Lord, that was ages ago. You're a different person.'

'You too.' She put a hand to his cheek. 'Where is the man in the waiter's pants and the braces? Playing games with his cohort? Do you miss your mates?'

'They'll keep. You're not still down?'

'I'm trying to pretend I'm not.'

He was silent for a while, staring at her. Then he said, 'I know this is a dump.'

'It's not that.'

'I told you why I took it. I can't share any more, and I'm trying to build up a bank. Would you like to go home?'

'Not to the girls I share with. Not yet.'

'Why not?'

'I'm still too weak to stand their perfection.'

'Ha! Anywhere else.'

Once, when she had sprained a wrist, Juliet had taken her in, and the others had come to visit, bringing magazines and board games. Miles was in London then, but he was not in London now. 'I don't think so,' she said, shaking her head in impatience as the cough rose again. 'No, nowhere else,' she said, when she could speak.

'Right, then I'll tell you what I'll do.' He got up as he spoke. 'I'll go out. And get that laundry done. And buy two newspapers. And some cough stuff. And two pizzas.'

The Telecom man came while Marcus was out, leaving a new socket on the baseboard, and the phone, attached by a long cord, squatting beside the mattress.

Beth dropped to her knees before it. It offered her melancholy the alleviation of small duties. She tapped out Kyrie's number, but Kyrie was not at home, and nor was her answering machine turned on. Neither Nicole nor Angela was at home. Beth rang Juliet. A train passed unnoticed while she waited. She was about to ring off when Juliet replied in a fast distracted voice.

'Juliet? This is Beth.'

'Beth. How nice.'

'I thought of you today.'

'How nice.'

'About how kind you were when I sprained my wrist.'

'Thank you. The girls say you have flu.'

'I'm nearly better.' But now Beth's cough took her by surprise, and when she turned again to the phone, Juliet said coldly, 'What a strange, contralto cough.'

'Juliet, I know I should have left an address.'

'As a courtesy, perhaps.'

'But I didn't know it.' Beth put her other hand over her mouth, then removed it and said in a burst, 'And I still don't know it. I still don't.' Her voice rose. 'I went with my lover.' Then, as Juliet responded only with a guarded *Oh*, she said, almost singing, 'I am with my lover.'

'You rang to tell me that?' Juliet rapped out.

'Did I? I think I must have.' Smiling broadly, Beth fell back on the mattress. 'Anyway, I liked saying it.'

'Well, now you've said it, you must excuse me. I'm preparing a dinner party.'

'Again!'

'Only a little one, but Mrs Ho has the flu, and they sent me a relation, who talks. So goodbye, my dear.'

Encouraged by this kinder tone, Beth said, 'Wait – wait.'

'What?'

'How is Miles?'

'Quite well, I hope.'

'I would like – ' said Beth restlessly.

'I am quite desperately busy,' said Juliet with force.

'I just want – '

'I'm sorry, Beth, but sometimes we must choose, which is evidently what you have done.'

'Of course,' said Beth, singing again. 'It doesn't really matter.'

'Goodbye, my dear. Take care of that cough.'

'Goodbye, Juliet.'

Beth took the newspapers from Marcus and dropped them on top of the phone. She carried the pizzas to the kitchen and came out replying, 'Yes, it just disappeared. I'm fine now.' Marcus was tipping the clean laundry on to the mattress. She took the plastic bag from his hands, threw it down, and put both arms round him. She said, 'You're my lover.'

'So you noticed?'

She laughed and said, 'I missed you.'

Returning her embrace, he rocked her to and fro. 'She missed me.'

'*I* missed you.'

'I missed her, too.'

She freed herself and lifted the newspapers from the phone. 'Look.'

'Lo!' He knelt, as she had done. 'I always make an incantation to a new phone.'

His ululation, coinciding with a passing train, was very convincing. Beth said. 'You can ring the cohort.'

'I rang them from the laundromat.'

'Well, now you can give them your number.'

'I'll just shove these pizzas in the oven first.'

'I will.'

From the kitchen, she heard him making the brief calls, and saying the names. Kirk. Andy. Stathos. Mil. She went in and said, 'I'll try Kyrie again.'

'She won't be home yet.'

'I'll try.'

Marcus stretched out on the mattress. 'It turns out

it takes some getting over. The laundromat took it out of me. Lord, what a wimp. Give Kyrie my number, will you? if she's home.'

Kyrie answered promptly. 'Beth! Where have you been?'

Beth was startled by her bluntness, her hint of accusation. She said in a childish voice, 'With Marcus Pirie.'

'That occured to me. I saw you leave the party.'

'I was just going to tell you,' complained Beth.

'Your Miles has been trying to find you.'

'He could have rung the flat. I left a note.'

'With no address.'

'I wasn't obliged to leave an address. And anyway, I didn't know it. Kyrie, hold on for a moment.'

Turning aside to cough, she saw Marcus's face, offended or bored. 'I still don't know it,' she said to Kyrie.

'Lucky I didn't, or your Miles would have got it out of me.'

'He's not mine, not any more. How many times did he ring?'

'Four.'

Marcus had raised himself. Kneeling, he leaned against Beth. She put an arm round his shoulders and said, 'Four!'

'Maybe five. Now listen, Beth, where are my bangles? I want my hat.'

'I'll bring them, Kyrie. I'll be home tomorrow.'

Marcus leaned close to the mouthpiece. 'Or the day after, Kyrie.'

Beth turned a shoulder to guard the phone. 'Is your man back yet, Kyrie?'

'He came back, but not to me.'

Before Beth could reply, Marcus took the phone. 'Hi, Kyrie, it's great to hear your voice. Here, take down my new number.'

He listened to Kyrie speaking. 'But you see,' he said,

'I didn't realise that. I didn't think what we said meant that much.'

He listened again. 'No,' he said, 'it wouldn't have made any difference. You know me, Kyrie.'

Beth struggled in Marcus's grasp. He had backed off at first from her hitting fists, trying to laugh, but had then, cursing, sprang forward and caught those fists in his hands. And now, holding them tightly confined between their two bodies, he said, in the vehement tone of his cursing, 'I didn't bloody know she was waiting for me.'

'You knew she was my cousin.'

'What's that got to do with it?'

'You ought to have told me.'

'You don't bloody own me.'

Her scorn was childishly emphatic. 'Who would want to!'

'What's all this shit, then?' He suddenly opened his arms. 'There!'

She had seen dogs turn away from each other like this. They scrapped, they snarled, they turned bridling away. But she continued to bridle, and to speak with the same scorn as she went to the kitchen.

'I can smell our junk food.'

His shout followed her. 'Junk nothing. Those are good pizzas. Made today.'

She kicked the kitchen door shut behind her. The oven released its heat full on her crouching body. She thought, *Scorch him out of my life.* But when she rose, and set the pizzas on the counter, and saw the slightly broken crust, the cheese still bubbling, the darkening strips of green pepper, and the shining ovals of black olives, saliva rushed into her mouth, and a light loving mildness relieved her anger.

Marcus opened the door. 'Right,' he said, 'I did think of telling you about Kyrie and me. In the car. But - this is the truth –I thought you mightn't have come if I did.'

She saw that he was not defensive. In each hand she held a pizza plate. His eyes exploring hers, and hers exploring his, were similarly fearful and curious. She said, 'Look at these, Marcus. Hot food. Let's eat it.'

They replaced the pink light in the reading lamp with a plain globe, Marcus saying that he hated to do it, and that it looked like bad timing, but Beth agreeing that it was necessary if they wanted to read the papers.

They sat on the floor, turning pages. Slowly, Beth's anger returned. She read, and turned pages, with a pretended interest, but would not reply to his comments. She felt his stare directed at the top of her bent head.

'Those are powerful sulks you've got there, Bethie.'

'Oh no,' she said, 'it was entirely my own fault, I know that, for not connecting you with Kyrie's Mark, and for still thinking it was Mark the cameraman.'

'Now listen, I get Mark. I get Marcus. I get Marco. It's all so simple. We've known each other for years, and there we were, both in Dubbo – '

'You told me that.'

' – and when I went on out west, and she left for Sydney, all we said was, See you.'

'But she told *me* she was going to stick with that one man. She must have told you that.'

'Not like that. We talked about herpes and aids. How rubbers can burst, and are desensitising, and all that stuff. And how we might be forced to that in the end, sticking to one person. Though, personally, I think that's an over-reaction.'

'Kyrie's really unusual. She's so beautiful. And she acts

as if she doesn't know it.'

'Yes, it's great the way she disregards it. In fact, unique.'

Beth lay back on the floor. She put a forearm across her forehead. 'Did you notice those low air fares? I could sell all my books and baubles and go to London.'

'Why not? That's what I'm getting a bank for. Wait till I get it and I'll come with you. My father's over there.'

'You said you didn't know where he was,' said Beth accusingly. 'You said he didn't write.'

'He was there last time he wrote, in Dorset, in a community.'

She turned her head aside, coughed, then said, 'What kind of community?'

'Buddhist of some sort. He went from Toomba to India, then to Thailand. He used to write me five-page lectures, and I used to winkle out the personal stuff and send back five lines. Then he wrote from this place in Dorset. And do you know what he said?'

'N-ho,' drawled Beth.

'He said I was part of the coarse hot world he regretfully had to leave behind.'

Beth raised herself on an elbow. 'Those words?'

'Those words.'

'Does that mean he's cool and refined?'

'He might be refined. How can you be cool and religious?'

'You can if your religion is the official kind.'

'His isn't. It can't be.'

'No,' agreed Beth.

Marcus lay on his propped arms beside her. She rolled her head so that her cheek touched his arm. She could hear the refrigerator, which had made them laugh at first by jumping with indignation at its load, but which had now settled into a nagging vibration. 'You must wonder what he's really like,' she said.

'Sure do. I wasn't four when we left Toomba, and about

all I remember is this big shadow moving over the reading and writing class he got together. And his hand coming down to guide ours. And his voice saying, Again. Ma says he believed that any child old enough to make a mark with a pencil was old enough to learn to read and write. We did learn, too. There were photos. Ma has photos. But somehow I don't connect them with the real Toomba. Jesus, I howled when we left.'

'Do you ever want to try something like it again?'

'Nup.'

'Why not?'

'Because I'm a trivial character. I went back once, and they were wearing flares. Nup. City's got me.'

She put an arm round his neck. 'Me too. Some city. Somewhere. I remember your mother so well in Rome, running through the traffic.'

'And screaming, you said. The truth is, they would have been a bit drunk, those two. Then a few years later, she suddenly gives up the grog, and starts saying her spirits are inborn. Oh, ma!'

She touched his hair lightly, here and there. 'Not much more than a week ago, I was weeping over a man.'

'The gay guy you told me about?'

She hesitated, but then said, 'Yes, Miles. His name is Miles.'

'Is he an older guy?'

'Nine years.'

'You like older guys? I can imagine that, somehow.'

'You're not older.'

'Ha! Younger.'

'Two months. And five years younger than Kyrie.'

He said, chanting, 'Mummy must have set a pattern.'

But Beth did not take this opportunity to say how long it seemed since they had crossed the two roads and the broken macadam of the car park. 'Miles used to call me

Sweet Reason,' she said. 'He used to say he could depend on my reason. He would say it to invoke it. And I'm trying to invoke it now.' She turned her head away to cough, then struck her chest with a fist and said hoarsely, 'When I'm hollow with jealousy.'

'It's always worse when it's someone you know. But it will muck us up if you let it.' He lay beside her, his face on her breast, an arm across her body. 'Don't let it. Let's get our banks and go to London together, like we said.'

'Yes.' She spoke into his hair. 'And split up there.'

'Don't harden the options,' he said lazily. 'See how we feel at the time.'

'All right. That's perfectly reasonable. And tomorrow, I'll go home.'

'It's not the full week.'

'No, but it's a good idea.' She looked down her cheeks at his hair, and again put a hand on his head. 'Don't you think so?'

'Right, Beth,' said his voice, 'I do.'

'So!' she said, feeling calm, and pleased with herself. 'And the next day, I'll go back to work.'

'How do you feel about that?'

Beth was in fact thinking with longing of the soothing precision of her work, and of the light limited company of her co-workers. 'Good,' she said. 'I quite like the work, and I quite like the people.'

'Aaaah,' said his sleepy voice. 'You're lucky to work with ordinary beasts, then. Not like me and my caryatids.'

Beth and Marcus, like Marcus and his cohort, were acquiring a store of common reference. People dependent on computers they called caryatids, or androgynous caryatids, because Marcus had told Beth how, in Rome, after much puzzlement, and argument with his mother and Gavin, he had decided *caryatid* did not belong in his list of fabulous animals, being compounded of the human and the inanimate, and so had deleted it from its place below *angel*, which he had insisted on leaving in.

'If I don't get out of that job soon . . .' Beth heard him murmur now.

'You'll become one yourself?' she said, very softly, to test whether he was asleep or not. There was no reply. She knew that soon they would be cold and uncomfortable, and that she would be forced to wake him, but in the meantime, it was wonderfully peaceful to lie like this, listening to his breathing, his head on her breast.

The mirror that had reflected Beth wearing Marcus's raincoat, and Marcus behind her in the black bowler hat, now reflected her figure in one of the pale and subtle dresses chosen by Miles. Her eyes, on this occasion, were as curious, as transfixed, as they had been on that.

The mirror was spotted and jaggedly edged with black. Behind her she could see part of the sofa bed, which Marcus and she had neatly returned to its function as a sofa. Marcus, in jeans, canvas shoes, and a thick pullover, stood beside it, opening mail from his last address. Beth tried the effect of lifting the hem. 'I've lost weight,' she said.

'We both have.' He was throwing coloured brochures on to the sofa. 'We've been very sick people,' he said, in the weak petulant voice they had affected.

'That's why this dress doesn't look good any more. *It* can't have changed. Do you like it?'

Marcus had come upon something that interested him. He said, 'What?'

'Do you like this dress?'

In the mirror, she watched him advance. He stood

behind her, his mouth again covered by her hair. 'It looks a bit daggy,' he said.

'Marcus,' she said gently, 'this is, I assure you, a very beautiful dress.'

'Well, you like it, or you wouldn't have bought it.'

'You liked that tarty black dress.'

'At first. Not now I know you. Look, forget that.' With both hands, he held a big photograph in front of her eyes. 'Look. With sea dog.'

Beth turned from the mirror. The photograph was glossy and limp. Beth also held it in both hands. Nita and her husband, wearing identical blue and white striped aprons and modified chef's hats, stood on a wharf, against a background of sunlit water, hugging each other and intensely smiling. Beth said, 'I believe I would have recognised her. Her smile's still exactly like yours.'

She looked at Marcus. He gave a quick embarrassed version of his smile, a grimace, and took the photograph. 'What do you think of Ralfe-Ralfe?'

'Swashbuckling?'

'What about that thirties movie moustache?' In a pantomime of lewdness, Marcus smirked and nudged her. 'Ay? Ay? And wouldn't you say he has more teeth than most people?'

'But of course. For the dog biscuits.'

'And the bones. 'Grrrr-*grrh*!'

'Does Nita often come to Sydney?'

'Not once since she went over there. She gets flight terror. Has to have hypnotherapy before every flight. And it's a hell of a drive over the Nullarbor. And anyway, she's sunk all her money into this fish-joint with the sea dog. Ma, once she gets started on something, she never lets up, she works like a maniac. She says here,' said Marcus, reading from the back of the photograph, 'that they're using this in their publicity.' He shook his head.

'Oh, ma, how could you!'

'The chef's hat. She cooks?'

'Cooks? Ma's a great cook,' said Marcus, as if Beth should have known this. 'Once on Toomba she cooked a goat.'

'Yuck. Do you miss her?'

'We ring now and then. It's always good to hear her voice.'

He spoke so dubiously, looking at the photograph with his head aslant, that Beth said, 'Coming from so far away?' He nodded. 'Like my father's voice,' said Beth. 'Quite acceptable, from down there.'

Marcus was still looking at the photograph. 'Yeah-yeah,' he said sadly. 'Show me a map of Australia, and I feel sort of soothed by the Nullarbor.'

She went and leaned against his shoulder. 'And comforted by the Great Australian Bight?'

'Yeah-yeah,' he said in his mourning voice. She rubbed her chin against his shoulder and said, 'I know. And you feel so helpless about it.'

'I would like to see her. Yes, fleetingly. That's how. For instance, Beth, if you and I went that way to London.'

Beth took the photograph, looked at it, and said with decision, 'Right. We will. Now let's go and see what it's like out there. Will the climate have changed?'

They had altered the route again by the time they left the building. Why not see India on the way? they asked each other as they thumped excitedly down the three flights of steps. India, they said, walking down the hill to Marcus's car, via Freemantle, to see ma. A cold wind was blowing. Beth wore a coat, and put both hands in the pockets as she turned her face to Marcus and spoke with sly amazement of Jammu and Kashmir, Jaipur and

Mount Abu. She felt she was physically growing, swelling, with this entirely unexpected delight in walking down the street at Marcus's side. Looking at his face as she said, Tanjore, Pondicherry, she could see that he too was possessed by the same lavish joy. Suddenly he gripped her shoulders and pulled them towards his own, and without pausing, and with the top half of her body half-shielding his, yet transcending awkwardness, they stepped downhill, laughing and saying, Bangalore, Hassan.

SEVEN •

<u>EXTENSION OF NOTES ON DREAM 22</u> = Always
provided, of course, that there is anything <u>in</u> this
business of commands in dreams, it does appear
that in "obeying" the first part of 22, I ought to
have paid more attention to the chair I couldn't
move. Dinner party not a disaster. No. Disasters at
least have some drama about them. Dinner party a
damn washout.
Ho-relation sent another Ho-relation to help. She
spoke a sort of birdy English and was quite quick
and skilled, and the ingredients I bought were
perfectly right, no compromises or making do,
which gave me that lucky feeling. It didn't last
through the cooking, since Beth chose that time to
ring me. Also the strain of listening to Ho-relation
birdy talk I couldn't <u>quite</u> comprehend. Once or
twice that wild lost feeling all cooks must control.
Did control it of course. Took myself in hand, told
Ho-relation no more talky-talky, and decided I had
no obligation to mention Beth's call to Miles, now or
ever. I am not a tittle-tattle. Clemmie and Conrad
came first and were marvellous as usual with the
drinks. Then Miles Victoria Bryan and Kate. And
me out of the kitchen, with my hair not quite right
but with a hold on myself and knowing the duck

perfect. Then to the table, and my lace, and the silver they all love and caress, camellias from the garden and truly that feeling of Aaaah as we sat down. Ho relation brought in little crabs and Aaaah again. Wine irreproachable and everything going swimmingly. And yes, duck perfect, and letdown could not have been caused by tart a mite hard. No, simply a dullness creeping over us, and worse because all of us straining to rise out of it, which we did of course, not being damn duds, but only up to a point. The Aaaah had gone. Expertise not the answer. It is the spirit, the damn spirit was wanting. When I went to make the coffee, which I trust NO Asian with, Miles came after me. He stood with me at the bench and said, It is her absence, Juliet. She defined us. I said, Oh Miles really. She did that to you, perhaps, but it is you who do that to us. But someone else will take her place, and we will get back to normal. He shook his head and said in voice of doom, No, Juliet, no one will take her place. After all my trouble, voice of doom. I was so enraged that I just burst out and said, Oh Miles you ARE A BORE. He said, actually WHISPERED, I seem to have lost my nerve. I was furious, I pretended not to hear. And when we took in the coffee I was still cross, and everyone noticed it, and bucked up no end for a while, until Miles's mood made itself felt, as only Miles's moods can, and down came that pall again.

They went. They went home. At the end I stopped pretending and almost shooed them out, laughing but wanting to say, Go, go. He was the last. I put my hand on his arm and said, Beth rang me today. She is nearly better, she has spent the week with her lover. He started to say something,

but I said, That is absolutely all I know. And then I
did say it. Go. Go. And I saw his back, as he hurried
to join Victoria, and he half-turned as if he wanted
to say something, but Victoria laughing pulled him
up the path between my darling camellia bushes. I
remembered Cable House, and how he kept all the
others away, and in the end forced me to sell. Yes
he did. He made me sell Cable House. When they all
went I hated him. The Ho-relation cleaning up
broke one of mother's dinner plates, and when she
showed me the pieces I just shrugged and said, But
of course. And after that she kept smiling at me and
tweeting and saying, So kind, so kind.

Mixed flowers would have been better. Camellias
so fixed and formal.

I couldn't sleep, of course not, and lying there
wondered if it is significant that I've had no dreams
since 22. In that book I tried to read, the green one,
it says science proves that we all dream every night,
but science is always changing its opinions, and I
can't help thinking that at least the shopgirl one
has some folksy wisdom.

I have just read 22 through very carefully. After
the part about trying to catch Solly-Beth, there is
that blank. Noticed I didn't have the bridle when
running up hill. Therefore, did I catch Solly-Beth in
that blank, and is the happiness, the soft green
grass, the snake that turns out to be only a fish, and
the beautiful swimming, so cool and silent, does all
that stand for my reward for obeying the voice, and
during that blank, catching Solly-Beth?

I realise that I am over-tired, but there are times
when any guidance is better than none. When I
learned that John had not survived, and that
Daddy's affairs were in such a mess, I let Fergie

93

take over, take me over, and I must say I never regretted it. And since Fergie died, I have rather looked to Miles.

It is the figure. It is the figure at one's side. It is nothing else. It is the figure. And since the fright I had with John, not being ostracised exactly, but there was humiliation, Fergie was perfect.

I have put so much into the group, first for Miles, then for us all. And now I ask what I would have without them. Answer = My bridge people, who are quite sweet, bless them. And my family. Yes, the damn McCrackens, and although, naturally, I have the greatest respect, and hope I shall always do my duty, the only damn one I give a hoot about is Aunt Bobbie, and Andrew slightly. But Aunt Bob has just had another of her tiny strokes, and it is only a matter of time, and not much of it, and as for Andrew, he seems quite pleased to be taken up by the glitterati, to whose level I shall never, please God, never descend.

Miles would keep coming, of course, alone.

Clemmie would come occasionally, I believe.

All groups break up sooner or later. It is a law of nature, though when I said that to Miles, after Philip and Gilda deserted, he said that laws of nature may be resisted, and that groups, like marriages, could be kept together by commitment and hard work. Now that those two have gone, he said, we have a very promising nucleus. That was just after he met Beth.

Fergie used to say my character had "crystallised" in the fourth form. He used to talk to me about business problems. Now Juliet, he used to say, let us have some of those machinations of the fourth form, uncorrupted by intelligence or education. He really was a toad.

Heaven knows, I am no authority on sexual attraction, but when it is blatantly displayed, as with Fergie and that big-headed Korean lad, and as when that man ran round grinning and threw Beth's bag into his car, and Beth bent to get in, yes, then it doesn't escape even me.

I see that man clearly. Aunt Bob would say, Not exactly common BUT. And the car was – well – and that was a week ago, and perhaps now, or in another week or two, she will be glad to come back to us. And then we would see if Miles would have her back. As for Miles "losing his nerve", I do not for a moment believe it.

Reflecting on the dream is only a way into the problem. That's what the books should tell us. And who knows if my "reward", the lovely swimming and so on, was not earned by my throwing down the bridle and leaving Solly-Beth alone. Alternatives are so confusing.

Wait and see. Time will tell.

When my damn hair isn't right, nothing is right. They'll have to fit me in before I go to see Aunt Bob. I'll ask for Carmen this time. Vincent treats me as he does all the old ones, like a slightly naughty pet dog. Vincent does not distinguish. He does not have the nous.

Barbara Philp – née McCracken – propped on her pillows, looked through her thick spectacles at the little dish Juliet was displaying. On this latest, most extended, most reluctant of her visits to her home country, Barbara Philp had turned her chair away from the window, saying there was nothing out there she wanted to see. She said to Juliet, 'Your crème caramel. Well, put it in the – ' She waved towards the kitchen. 'If I don't eat it, Mrs Silver will.'

'Is she good, Aunt Bob?'

'What, she does what's necessary, you know. Lorna and Matthew got her from that angel place. You ring up.'

'Dial-an-angel.'

'Ff, I suppose so. Quite a civil little woman.'

'But?' enquired Juliet.

'Yes, but but but,' said Barbara Philp, laughing. 'Her food, you know.'

Returning from the kitchen with the vase for the flowers she had brought, Juliet said, 'Is there any food you would especially like?'

'Broth. Made with good gravy beef and a marrow bone. Put to one side of the wood stove.'

'Those big hot kitchens,' said Juliet, unwrapping her flowers, 'with pepperina trees in the windows.'

'Mother's Mrs Hope used to put in one bay leaf and one small onion. She was positively snobbish about cooks who put in a big onion. Ff. Those are from your own garden.'

'Yes,' said Juliet, satisfied with her hands arranging the flowers.

'They look it. Thank you. Those native flowers were brought by Miles Silver. Oh-oh-oh, Ligard. That's one of the old names. They don't often desert.'

'No,' said Juliet, seeming to be worried only for the flowers under her hands.

'Ligard. Ligard. Matthew and Lorna Ligard came. Then Miles Ligard came. Though it's naive to think that repetition will help. I find it best to fix on something from the start, and just say that, and then sometimes the right name comes. This time when they desert I look quickly at those picture frames and say Silver. Better than last time,' said Barbara Philp, laughing, 'when everyone was Clock. Your hair looks ravishing, my dear – '

Juliet leaned across the flowers and kissed her aunt's cheek. 'Juliet,' she whispered.

Her aunt laughed. 'Juliet.'

'I've just had it done.'

'I don't care for it, Juliet, the desertion of the names.'

'They came back last time, Aunt Bob.'

'Up to a point.'

'When did Miles visit you? Miles Ligard.'

'Yes, Miles. First his parents came. Matthew and Lorna came first. Two or three days ago. Matthew is still a good-looking man. But not a patch on his father. At my wedding I looked up at Matthew's father and thought, I wouldn't mind you as well. But that little Lorna is a duffer. Snivelling and whining because Miles has lost some little girl. Matthew told Lorna to stop worrying about it, but I told her to go on. At least it was a bit of gossip. Better than all that insipid caring and supporting. Fff. I suppose you know about it.'

'Yes. The girl's name is Beth. She's very sweet, but Miles will get over it.'

'That's what Matthew and I said, but Lorna said it was like that breakdown he had at school.'

'I don't know all about *that*.'

'Why should you? It was nothing. He had a, you know, a thing on a boy. A lad of his own age, and when the boy went on to someone else, he had that so-called breakdown. It was a, you know, a *fixation*, like you had on what's-his-name – I'm sorry – John. Who was really, you know, hardly presentable.'

'Go on about Miles, Aunt Bob.'

'He brought those bush flowers. He does everything

so well, you know. The entrance, the flowers, the kiss, the chat. And he must know I have only my annuity. Mrs Silver was almost licking his boots.'

'Yes, but go on about – '

'And isn't he wonderful at the funerals? He has only to appear to make everything seem so – how shall I put it – '

'Seemly.'

'Seemly. Thank you. And ceremonial. That's what Miles is good at. The ceremonies. I made him promise to come to mine. He said in that case I mustn't die while he is in London. I suppose Matthew will put me in. And the ancients will come – I can see them – out of the last of the nests of gentlefolk – and the young who like to do the right thing. You will come.'

'I am not young,' said Juliet, laughing.

'But you do like to do the right thing. And Matthew won't say a word about the scandals and bankruptcies and divorces. He will excuse them by saying something ridiculous like, She had the gift of life.'

'Aunt Bob! He wouldn't be so banal.'

'Nothing surprises me in this country,' muttered her aunt.

'I wish you would tell me about Miles's breakdown at school.'

'Fff, in my opinion it was nothing to fuss about. I remember it well. It was when I had to come back to sell Werrindoo Downs. He stayed in bed. Wouldn't do anything, got very fat – '

'*Fat!*'

'Fat as a tub. And at the same time he had that, you know, acne. And if anyone came to the house he used to hide, I remember. He fell behind a full year at school. All he did was read, Russians and so on. Matthew and Lorna did it, you know. They did that to him. They brought him up to be too tightly controlled and idealistic. Lucky for him he met your Fergie.'

'He was still idealistic.'

'What, he was sensible. No more singles for him, but groups, always groups.'

'But he made an ideal of that,' said Juliet. 'Would you like me to put his flowers in another vase?'

'Leave those flowers alone,' said Barbara Philp sharply.

Juliet let the bracts and grasses drop back into the wide vase, and her hands back into her lap. 'I didn't know he was making an ideal of Beth. I thought his intention to marry her was simply sensible.'

'What, yes, very sensible. Not the best choice, according to Lorna, but good in the, you know, circumstances. The girl's mother died young, but not of disease, she was killed on one of those dreadful glaring highways you have in this country. He inspected the family. Extremely fecund. Not like you and me, my dear – '

'Juliet.'

'Juliet. Your Fergie was a devil, Juliet.'

'Yes,' said Juliet absently.

'No one was safe – '

'Except me.'

' – and your first was hardly presentable.'

'I loved them both,' said Juliet.

'You've got that off pat, haven't you. Yet you do go on about being frigid.'

'Yes,' said Juliet calmly.

'Frigid women are over-possessive,' said Barbara Philp, 'in my experience.'

'Please, darling Aunt Bob,' said Juliet, 'don't tell me all Mother's stories. Not about my jealous screaming fits, please, nor how I refused to share my toys. One does grow up. I suppose those roses came from Andrew.'

'Yes. Thoroughly dull, aren't they?'

'Horrid. Rosebuds were never meant to be wrapped so tightly. They look like some nasty Japanese food.'

'And he always sends so many. You should have seen Mrs Silver's face. Still, Andrew is the one I wish would visit.'

'Aunt Bob! When you say he's so vulgar.'

'So he is. But he's jolly. I would like a visit from someone jolly,' complained Barbara Philp, 'and not someone like you and Lorna and Matthew, all worried about this girl, and not having the manners to hide it.'

'But Miles did,' said Juliet in alarm. 'Miles hid it.'

'What, with me he did,' grumbled her aunt, 'but after Mrs Donnelly let him out, she looked out of the window, and saw him bent over the wheel of his car, and she said she could tell he was crying, and that he had a weight on his mind even when he was here.'

'Oh, but women like that always say things like that.'

'True, they are inclined – Juliet, Juliet, Donnelly, Donnelly. I got the name right. Donnelly.'

Juliet put the palms of her hands together, partly concealing her worried face. 'There you are, Aunt Bob. They are coming back.'

Across the road from Barbara Philp's flat was a narrow park, and beyond that, the harbour on which she had turned her back. Juliet, in the red telephone box beside the park, listening to Lorna, then to Matthew, watched through the glass panels children on a play structure in the park, and even as she widened her eyes in alarm at what she heard, she approved the determination of one small boy as he climbed, slid, crawled, swung, and jostled other small bodies out of their places in the queue.

'He's a bit young for me, anyway,' said Kyrie.

She tossed the bowler hat, with the bangles in its crown, into the bedroom as she and Beth passed the open door. It landed on the bed, the bangles hardly jingling. In the kitchen she said flatly, 'Coffee.'

'You see,' said Beth, slowly sitting, 'you called him Mark.'

'And the connection never occurred to you.'

'Kyrie, believe me, not once.'

'Not when you caught my eye as you left with him, and looked away so fast?'

Beth drew her eyebrows together, thinking of other occasions when her instinct had grasped the whole, leaving her slow reason to laboriously assemble the components. She said, 'It did not enter my mind.'

'Right, forget it. With him and me it was partly business anyway. We bounce ideas off each other. I want to expand. I thought of him for sales.'

'He's not a salesman.'

'Born to sell. Get him to tell you about being the rep for those false fingernails.'

Beth did not like Kyrie's reminiscent laugh. She said, 'Next March or April, we're going to London, via India.'

'Six months to go? You expect it to last that long? With Marco. The joy-boy?'

Feeling her face flush, Beth dropped her eyes and said stubbornly, 'I won't be surprised if it doesn't.'

'Won't you?' Kyrie put coffee in front of Beth, sat down opposite, and lit a cigarette. 'Best cosmetic there is,' she said softly. 'What do you *really* expect?'

'Nothing but what we have. Though I hope that next March or April, we'll go away, as I said.'

'Nothing after that?'

'We'll see how we feel then.'

Kyrie smoked for a while, then said, 'Beth, whatever

you do, don't give up your flat.'

'Of course I won't. Where else would I live? Marcus and I have agreed to cool it, take it easy for a while.'

'I want to remind you of something.'

'What?'

'Eight days ago, it was Miles, Miles, Miles.'

'You can't compare this and that. That was only compatibility.'

'Oh, really!'

'As it turned out.'

'Will you see Miles?'

'Well, it's over.'

'What about the others you were so wrapped in?'

'I rang Juliet yesterday. I guess I'll ring her again soon.'

'Right, don't drop everyone, Beth. I did that once. Big mistake. Drop me, though, for a while, please.'

'Oh, Kyrie – '

'Just till the worm stops gnawing. It never takes long. I'll get down to serious work on those qualifications. In eighteen months I'll be a sound engineer.' Kyrie put out her cigarette. 'It serves me right, anyway, for getting personal about sex.'

Ah-ha, said Nicole and Angela. This is the way it always happens. First you leave your bathrobe there, then your gel and bodywash, then your raincoat ... Nicole and Angela let fall that they had a friend, Kate, who would be glad to move in when Beth followed her things to this mysterious lover's place.

'Don't you dare,' said Beth. 'This is where I live. I've learned from you two how quickly these things can end.'

'As long as you're quite happy with the way you're handling it,' said Nicole.

'I'll be sleeping at home for the next three nights. For sure. He and I agreed on that.'

'Your period,' said Angela.

'Not my period,' said Beth fiercely. 'My common sense, advising moderation. And *his* common sense, too.'

On the second night, Beth, unable to sleep, stood at the window watching the winter rain. Marcus rang at midnight.

'Oh, Bethie, this is bloody silly.'

Beth, leaning against the wall, hearing the ache in his voice, could not reply. He said, as if on sudden inspiration, 'Beth! Ten minutes! I'll come and get you.'

In ten minutes, the drizzle had become a downpour. Beth, without a raincoat, took from the hall cupboard the plastic bag Nicole's new upholstered chair had come in. She waited in the porch until she saw the headlamps of Marcus's car, then enveloped herself in the bag and ran, pointing forward with her fingers to let in some air.

There was room for two in the bag. From Marcus's car they ran in unison, each with arms extended and fingers peaking the plastic. In his room, they struggled out of the steaming bag, kicked off their wet shoes, and dropped, clammy and fully dressed, to the mattress, where Beth quickly plucked her pants loose, then hooked them off with her toes.

Nothing had yet equalled this grave, unerring, silent act. A pair of blue shoes, an umbrella, and a pullover followed Beth's other things to Marcus's room. At her own flat, she often encountered Kate. Kate even looked like Nicole and Angela: a tall soft conservative young woman who often stroked her own hands, or held them at a distance to scrutinise their attitudes. One day Beth found Kate inspecting her room. 'I simply adore your Hockney, Beth,' said Kate kindly. But it was Beth who felt an intruder. Behind the kindly tones, the aloof amusement, of all three, she sensed disgust. When Marcus heard of a bigger flat in a building nearby, Beth packed the rest of her things and ordered a taxi truck.

Packing, she came across the cameo brooch Juliet had given her. Her immediate impulse to return it defined the formerly unacknowledged condition on which it had been given to her. It was Miles's wife who would have worn Juliet's grandmother's cameo. As she put it in its velvet-lined case, ready to return, she experienced an overflow of tenderness in which she wanted to lay her cheek against Juliet's cheek, and to hold Miles's head, in understanding of all his deceit and frustration, against her breast. She went at once to the phone in the hall and dialled Juliet's number; but there was no reply, and the repetition of the hooting melodious bell rebuked her mood, so that she was pleased, after all, to ring off.

EIGHT ·

The flat Beth and Marcus rented was again in an old building, again on the third floor; but as it was further south, the trains were seldom audible, and nor, through its stouter structure, were the other tenants, except for the cough of their immediate neighbour, which they supposed would be as temporary as Beth's had proved to be.

Perhaps it was an addition to the building; there was an improvised look about it. The long narrow living room reminded them of a foyer. Three steps led up to it from the hall, and at its other end, one step led down to a kitchen, a bathroom, and a small bedroom. From the long room they overlooked, through a continuous strip of windows above a broad window sill, the roofs of Darlinghurst and the conglomerate buildings of St Vincent's Hospital. In the blank wall opposite the windows they could imagine curtained entrances to a cinema, or a bank of elevators, but behind it, the neighbour coughed.

While they were buying the necessities not supplied, they saw a red geranium in a terracotta pot, and simultaneously coveted it for the window sill. The nursery man remarked that it would need a warm sunny spot, but they chose not to hear him. They knew no winter sun would enter those southern windows, but in their covetousness they trusted that for this geranium, an exception would be made. They put it on the end of the window sill nearer the front door, where, by providing a focal point for the broad view, it pulled it in, and made it their own.

A Telecom man came and put the phone on the other end of the window sill. Chairs were drawn up to a blue cuboid table inclined to move on its castors, but were turned just as often to the window sill. Coffee and tea mugs were set down there. The bowls of wine glasses collected and miniaturised rooftops and lines of clothes drying on balconies. Big ashtrays were put there for Andy and Kirk.

Mil, Kirk, Andy, and Stathos came. Mil, with his girl Annette, and the others, with varying girls, observed Beth while pretending not to. Beth had put away most of her dresses and all of her Victorian jewellery except for Juliet's cameo, which was still in its box, in her bag, ready to return. Now she usually wore jeans, with a shirt or pullover, and sometimes a necklace of lacquered papier mâché leaves. She had made this herself, but it had been regarded coolly by Miles.

Kirk and Stathos were engineering students, though Kirk had lately been earning money as a clothes model and in television advertising. Mil was a part-time design student who also worked with his father, a Czech house-painter. Annette was a printer's proof reader, but all the other girls were travellers, working only until a courier's job turned up, or they had saved another fare.

Beth learned that Marcus, Mil, Kirk, Andy, and Stathos had come together in the rock band at Brigden High, and had remained united by their sharing an amazed conviction that the world was governed by solemn lunatics. Nor did they see any hope of themselves escaping the general lunacy. Once they had come to the conclusion that whatever they did, however they wriggled and protested, they would be squeezed or shepherded into the mass of sober lunatics, they had stopped working in the idealistic causes, the peace and anti-uranium movements, and had declared their interest only in this waiting, this space, this meantime. All had been at the party in the warehouse.

At first Beth wondered if there was something quelling about her, in her role of Marcus's companion. They, and the girls, were awkward and quiet with her, and she with them, by contagion. Then one night, when they were sitting about drinking wine, Andy described how his father, after a quarrel with Andy's Malaysian mother, had called her a black whore, and had gone out, got into his car, and driven it into an embankment. Andy was haunted by the question of whether his father had meant to kill himself, or only to go back to the pub. Andy cried, and listened gratefully to the opinions of the others, which strongly favoured accident, as it had been Andy's father's practice, after a quarrel, to go back to the pub. Then Beth was moved to tell them of the fate of Debbie Youdall, and the questions it had left in her mind, and how Doctor Gelthartz had tried to persuade her that Debbie was more likely to have been forced or tricked into entering her murderer's car than to have entered it of her own accord. Looking round the circle of engrossed faces, she repeated Doctor Gelthartz's opinion that it was better for Beth herself to accept the more reasonable solution than to keep injuring herself with the one less likely.

All her audience agreed. They said that everyone had to live somehow, and asked, Why be hard on yourself? Marcus said, 'You've never told me about this shrink.'

Beth drew a deep breath, then smiled. As with Miles, so with Marcus: there was always something she lacked time or opportunity to say. She said with relief, 'I am telling you now.'

So drinking and talk drew Beth in. The game in the warehouse, which they had never been able to explain to her, had its counterparts here in the burlesques, led by Kirk, of the TV ads he appeared in. These were disciplined, excesses being checked by hisses, thumbs turned down, or cries of *Too far, too far*.

'Too far,' Beth heard herself chanting. 'Too far.' Beth enjoyed the relaxation of the drunken state. One night they made a little music, a drum and a clarinet. The coughing neighbour banged on the wall. As Beth joined in the mirthful shouted reply, it occurred to her that she had joined the jeering society.

When alone, or at her drafting table at work, Beth often found herself wanting to discuss them with Miles. In all such imaginary discussion, she was defensive of them. She would have liked him to understand them. She wanted him to be invisibly present, watching, when she and Mil painted a cinema door on the long wall opposite the windows. Mil was an experienced street painter. In a week, there appeared the half-curtained door, the dummy in the stove-pipe pants taking a ticket from a girl, who bent slightly as she entered, and, in the dim interior, the suggestion of seated patrons, the nearest of whom held to his mouth the tent of a big white handkerchief.

Though the neighbour no longer coughed.

Beth also found herself, at work, silently telling Miles about the commune at Toomba. It had become clear that the cohort was very familiar with Toomba. They had heard about the river, the mud slides, the leeches, the fires, the lanterns bobbing in the dark night, and the time – the time to spare, the talk going on and on.

'And the quarrels,' said Stathos.

'Yeah-yeah,' mourned Marcus.

'And the split-ups,' said Kirk. 'Like when you share a house, and every time it fails, you feel so rotten.'

Recalling Miles's need to share, Beth said, 'If there's such a longing, there must be a way.'

'Submission,' said Marcus. 'My father said, in one of those lectures he used to write to me, that submission is the way.'

'But he means God,' protested Mil.

'Yeah-yeah.'

Marcus and Beth were saving money towards their journey. They had enthusiastic swings away from their intended destination. Fired by the wandering girls, they would change it to Argentina, China, West Africa, and for a few days would feed this new passion with brochures and information, until Marcus's talk of his father, and Beth's of her mother, would revive their original destination: to England, via Freemantle, to see ma.

In the small bedroom, Beth put her Afghan prayer rug beside the bed to cover the thin area of carpet where other feet had reached down on innumerable mornings. The only window looked into a bathroom in the building next door; they bought a white paper shade and kept it always drawn. Ribbed paper also covered the light hanging from the ceiling. Beth, waking at night, would look up at this white sphere, would hear Marcus breathing beside her, and would feel such a profound yet aerial satisfaction that she wondered (half-asleep) why they wanted to go anywhere.

The bed was high and old-fashioned. Marcus called it a genuine quadruped. Its original wire had been replaced with boards, and on its wide solid mattress, Marcus and Beth continued the explorations and loving exertions which fuelled their life together. Beneath the bed, they stowed their suitcases and cartons. Beth's dresses were there, and so were her cartons of books. She thought of her books with a passive affection. They were like a hearth in a house she owned; they would always be there, waiting.

There, in wine cartons, were her architectural works, her mythologies, her novels, her childhood copies of Lewis Carroll and May Gibbs, the beautiful edition of *The Golden Bough* given to her by Miles, and the paperbacks on Art Nouveau presented one Christmas by Clem and Conrad. Beth reflected with pleasure on their differing sizes and weights, their cover designs, the markers she had left in them, but was never tempted to kneel by the bed and draw them out.

Though their references in common had expanded, they still often returned, on the high bed, to their first meeting in the cloister. Under cover of prompting Marcus's memory, Beth indulged in surmise on the two children, the stone animals, the parents and stepparents, the two paths bisecting the ground of the cloister, and at their junction, the rhino's head raised against the blue sky. But when she suggested that she and Marcus, in their care for each other now, were compensating for the lack of care shown for them then, Marcus lost his playful indulgence and said that she spoke without regard for the facts, that he had not been neglected at all, and that ma was all right.

Marcus discovered a few photographs in a big envelope and showed them to Beth. Here was Nita, wearing a mini-skirt and very high heels, walking in profile, smiling along one shoulder. Here was his father, alone, an exceptionally handsome man, serious and aggressive. And here Marcus, eleven, stood with Gavin, both in shorts, each holding a fish by the tail. There were none of Toomba.

'Good,' said Beth. 'Green paradises are best kept away from the light.'

'There are lots of them somewhere. Ma must have them.'

Beth had left her carefully assembled childhood albums at the house in Melbourne, and had put away, with the books, all photographs of Miles, Juliet, Clem and Conrad and the others. Beth was learning that physical intimacy engenders its own little pockets of privacy: she did not avoid saying Miles's name, but pronounced it with an airiness, a detachment – as, she noticed – Marcus pronounced Kyrie's name. She showed Marcus the few photographs she wanted him to see: her grandmother; herself at fifteen, standing beside a *trompe l'oeil* mural she had painted on her bedroom wall; and, last, her mother at twenty-one, wearing a dress with a frilled collar.

'Don't you think she has an enigmatic face?'

'No,' said Marcus, 'She looks exactly like you.'

(Miles had said, 'She left herself behind, Beth.')

Beth took the photograph from Marcus. 'I see that, yes. But one moment she seems to be looking straight at me, telling me something, and in the next moment, there's nothing.' She held the photograph at arm's length and said, 'Her name was Cynthia.'

The only other photograph she showed him was one sent recently by Judy, showing the latest additions to the house in Melbourne. It had once been a big bungalow with jutting porches, but was now a square two-storeyed house with cars parked about it at impulsive angles.

Marcus had sent his mother a card. Beth and he had chosen it together. But Beth had not written to or rung her father since before her break with Miles. She took pleasure in her unashamed neglect, as if she needed this proof of her independence from them. When Bill rang her at work, and rebuked her, she coolly replied that she was quite all right, and that she could always be rung at work if she were needed for anything, though she could not imagine what thing that could be. Her neglect of Juliet McCracken caused her more discomfort. She recalled Juliet's many kindnesses, especially her pampering of that sprained wrist, and the cameo, in its box in her bag, its return postponed every day, was a constant reminder.

At that time, talk of aids and other sexually transmitted diseases was gathering momentum. Aids dominated. Sensationalism throve, and was resisted with much mockery by the cohort. But one night, Mil and Annette arrived, after having met, in the street outside, one of the class at Brigden High. He was a heroin addict. He told them he had aids. When Annette and Mil commiserated, he shrugged and said it wasn't bad yet. 'I keep forgetting I have it.'

'Keeps forgetting he has it,' they all repeated, with horror and amusement.

When Marcus and Beth had been living together for three weeks, a television programme on the crossover of aids into the heterosexual community provoked another outbreak of jeering in the foyer-like room. At its height, Stathos proposed to Mil that he paint a few black spots on the face of the cinema attendant. There were immediate cries of, 'Too far! Too far!' Then there were silences, and desultory talk with undertones of sullenness, until presently Andy and Mil said they wouldn't mind going over to Albion Street and taking the test.

Beth and Marcus, because it was rumoured that certified freedom from aids would soon be a passport requirement, went with them. All gave a sample of blood, and were told that the results would be known in about a week. All were questioned about their sexual history. Marcus was kept longest and questioned most closely. As he and Beth walked home, his amusement gave way to offendedness.

'They kept going on at me about men.'

'They must have thought they had a reason,' said Beth.

'In that case, why me, and not you?'

He was truculent now. Beth said, 'Because they believed

what I told them. About Miles.' She gave the name its usual cool distance. 'My man said that if Miles told me he was celibate, apart from me, it was likely to be the truth. He said responsible people don't lie about it.'

'Then my guy can't have thought I was a responsible person. I told him I had never been with a man, but then he kept coming back to the general promiscuity.'

'I suppose so.'

'Right, you needn't sound so smug.'

'Smug!' echoed Beth in anger.

'Yes, smug. The general promiscuity was a great thing while it lasted. Especially the group sex, if you must have the details.'

'I mustn't,' said Beth with ferocity.

'Why, what's wrong with them? Kyrie – ' He pronounced the name with force ' – Kyrie used to be in it.'

'I see.'

'No, you don't, or you wouldn't use that tone. Right, it's over for all but the crazies. So okay, goodbye. But nobody knows how good it was for those few years, nobody who wasn't there.'

They did not speak, or even look at each other, for the rest of that day. When Beth felt him near her, her joints turned stiff, as if made of metal. That night, he slept on a li-lo below the broad window sill, while Beth, alone in the wide bed, tried to keep her lids lowered over dry burning eyes. At work next day, she again bent low over her drafting table, and spoke only when spoken to. Then, on the way home, she started to shake with a fury she had never experienced before, a subtle trembling throughout her body. Marcus was the object of this fury, but her pride diverted it from him. She would set him contemptuously aside; she would pack her things and leave. If she failed to find a hotel, Juliet would not refuse her. She ran up the three steps from the hall, and opened the door just as he mounted the single step from the kitchen, a paring knife in his hand. He dropped the knife onto the window sill and came towards her in the half-dark of the long room saying, 'Beth – ' She threw her keys at him and retreated to the other side of the cuboid table. As they dodged around this table, Marcus coaxing, Beth furious, it shifted, running this way and that on its castors, like a third person in the dispute. Marcus began to laugh, which weakened him, and incensed Beth into kicking the table aside and running at him with pummelling fists, as she had once done in the room. But as soon as she touched him, laughter entered her cries. She put both arms around him. The metal left her joints, and as she stood in his embrace, choking with laughter and tears, she saw, in swift recollection, his figure coming up from the kitchen, his eyes pleading, his mouth saying, 'Beth,' and his hand instinctively, prudently, casting the knife away. She took a deep sobbing breath and said, 'You shouldn't have told me.'

'What? I don't have any damn disease, Beth.'

'No, about Kyrie.'

'Not the aids thing, then?'

'I didn't even think of it.'

The tests showed none of them to be antibody positive. Nor were any of them advised to return for later tests. Andy and Mil were abashed at having taken them.

It was now more than five weeks since the party in the warehouse, three weeks since they had moved into the flat. Beth had not had a period, but assured Marcus that it was often late. It was true that it had been late four or five times, and moreover, having grown up hearing the cheerful catalogue of Judy's early symptoms, she knew she had none of them. She let another week pass before taking a walk, alone this time, south-east and uphill, to the Women's Hospital in Paddington, where she was given another test, and learned that she was pregnant.

'Possibly five weeks,' she told Marcus that night. 'It must have been when I was so sick with flu. I was certain I took a pill every day, but I must have missed a day. Or perhaps this is what comes of pinching them, instead of having them prescribed.'

She was disturbed because he stood immobile, his arms hanging, as if clowning incomprehension, though she sensed that he was not. 'It might delay us going,' she said. 'We must find out what it costs.'

'What what costs?'

'Well,' she said, 'the abortion.'

It was hard for her to understand how much he wanted the baby. She had never seen him so serious before. After she dubiously agreed to consider it, if he would only stop talking, and give her some time to think, he became practical. With the same business-like zeal with which he had cleared the back of his car, and bought food, champagne, medicine, and pink light globes, he rang the aids clinic for information about transmission to infants. He took careful notes, read them to Beth, and put it to her that the first thing she must do was to get Miles's solemn assurance, in these changed circumstances, of his celibacy as a homosexual. He pronounced Miles's name with a restraint like Beth's own, but was solemn himself when he spoke of that solemn assurance, and would not laugh when Beth assumed a slow deep voice, and went around intoning, 'I want your *solemn assurance*!'

NINE •

Beth laid a cheek against Juliet's cheek, and then, leaving a hand in Juliet's two hands, submitted to scrutiny. Juliet, she saw, respected her face, approved her familiar tweed jacket, and snubbed her jeans. Marcus, at Beth's side, having acknowledged introductions, was now poised to depart with Andy and Mil. They all stood in the street, where Juliet had once again accosted Beth as she came out of work.

'We'll be at the Regent,' said Juliet to Marcus, while retaining Beth's hand. 'You could pick Beth up in your little car.'

Beth supposed Juliet's suddenly flustered look to have been caused by her catching herself out in the unimaginative assumption (often pointed out by Miles) that everyone had a car. She said, 'Marcus doesn't bring his car into the city,' and to Marcus she said, 'See you at home.'

'So kind of him to let me carry you off without notice,' said Juliet, releasing Beth's hand as they watched Marcus speed away with Andy and Mil. 'Is Mal the dark one?'

'No, that's Andy. His mother's Malaysian. And it's not Mal. It's Mil. Short for Milan.'

'Well, Marcus is a good name. You don't object to the Regent? I suppose you know any number of fascinating little ethnic restaurants.'

'Not around here,' said Beth kindly.

'Then it will have to be the poor old Regent. Your jeans don't matter. You're with me.'

In the luxurious restaurant of the Regent Hotel, then about three years old, they read their menus. Juliet said, 'You can depend on their fish. I must apologise for routing you out at work, but I felt I had to see you.'

'I'm the one who ought to apologise,' said Beth. 'Every day I've meant to ring you. Not the lobster. They scream while they're being cooked.'

'Only neurotics can hear. Speaking of which, though the connection is ludicrous, Miles has had some sort of breakdown.'

'Yes, I *said* breakdown,' said Juliet with irritation, as Beth raised her head from the menu and began to echo the word. 'Just listen, would you, please? Miles says it's because of the break with you, but now it emerges that he had it before, as a schoolboy. It takes the form of an extreme listlessness, an inability to act. He calls it Oblomovism, after some lazy hound in a Russian novel. But I persuaded him to see my cousin Paul, and he's taking some little pills, and is getting better every day. I'm afraid I had to be more intrusive than I would have liked. Or than an old spare godmother ought to be. But what could I do? If he had gone to some sort of hospital, it would have got around in no damn time, and I couldn't allow him just to lie about in his flat, it was too sordid for words, and you know what his parents' house is like.'

Beth, still astonished, watching Juliet's face, noting her unusually belligerent tone, said absently, 'Yes, it's very glum.'

'Quite. So I took him in. And he is supposed to have the flu. And I do believe I have made him comfortable.'

'I'm certain you have,' said Beth with admiration, recalling her pampered wrist. The waiter was standing beside them. 'I'll have ocean trout, Juliet.' Beth was reaching sideways into her bag to extract the cameo in its little padded box. When the waiter had turned away, she passed it to Juliet. 'I know you'll understand, Juliet. I want to return this.'

'I certainly don't understand.' Juliet took out the cameo and held it between a thumb and forefinger. 'You don't often see such an example. It's the quality of the shell. Beth, Miles wants to see you. He has been begging me to ask you to see him, and of course, not understanding his strange paralysis, I've been telling him to ask you himself. But once I understood that it was psychosomatic, as they call it, I agreed, and here I am.'

'Well, I'm so pleased,' said Beth, 'because I want to see him, too.'

'Oh?'

'I rang him last night, but of course he wasn't there.'

'I shan't ask why you want to see him, Beth. Though in the circumstances perhaps I am entitled to. But I shan't conceal from you, Beth, that in my opinion, it would do more harm than good, and now that he is recovering so nicely, I was counting on you to refuse.' Juliet put the cameo back into its box and pushed it with a forefinger towards Beth. 'My gifts are unconditional, and I must say I feel damn insulted that you could think otherwise.' The wine waiter was at her side. 'Oh,' she said crossly, 'this Petaluma chardonnay.'

'I can't have much,' said Beth, as the waiter moved away, 'because I'm pregnant.'

'Goodness gracious,' whispered Juliet. She pushed the box aside. 'Does that mean you intend to have it?' And she repeated in an incredulous whisper, '*Have* it?'

'I don't know,' said Beth.

'I thought you girls these days just toddled off and had little terminations.'

118

'So did I,' said Beth. 'I just took it for granted. But Marcus opposed it.'

'What damn cheek,' said Juliet. 'It's your body.'

'I said that, too. But Marcus said the baby in there is half his. And he's so determined about it – I couldn't believe it. And I can't help but be influenced. Have you noticed that when anyone wants anything very passionately, and persists in wanting it against all the sensible arguments, that it turns sense on its head? And it starts to seem reasonable to give it to them?'

'I can't say I have. In fact, it reminds me of the tales a very dear friend of mine tells me. Liz Ballard. She works for victims of rape or some such thing.'

'I see what you mean. Yes, it's easy to imagine, just for that one second, giving in.'

'Not easy for me, I'm glad to say.'

'Of course, your frigidity,' said Beth, smiling. But she wondered if Juliet's proclamations were, after all, true, and if she had really spent a life unhampered by a part of her being that wished only to be subjugated by love. She said carefully, 'But we're not talking about rape, or forcible seduction. We're talking about being asked to have a baby, and being able to refuse.'

Juliet looked down at her lap, moved the rings on her fingers. 'It's all very mysterious, I must say.' But she spoke now in a mild and thoughtful tone. 'What does Marcus do?'

'He's a computer operator,' said Beth, laughing. 'But he's had so many jobs, I've lost count. He was an international courier, that's what he liked best. He liked moving about. But now he says he will change. Now he's talking about opportunities in sales, and a retail outlet.'

'A retail outlet,' said Juliet, as if pronouncing a foreign language.

'A shop. And I would keep working. Your nephew

doesn't sack women for pregnancy or motherhood.'

'They don't, these days. How old is Marcus?'

'Twenty. Twenty-one in December.

'You are both only twenty.' Juliet, silent, abstracted, laid a hand on her left cheek and surveyed the restaurant. 'Well,' she said then, as if slowly drawing the words from the air, 'they say the healthiest and most clever and beautiful babies are born to young parents.'

'I saw all my halfbrothers when they were babies,' said Beth, 'and I don't think that's true.'

'All the same,' said Juliet, still in that remote reflective voice, 'what a charming sight it is, a young married couple with a baby.'

'Nobody mentioned marriage.'

'A young couple with a baby,' said Juliet, without variation of tone. 'When is it to be born?'

'Juliet, it isn't decided that it will be.'

'How can you say that?'

'Only without thinking,' said Beth, worried. 'It does sound . . .'

'Surely you've had enough time to decide.'

'One week?'

'Obey your heart.'

'My heart is strangely silent. I ask myself if it remembers all those years of watching Judy.'

'Well, I suppose I'm a sentimental old thing. Having been deprived myself, and babies being such a feature of my dreams.'

'Because you see them all the time, in shops, strapped into cars . . . Debris from the day before. Remember? You'll dream of them tonight, because of this talk.'

Juliet said softly, 'They are so hard to capture, just lately.'

'Do you still write them down?'

'Good heavens no! What do you take me for? You agreed

with me about the debris, I think. Spreading your sweet reason, which you proceeded to throw overboard a week or so later.'

'I did. I did, too,' said Beth, laughing and blushing.

'And do you regret it?'

'I'll never regret it,' said Beth seriously, 'whatever happens.'

'I've thrown overboard some of that dream theory. We overestimate reason. Look at how beautiful the loss of yours has made you look.'

'Oh, Juliet, don't say I've lost my reason. Not now, when I need it so badly.'

'Certainly you must keep enough for practical matters. For example, where would Marcus and you and the baby live?'

Beth gave a slight grimace. Putting their circumstances before Juliet had begun to make the baby seem as absurd a notion as when Marcus had first proposed it. 'I expect we would manage,' she said.

Juliet again turned her head to survey the restaurant. 'I happen to own a few little houses,' she murmured, 'though none are vacant at present . . . Well, here is our fish.'

While they ate, Beth asked for news of Conrad and Clem, of Victoria and Bryan and Kate. She was slightly offended when Juliet answered her evasively, almost as if saying, *Keep out*. She *was* out, and though often affected by nostalgia, had accepted her expulsion, and was speaking of the group only as a route to Miles, as a preparation for telling Juliet bluntly, since Juliet had made her opposition so clear, that she must see Miles.

'But that's enough of the so-called group,' Juliet was saying now. 'I want to hear about Marcus. Where did you meet him?'

'In Rome,' said Beth, diverted at once, 'fourteen years ago.'

Juliet's amazement delighted her. She told the story in detail, and was still speaking when their plates were taken away, and their coffee brought. Juliet listened in silence, sometimes slightly shaking her head, sometimes dilating her eyes, until Beth put down her cup and said, 'And so – here we are today.'

'It's as if it were ordained,' said Juliet.

'I let myself think so now and again,' said Beth, 'as a luxury.'

'Does Marcus think so?'

'As a sort of joke. Except when I said that in every coincidence there is a message. He wouldn't have that even as a joke.'

'I have a problem with messages,' Juliet said, 'myself.'

Juliet was scrutinising the account, taking the pen from the waiter's tray. Beth, as the waiter retreated, leaned forward and said, 'Oh, but listen, Juliet, I did mean it about seeing Miles. I must see Miles.'

Juliet met her eyes and said bluntly, 'Why?'

'He can help me.'

'To do what?'

'To decide.'

'To decide?' asked Juliet with scorn.

'Yes.'

'How?'

'I can't tell you. It's too private. Please believe me.'

'When he is making such progress,' said Juliet, with angry despair.

'I shan't hurt – '

'How can it help but hurt him?' asked Juliet bitterly.

'It may have the opposite effect. Please, Juliet, don't force me to go over your head.'

'You are really a hard little thing.'

Beth knew that offensiveness was Juliet's last resource. 'You have been so kind before, Juliet,' she said, 'in lending us your garden. Please do it once more. It will be lovely to see it again. Are your camellias still in bloom? Does Mrs Ho's mother still like sitting in cars?'

Juliet put the cameo box into her bag. 'No,' she said, 'Miles insists on her being accommodated inside.'

'Well, he could hardly take a legal interest in human rights,' said Beth, 'without trying to apply them. I'll ring him, Juliet, and arrange a time to suit us all.'

Beth, to forestall any argument Juliet might put to Miles, rang Juliet's number from a public phone at the Quay. She was sorry that Miles sounded so happy to hear her voice, and quickly told him that it was a practical matter she was forced to consult him on. She was sorry that he sounded even more happy when they decided on Saturday at three, and that he should ring her at work if that time were not convenient to Juliet. Bearing this light regret, which did not stop her beginning to smile, she ran to catch one of the Eastern Suburbs buses.

She got out at the Cross and hurried along Victoria Street, repressing her expectant smile. She hurried, and wanted to smile, because no event felt complete, no news confirmed, until she had told Marcus of it. Now she was getting ready to say, 'Well, I've fixed it so that I can get that *solemn assurance*, and we can take it from there.'

She had left her keys in the flat, as she often did. It had not mattered before, because she and Marcus had not arrived home separately before. When she saw the light under the door, she put an ear against the wood, her smile breaking out, and tapped with one knuckle.

There was no response. She called, 'Marcus!' and tapped loud enough to bring him from the kitchen.

She saw the light brighten. The door opened a chink, and in the aperture, dark fur appeared. The animals of childhood stories, the wolf and the grizzly bear, flashed terror through Beth before she saw that the fur encased an arm now moving down from the high light switch, and then the door opened to disclose Marcus's mother, shoeless, in black pants and a fur jacket.

'If you want Marcus,' said Nita, 'I'm sorry, he's not home.'

Beth pointed at herself. 'I live here too.'

'So you're the one.' Nita opened the door wide, stepping back and smiling. Beth came in, slowly easing the bag from her shoulder. Nita said, 'I could see he had one of his girls here. There's the evidence all over. I'm his mother.'

Beth had not expected Nita to speak in this sweet, pensive voice. Her eyes, as Juliet's had done, approved Beth's green jacket. Her familiar, intense smile showed many tiny flecks of gold. Beth, slowly letting her bag come to rest on the cuboid table, wanted to tell Nita she had once seen her in Rome, while simultaneously she wanted to ask how, without a key, Nita had got into the flat. Her bag came to rest beside a bulging grey bag with a long thin strap. She said, 'I'm Beth Jeams. When did you see Marcus?'

'I didn't. That's what I'm waiting here for.'

'I thought he must have given you his key.'

But when Nita only shook her head, and absently smiled, Beth rushed on to say, 'I don't think he'll be long. You know, I recognised you straight away. Marcus showed me a photo of you and Ralfe.'

Nita clapped a hand to her mouth for a moment, then gave her smile, then several little bobs of her curly head. She took off her fur jacket, slung it instead over her shoulders, and sat down, sighing deeply, in one of the two low chairs. Beth respectfully wondered if she were stoned. A pair of black running shoes lay on their sides by the chair, and she had drawn up a small radiator, towards which she now extended her stockinged feet. 'Sydney's a cold place,' she said reflectively, 'after the West.'

Beth sat on the arm of the opposite chair. 'May I call you Nita? In fact, I'm not sure of your last name.'

'I'm not sure of it myself,' said Nita, with wryness in her sweetness. 'I suppose it's Vyner-Unwin. Before that I remember it was Court, and before that Pirie, and I was born Poussard, which I've gone back to in between. So don't ask me.'

She added something Beth failed to hear, then sat in her chair, dropped her hands to her lap, and appeared to fall into silent musing, smiling slightly and shifting her eyebrows. It was like watching a sleeping person respond to a bad dream. Beth, feeling it discourteous to stare, looked at the grey handbag on the table. It was crammed so tight that through its soft leather the shape of some of its contents was discernible – a wallet, a stiff hairbrush, a cosmetic jar. Through the stockings on Nita's feet, stretched out to the radiator, distortions were also visible – humped toes jostling, lumps at the base of each big toe, and on one heel, a ridge of bone. Beth said lightly, 'I keep wondering how you got in.'

'Opened the door with a credit card.'

Her muffled voice explained the repressing twitching of her face. Beth jumped up, knelt by her chair, and took one of her hands. It was a worn knuckly little hand, though the body in the opening of the fur jacket was shapely and sleek, and her neck plump and suntanned. Beth asked the questions of mystified sympathy. Could she get her anything? How could she help?

Nita shook her head. The tears glazing her big blue

frightened eyes had not wet her cheeks, but sorrow muffled her voice when she replied that Beth could not help her.

'And it's no use telling you the story, darling. If he'll soon be home, it will only mean telling it twice.'

Marcus and Nita sat at the cuboid table. Beth had set a canvas chair back a little, and sat with one elbow on the window sill. Marcus and she watched in silence as Nita drew out of the grey bag a wallet, then a change purse. She took notes from the wallet, and spread them to reveal their denominations – two twenties, three tens, three fives. Though Marcus flicked an impatient hand, she tipped up the purse and spilled out a pile of coins. Beside this, she tossed two credit cards.

'Those,' she said. 'I owe on those, darling. I don't know how much.'

Marcus took a big bite of the sandwich which Beth, to give Nita and him time alone, had lingered over preparing for him in the kitchen. She had left mother and son jubilantly embracing and exclaiming, but had returned five minutes later, with food and wine, to find Marcus in his present mood, dogged and hostile while Nita, perhaps to adapt to it, had assumed a character more in accord with the Nita of the photograph or of the woman who had run through the Roman traffic. She was defiant and flippant, ostentatious and sometimes nonchalant. Now, from the heap of coins, she picked up a button and the stub of a theatre ticket and dropped them daintily into the ash tray.

Marcus finished his sandwich. 'That can't be all,' he said.

'I told you, darling. 'Tis all.'

'Well, then, listen, ma. When can you raise money on your share of the restaurant?'

'In the never-never, actually.'

'Why's that, mum?'

'Marco, I would like to know where you get all this ma and mum from. When are you going to start on the Nita?'

'Come on, ma. Why can't you?'

'It took you long enough to stop the mummy. Is it going to take you as long to start the Nita?'

'Right, Nita. Why can't you raise money on your half-share of the restaurant?'

'In the first place, I won't need to, because I won't be away for as long as all that. And in the second place, because I made my share over to Ralfe, actually.'

Marcus sprang from his chair and walked about the room, swearing. Nita pursed her lips and began idly to separate the dollar coins from the pile. 'God-god-god,' Marcus was saying. Beth leaned out of her chair and said softly to Nita, 'Do have something to eat, Nita.'

'I couldn't eat, darling.'

'A drink, then.'

'I never drink, darling. My spirits are inborn.'

'These men!' said Marcus.

'You ought to know, darling. You're one yourself.'

Marcus sat down. 'These men of yours!'

Nita said to Beth, 'What men does he mean? I was married, wasn't I?'

'Mum, *why* did you make it over to him?'

'Because I was putty in his hands, that's why. Because I loved and trusted him. And I still do love and trust him. He'll soon get tired of that lazy little Karen, you'll see. He'll soon find out how much business he does without me there. It was my cooking, and my personality – oh, his personality, too – well, I sent you that photograph – but you don't get far on the personality without the cooking. You wait and see, one day, any day, that phone will ring. I left him this number.'

Beth forestalled Marcus's outburst. 'But Nita, that may take some time.'

'Let it,' said Nita. 'See this.' She drew back her cuff and displayed the watch on her wrist, passing it through the air between Beth and Marcus. 'When Ralfe gave me this, just before our wedding, I said to him, "My darling husband, as long as this still ticks, my heart will beat for you." You see what it is, don't you? It's a Tissot.'

'Oh, mum,' said Marcus, sadly and gently.

Beth said, as gently, 'Nita, if you felt like that, why did you leave?'

'Because I couldn't bear it, what I saw, and what he said I would have to put up with seeing. You're probably too young to understand – ' Nita pressed both hands flat and hard against her breasts – 'the hurt, when I saw them like that. I told you about her legs, sticking straight up in the air, and him between them. Still fully dressed. It's not the first time. Well – thirty I could stand. Twenty-five. But seventeen – well – this time I thought, well, teach him a lesson. I left a note. Just this address and number. And a message, well, he'll understand. Tissot still ticking.'

Beth thought those big wet frightened eyes, looking from one to the other, must have reminded Marcus of another of Nita's fears. He said, 'Did you get your hypnotherapy before the flight, ma?'

'Darling, do you know, I didn't give it a thought. Well, one fear drove out the other.' She nodded her head; the tears fell. 'It did. It did.'

TEN •

This was a morning dream, so Juliet wrote in the first light of a damp day. Dew had slipped to the lower part of the window, where it clung in a shining sling, obscuring the bare maple branch.

<u>DREAM 23</u> = With Mother trying to rent house in Italy. Urgent. Then both stand in little house. I say Cheerful just the thing. Mother says But it's bloody fibro. Big table Italian family beautiful little children. I say Like in the paintings. Italian woman in apron gives me parcel. Says Here is pig's liver for your dinner. Blood on parcel. I take and put in pocket. I say It doesn't make a damn bit of difference to me. Blank then standing in paddock. Shadowy man with me says Look. Couple on grass man on top moving up and down up and down. Tails of man's jacket drops away see big bottom rising falling. I won't look turn away. Woman under man screams. Shadowy man laughs. I turn away saying But I must rent house. Then in house alone. Stone but no roof no window panes. Know good house is through archway so walk towards. But floor mud like shallow trench keep slipping. Call out crying Let me through. Wake struggling mumbling something.

After breakfast with Miles, Juliet took the ledger from the locked drawer where she now kept it. She opened the window before she sat down, and as she picked up her pen, noticed three swollen nodes on the maple branch. *But it is hardly August!* She always had some much amazed response, as if she really did not expect them at all. Impulsively she reached out with her pen, but, always respectful of vegetation, she did not, after all, mark the nodes, but, after contriving a few more delays, bent to the ledger.

ORIGINS DREAM 23 = Debris. One clear message, or command. House = Saying to Beth that I own a few little houses, and the one that came to mind was the little one near the cemetery that Fergie bought, with the fibro bathroom addition. Mother would be furious that I even dreamed of her saying bloody. Can hear her now. Kindly leave the swearing to the men. Italian family = Beth-Marcus-Rome. How she went back to hotel pretending to lose her way and asking directions of old Romans strolling about during the siesta. She said, From those tightknit Italian families.
Beautiful little children = Me coming to decision that it would be a very good thing if Beth has this baby. She looks so well and beautiful that it must be the right thing. She is "in love" with Marcus, but once the sex thing wears off anything can happen, as I saw too often with Fergie. And if Miles remains in this mood of almost disgusting humility, I would not put it past him to take her back, which would not be a good thing for anyone, Beth included. I am far from being unmindful of her interests. I am very fond of Beth.

Like in the paintings = Close up Marcus really is like the wicked one of those pairs of cupids. And so springy and bouncy. One sees the attraction. But no money, can't stick at a job, and as for his family, Beth's story of the mother in Rome, and her career since, and the "religious" father, is hardly promising. However, two young people pulling together can overcome many obstacles, and fortunately, the mother is on the other side of the continent. Also, in certain circumstances, I would not withold a little discreet assistance, such as the house. Check when that lease is up.

Taking parcel and putting in pocket = Nothing. Damn bit of difference = Nothing. Unless it was what I said to Clem. Irrelevant. And in any case details not to be put down here.

Couple on grass = Nothing. Unless impression Beth gave me of Marcus's mother, who <u>screamed</u> as she ran through the traffic to collect the child she had actually left alone in that dangerous city.

Must find the house etc. = Quite clearly, the <u>house</u> for Beth and Marcus, to give their marriage a chance. That is, if they have the baby, which I do feel they will.

Roofless house etc. = Must face up to this. The green book is right. Those broken houses appear in my dreams when I feel very uncertain. To be meticulous, the green book says insecure, but in my case, uncertain is nearer the mark. In Dream 20 at Cable House I felt uncertain whether Miles was doing the right thing in taking up with Beth, and I must say events have proved me right. And now I feel uncertain because he is to see her again, and I am so afraid of the effect it will have on him. Fond as I am of Beth, I must say she was rather sly in

ringing Miles straight after leaving me at the
Regent, and giving me no time to break it to him
gently. As he was so pathetically grateful and
humble, just to have the chance to see her again.
But also so ready to accept it when I told him how
right, how beautiful, she and Marcus looked
together. It's very mysterious. Saturday at three. I
shall go and play bridge.

NOTES DREAM 23 = I seem to have put it all in
ORIGINS. And I meant to be so scientific. Having
Miles in the house distracts me. Also, there is
something about this dream, so nasty and coarse,
with none of those little amusing or elegant
touches. It has made me quite depressed. Colour?
Voices? What do they matter?

Resolute, as on that other Saturday, and again with some
dread, Beth walked from the bus to Juliet's house. First,
she passed the thirties blocks of flats Miles called the
bungaloids, then she walked beside the high old sandstone
walls beneath the lower boughs of evergreens, and then
into those quiet winding streets where the only
pedestrians were the aged or the young and carless like
herself.

She was wearing jeans, a cotton shirt under a pullover,
and canvas shoes. Though still delighting in this
stereotype that had set her free, now, advancing into
Miles's orbit, she was dismayed to find herself braced
against his critical habit, which, she was sure, would
have survived the crisis of nerves described by Juliet.

Again, as on that other Saturday, the shining Holden,
though unoccupied now, stood outside Juliet's house.

Miles's car, Beth supposed, was in Juliet's garage. The camellias beside the path were in fading bloom. She did not pass between them to ring at the door, but hurried round the side of the house to the garden.

Again Miles was sitting at the table Juliet had brought from Cable House, and when he saw her, he got to his feet, rather awkwardly, as he had done then. And now Beth surprised herself by running across the grass towards him. She saw his expression change from uncertainty to joy. He flung his arms apart to receive her.

He did not rock with her, as Marcus so often did, but stood still, holding her, his lips lightly on her hair. She rested a cheek against his chest, delighting in every small familiarity. She said, 'It's such a *relief*, liking you again.'

'Thank you. Thank you.'

She did not quite like the reverential tone of this. She said, 'But I had forgotten you were so tall.'

'Marcus is near your own size, then?'

'Nearer. Juliet told you about him, of course.'

'Yes. And that you're pregnant, too. So I guessed why you wanted to see me.'

They released each other and turned in unison to the table. 'Did Juliet guess?'

'Oh, Juliet and I – ' he said, laughing. 'There is so much we don't mention. And there are so many connections Juliet fails to make. Or perhaps rejects. Perhaps rejects.'

It was also a relief to Beth to learn that Juliet was out. It was Mrs Ho who, a little later, crossed the grass with their tea tray, and who, to Beth's surprise, passed a hand across Miles's hair and gave her babbling laugh.

'Mrs Ho on a Saturday afternoon?' said Beth, watching her go back to the house. 'Not another dinner party?'

133

'Not this time.' Miles looked amused as he set the cups upright. 'This time, because I am here. Juliet insists on my absolute comfort. It makes her very happy. Mrs Ho's mother has a chair in the ironing room. We couldn't entice her further into the house.'

He had given Beth the assurance she asked for, saying that Marcus was right to demand it, and that in the circumstances, it couldn't be less than solemn, and that the cliché was justified. To Beth, his playful affectionate mood seemed attuned to Mrs Ho's gesture of passing her hand over his hair. She picked up the teapot, and as she poured the tea, said she had not expected him to look sick, exactly –

'But Juliet did use the word breakdown.'

'And you expected me to look depressed. So I have been, and was, in fact, to a degree, until you started to run across that grass.'

Now Mrs Ho's gesture took on another meaning. It was maternal, encouraging. Beth had set her teeth into a biscuit. She withdrew it and held its disc between them as she looked into his eyes. They were as deep and soft and eager as when he had encompassed her life. Casting her own eyes down, she warily took that bite. Miles said, 'You find your influence on me a burden, Beth?'

'Could so much have depended on me?'

'It did, Beth. I deceived you, and I exercised my deceit by manipulation and bullying.'

'I collaborated,' said Beth.

'Not at first, dear girl. I did that to you, too. I put down your resistance.'

'That letter I wrote you. I wouldn't even apologise.'

'Your letter was in the range of behaviour it's possible to apologise for and forget. My deception and bullying weren't. I very badly needed your forgiveness. Thank you. Thank you.'

The reverential tone being explained, Beth could smile. 'And you'll really be better because you have it?'

'Yes. Your leaving me, and the questions you asked me here in this garden, began what Juliet calls my breakdown. I think of it more as a process of stripping. I was clothed in lies and pretence. I had armoured myself like that to go to war for what I wanted. I was so busy armouring and enforcing that I didn't stop to assess the extent of my corruption. No, that's wrong, occasionally I did, but I forced myself on because I couldn't face the reversal. You made me stop. The process of stripping is rapid once it really starts. I would wake up at night, and get up and feel it fall away, piece by piece. And I would cry, Beth. It was painful in the extreme, being left with only my sins.'

'Sins?' said Beth. The word sharply questioned her sympathy. She wondered what Marcus would make of all this. But Miles, agitated now, got to his feet, clasped his hands at his back, and said, 'Yes, sins. I know you have never shared my religion.'

'I used rather to like going to church,' said Beth. 'The dressing, the music, the unusual acoustics. And coming out together under the plane trees, the nods and half-bows and salutations. I liked that. But I saw it as only one of your ceremonies. Almost as one of your games.'

'I nearly allowed it to become one.'

'I suppose it is impossible to put your belief into words,' said Beth, in the eagerly hopeful voice adopted by Miles's group when faced with those who threatened boredom by struggling to express their beliefs.

Miles gave the voice the recognition of a smile, but refused its diversion. 'It *is* impossible, in fact. Any experience I've had that seemed to have a mystical element – no, why do I put it like that, as if I want to keep my doubt – any mystical experience I've had has proved not useable in words without inflating it to the point of destroying it. It's said that poetry can do it, music can do it, indirectly, through their harmonies. I am a lawyer. I can't express the mysteries, but if I keep my awareness of them, and never stop reflecting on them, some part may attach to what I do, no matter how mundane the material I work with may be.'

His dark head against the sunlit web, his fervent eyes, his straight stance and vigorous movements of the head, all served his voice, which had on Beth a mesmeric effect that placed his words deep in her mind. She knew this was happening, and knew it to be one of those occasions her memory would never let go. Yet she felt an obscure anger, too, and when he came back to the table and said earnestly, 'Do you understand?' she took another biscuit and said lightly, 'All I understand is that you want me to understand.'

He sat down. 'My darling girl, I have taught you too well.'

'Well – ' she said, laughing and gripping his hand for a moment – 'I did understand, yes. But I can't be bothered with things like that at the moment. It's enough for me that I love Marcus. Do *you* understand that?'

'Oh yes,' he said, with a series of staid little nods, 'I understand that.'

'And that I'm pregnant. Which is slightly more than enough, in fact. Now that I've got this solemn assurance, I can't put off deciding for much longer. Oh – ' She gripped his hand again – 'don't think I'm asking for advice. I know it's up to me.'

'You and Marcus.'

'As I am constantly reminded.'

'He wants you to have it.'

'Juliet told you?'

'Yes.'

'Oh, right, of course, she thinks it's a great idea. That's her sentimentality, because she had no children herself. But me, I'm always seeing Judy, going about rubbing her belly in that self-congratulatory way. And dad and her being so coy about the number of them. *And all boys*! No. No, thank you. Besides, just when I've come to enjoy my body . . .'

Beth's voice trailed away into reflection as she ate the biscuit and looked down at the body she spoke of. It gave her a special pleasure, when dressing, to survey the firm low mound of her belly between the two cushioned hip bones, and then to zip up her jeans tightly, neatly, over it. She brushed biscuit crumbs off this cherished area and said, 'No, I haven't the slightest moral objection to abortion. If they're willing to tinker with nature at one end, to prolong life, they haven't a reasonable argument against tinkering with it at the beginning. And anyhow, being a mother's not much of a cop, if you're truthful. Never having had a mother, I'll give you an impartial opinion. Mothers become obstacles, and are put aside. Did you appeal to your mother, Miles, in your trouble?'

'Juliet did rather take over. But I confess I allowed it. All the same, you're unfair, Beth. I've never put my mother aside.'

'No, you do your duty. I know how scrupulous you are. Perhaps that's the only answer, but it's not very enticing. Marcus's mother arrived on our doorstep last Tuesday night.'

Miles was silent. Beth looked aside and said, 'Nita. Her name is Nita. Did Juliet tell you Marcus was the boy I met in Rome?'

'Yes. The boy with the list. It's wonderful. The boy who wrote, And the rhino has ivy growing out of his mouth.'

Beth remembered how she had longed to tell Miles about

Marcus's gesture, at the party, of putting his fingers to his lips and drawing out the ivy. She hesitated, but her current preoccupation prevailed. 'But I didn't tell Juliet about how much Marcus loved his mother. I watched her squat on the footpath to coax him back into a good temper. He adored her. You could see him adoring her. And now she gets on his nerves so much; it's painful to watch, especially as she gets on mine too. She's sleeping on a li-lo on our floor, and apart from having to *let* her sleep on a li-lo, the indignity, for her, we can hear every rustle, every sigh. We have to whisper in bed.'

Seeing that Miles was about to ask a question, Beth said impatiently, 'Oh, she ran away from her husband in Western Australia because he got off with a girl, and now she lies or sits by our phone waiting for him to ring and beg her to come back to him. I can't stand seeing her there, and yet, the really painful part is that I can't help feeling so miserably sorry for her, and hating Marcus for being so mean to her, and yet, for not being able to resist her demands. She has no money, not a penny.'

'Beth, this is a temporary worry.'

'That's what I tell myself. But that's not the point. The point is, the fate of mothers. And now everyone wants me to become one.'

'Nita, too?'

'No, not Nita. She says being a granny would be the last straw. And that she's too young. Forty-seven.'

'Can't she get a job?'

'She has been cook and part-owner of a successful restaurant for three years. I'm sure she could. But I told you – she won't leave our phone.'

'But that's ridiculous. Have a answering service put in.'

'We got the gadget, and Kirk – a friend – put in a socket, which I suppose is illegal. Anyway, it doesn't work, and we have to wait another week for Telecom.'

'Only a week. This is a practical woman, Beth, who is in shock. Before the week's out, if she hasn't gone back, she'll face her predicament, and start looking for a job and her own place to live. I'll speak to Juliet. There must be someone we know.'

'There was always someone you knew, you two.'

'And you never quite liked it.'

'But was often glad of it. I would be glad of it now. Thank you. The reason she has no money, by the way, is that she made over her half of the restaurant to her husband. Which doesn't seem very practical to me.'

'An aberration of passion.'

'Or the need to be subjugated,' said Beth glumly.

'This husband isn't Marcus's father?'

'No. Thank heaven no. She left his father on a commune up north, when Marcus was four. Toomba. Marcus thinks of it as a green paradise.'

'Really? There are so many disappointed communards. Country communes, city communes, even extended households. They nearly always fail. Even one so lightly bound as the group. Something happens, a crack appears, and after that, the break can be delayed, perhaps, but not stopped.'

Beth, understanding that the group had broken up, wanted to console Miles, but her spirit and her body had begun to leave him, and were speeding her back to Marcus. She said, 'I'm sorry if the group's broken up. You put so much into it. But you're well and strong. You'll make other friends, and go on to fulfil your ambition.'

'My ambition,' he said with a laugh.

Beth was arrested on her flight towards Marcus. 'You've given it up?'

'Of course.'

'But what will you do?'

'Oh, I'll continue in the law. It's the hope of high office I've given up.'

'Why?'

'Beth, I can no longer face disguise and betrayal.'

'Betrayal of your nature?'

'Yes, at one point I decided to give up the whole caboodle, the law too. Last week – '

He set his head back, half shut his eyes, and Beth saw that almost forgotten sign of his foolery, the lip curling back from the teeth. The foreshortening of his face let the sunlight catch the tender skin of his exposed lip, the white lowered eyelids, and the pocked and roughened area of cheek she had once thought of as a moonscape.

'Last week, at my very lowest point, I thought of running away, going to a small country town, and buying a shop. The kind of town where when business is slow, the shopkeepers come out and stand in their doorways.'

Beth laughed with surprise. It was Marcus she could see at the door of such a shop, one arm against the door jamb, one knee flexed, one hand in a pocket. She said, 'What kind of a shop?'

'I fancied hardware.'

'That's it exactly. You could wear a knee-length grey cotton coat.'

'Yes, with *Ligards* embroidered in red on one lapel. So would my assistant, a woman who would also do the books and take our coats home to wash and iron in the weekend. At a quarter to nine every morning, I would sweep the footpath outside the shop.'

'I think this town would be on a train line.'

'Yes. When I heard a train pass I would look at the big round clock on the wall. There would be a backyard, but I wouldn't make a garden. I would live over the shop, and read prodigiously. From my back window I would see a paddock, with tussocks of grass, barbed wire, and cowclaps.'

Beth peeked at her watch. This shopkeeper was not, after all, Marcus. 'And you would be active in the church.'

'Of course, I would be most correct in every way. I would not know how to dispose of the seven Christmas cakes left by pitying women with large families.'

Miles's laugh had not broken out. His lip no longer curled from his teeth. He opened his eyes and said tartly, 'They would get me in the end, of course. I would be suspected of sexual interference with boys. Perhaps I would be guilty. Or perhaps I would go mad with loneliness.'

Beth resisted the rush of sympathy that would detain her, perhaps even entrap her. 'Miles,' she said, 'last time we talked here, you said marriage was possible for you. Isn't it still possible?'

'I said marriage to you was possible. Only to you, Beth. If Marcus and you don't make a go of it, I would like to marry you, with or without the baby. Try not to mind my saying that. Try not to feel my attachment as too sticky. I do want you to know about it.'

Beth might have felt it as too sticky if she had been able to believe in it, but, instructed by the changes in herself, she perceived how resistant Miles was to change, both by nature and by training, how change would hurt him, and by what elaborate means he might ward it off or render it harmless. She set herself to subdue her impatience and to put all this to Miles, reasonably and gently. She did not mean to smile and say, 'Could we both live over the shop?'

He clapped both hands flat on the table. Then he laughed, 'Why not?'

'And in the mean time,' she pleaded, 'you still have Juliet. And surely, Clem and Conrad.'

'I will depend on your discretion, Beth. It will make this whole thing more explicable if I tell you that Clem has been diagnosed as antibody positive.'

Beth jumped to her feet, wailing, 'Oh – oh – oh – ' while Miles also quickly stood, saying, 'Don't over-react.'

'I'm sorry.'

'It doesn't mean that he'll go on to develop the condition.'

'Of course not. He won't. He won't.'

'The chances simply haven't been assessed, neither generally nor in his particular case.'

'He won't. He mustn't.'

'We hope not. Clem himself is very indiscreet about it, even though there's his job to consider. And entirely flippant, I'm afraid.'

'That was the crack in the group.'

'No. That was when you left.'

'As if I – ' She spread a hand on her breast – 'were half so important – '

'It has nothing to do with individual importance. Clem's diagnosis came later, and was the end of my ambition, and the beginning of my recovery. Which your forgiveness completed, my dear girl. As for the group, Clem's disclosure did hasten its disintegration. Conrad will continue to share their flat, of course. But of the others, only Juliet said it didn't make a damn bit of difference to her.'

Beth wanted to say that it didn't make a damn bit of difference to her, either, but knew she would have to add, 'Unless I have the baby.' She had rebelled at the occupation of her body, but had not expected an occupation of her mind. She said weakly, 'There is so much superstition about it.'

'Naturally, when so little is known. I hope you'll let me drive you home.'

'No-no-no.' It was a substitution of her wail.

'To the bus, then.'

'No, no. I need to walk.'

'Very well. But don't rush off like that. Come through the house. If we are to do anything about Nita, we'll need her full name, and your phone number.'

They said goodbye at the front door, pressing hands, not smiling, kissing solemnly and sedately. As Beth hurried up the path, between the camellias, he called her name, and said when she turned, 'That is the *only* other way.'

Not understanding, Beth gave a nod and a mechanical smile and hurried on. In the street, she saw that Mrs Ho's mother was now sitting in the front passenger seat of the Holden. She has escaped to the car, thought Beth, and responded to that smile, to that incisively delineated mask, by raising a hand and laughing. As she laughed, a protective conviction took hold of her, and she said blithely to herself, Oh, but he won't get it, he won't, and let joy take her quickly on her way.

But going home to Marcus was not the spontaneously joyous event it had been before the arrival of Nita. A little dread lay at this end of the journey, too. She was nearly there before she realised that Miles's last remark had been the expected judgement on her clothes. She could not help her gratification. It straightened her back and lightened her step. Passing at that moment their local cash-and-carry, and seeing Marcus at the far end, facing the wall of refrigerators, she hurried past the Lebanese couple at the cash register and down the narrow shop, sliding past standing customers. She said Marcus's name, and as soon as he turned, took his head in both hands and kissed him all over his face. He stood with a packet of butter in one hand and a carton of sour cream in the other, trying to speak. The soft white light and cold air flowed over them. The Lebanese couple watched impassively. An old woman passing close by, carrying her goods in a precarious embrace, seemed to send a smile into herself, deep into her eyes. But Beth could not stifle Marcus's voice for ever, and at last he managed to say, 'How was he?'

'Ineffably condescending, as always.'

'Ha! But what did he say?'

'He gave me his solemn assurance, and said in the circumstances it ought to be solemn.'

'Great. Then we can go ahead.'

'We can think about it. Come and give me a driving lesson.'

'She wants to make us her chicken breasts bloody Dijon. What else is there to think about?'

'Having a child who will call me *she*, for one thing.'

'Okay. Nita. Ma. Do it, Bethie, do it for us.'

'Has he rung?'

'Bow-wow? You're kidding.'

They were going slowly to the cash register. 'I don't believe Nita could have such faith in him without cause.'

'You don't know ma.'

'He might be ringing right now.'

'Tarragon vinegar,' he said gloomily, taking it from the shelf as they passed.

Outside the shop, he took an envelope from his pocket, 'And I've got to post this.'

Beth, having posted them herself, could have read the message through the envelope. *Tissot still ticking*. She took it from Marcus and said, 'I'll post it while you take those things upstairs. Please. Tell Nita we're looking forward to her chicken Dijon, and that we'll be back to eat it at eight. Then come and give me a driving lesson.'

'It's a bit difficult,' said Marcus.

Marcus was a collaborator too. There he was, standing perplexed, holding the butter, the cream, and the vinegar, and saying, 'She has started to prepare – '

'She won't mind a bit,' said Beth, and actually gave him a little push with her fingertips. 'Please. I love sitting in cars.'

ELEVEN ·

'Waiting for her,' said Barbara Philp. 'What a scream.'

'He seems to mean it, Aunt Bob.'

'Fff, it's a pose.'

'He has made it so public.'

'People must be laughing.'

'Aunt Bob, they're not. People don't expect Miles to be commonplace.'

'It's commonplace for most of them to have some unattainable female in the background. People simply laugh.'

'Were Lorna and Matthew laughing when they told you?'

'What, they never laugh. I put this to them. Suppose the girl takes him seriously, and gets tired of her little man, and comes back to Miles huge with child. They were quite unshaken. They said they would regard it as their grandchild. Fff, they're mad.'

Barbara Philp was in an armchair, her swollen feet on a stool, her stick by her side. She twitched a shoulder and said, 'Not that it matters, any of it. To think I am reduced to this. Chattering about nobodies.'

'But the names have come back, Aunt Bob.'

'Nobody visits. Only Lorna and Matthew. It's their religion. What, the names? They come and go. I'm sorry

I said that about nobody visiting. I didn't mean you. You've been very good. You had better go and put those flowers in water.'

Juliet picked up the flowers and took them, with a vase of dying daffodils, into the kitchen. On the sunny window sill stood a pot holding a dead ivy geranium. Juliet examined the tea-stained cups in the draining basket. She opened the refrigerator and looked with distaste at its contents.

As she came into the sitting-room, holding the fresh flowers in a clean vase, her aunt said robustly, 'At least, this time, Miles didn't get fat.'

Juliet laughed and said, displaying the flowers, 'It didn't last long enough for that.'

'It wasn't a real breakdown. I've known breakdowns.'

'Do look, Aunt Bob.'

Barbara Philp looked at the flowers. 'They are very beautiful. Thank you.'

'Aunt Bob, is Mrs Donnelly still coming?'

'Mrs who?'

Juliet glanced at the silver-framed photographs. 'Mrs Silver.'

'Oh, Mrs Donnelly. She went with her husband to Disneyland for a second honeymoon. The money they all have. A Dutch girl is coming now. She's here to improve her English. What a scream.'

'One of those frames is empty, Aunt Bob.'

'Malcolm and Janet. I tore them up.'

'You know how busy Malcolm and Janet are.'

'They could ring. Even Andrew rings.'

'Malcolm is standing for parliament. And Janet – '

'I hope he gets in. I can see him on that thing.' Barbara Philp pointed with her stick to the television. 'In his grey suit. One of the grey beetles, all in their grey suits. The grey beetles who run this country.'

147

'They run the world. You see them in Geneva, Paris, London – I simply turn them off.'

'At least over there, they have a bit of style. Look here, Juliet, you may have that frame. It's silver.'

Juliet picked up the frame. 'Such a nice big heavy one.'

'Go on, take it. I'm not likely to meet anyone else I want to put into it, and I've got the rest of you. I tore up Janet and Malcolm late one night, when one does that sort of thing.'

'When the bile is running, as Fergie used to say.'

'Your Fergie was a very amusing man.'

'I know.'

'Not like your little John.'

'I must go early today, Aunt Bob darling.'

'Fergie knew his mark. He knew that with me, he could say anything. He didn't think pap was good enough for Barbara Philp.'

'When is Mrs Donnelly coming back?'

'When Mickey Mouse lets her go.'

'But really?'

'I suspect she isn't, but didn't have the guts to tell me, so she made up the Mickey Mouse story.'

'Do you like the Dutch girl?'

'When I heard she was Dutch, my hopes rose. But actually, I don't think she's all there.'

Juliet had left her car near the Yacht Club. Carrying the silver frame, she walked up New Beach Road, her tread fastidious of cracks in the pavement and the rubble of building restorations. A few of the cars parked near the Yacht Club had personalised plates. BITCH. CAD. GROOVY. Suspicious of the sobriety of persons who would choose such plates, she had parked her treasured old Jaguar on the footpath. An old man, having been obliged to walk on the road, halted, as she came up with her keys, as if to remonstrate. She gave him a terrible smile. He raised his towelling hat.

'Every time it rings,' said Nita, 'I think it's him. There was this call just before yours. The STD pips, then this man's voice that could have been his. My heart! But it turned out it was a wrong number. For Apex Rent-a-Car. Then you rang. So if I sounded funny, that was why.'

'You didn't sound funny,' said Juliet.

'I try to control it.'

'You sounded very nice.'

'Thank you.'

'There's life in this yet,' said Juliet, plucking yellowed leaves from the geranium on the windowsill. 'I can't bear to leave the poor creature here with no sun. Would Beth and Marcus mind if I took it?'

'They're only going to throw it out. They were talking about it yesterday, saying how silly they were to expect it to live there. They'll love that maidenhair. Who wouldn't? At home,' said Nita, her sweet voice thickened by her recent tears, 'I have the dearest little fernery. He teases me about my ferns.'

'I wanted to bring Beth and Marcus something really beautiful,' said Juliet, standing back to regard the fern, in its blue glazed pot, on the broad window sill. 'I'll nurse the other poor old thing back to health and put it in my Aunt Bob's kitchen. She's eighty-six, and a perfect old dear.'

'Ralfe's mother died at eighty-six. It was her money and mine we started up with. Ralfe was her youngest. That's why he's spoiled. I don't dispute he's spoiled.'

Juliet came back to the cuboid table and sat down. Between them stood their empty coffee cups. It had been very good coffee, served with the almond bread Nita had made, she said, because she had nothing else to do while waiting for Ralfe to call. 'How old is Ralfe?' asked Juliet.

'Fifty last New Year's Day. Wait.' Nita took the bulging grey handbag from the floor beside her chair and bobbed her curls at it until she found a photograph. 'There.'

Juliet raised her eyebrows as she looked at it. When, silently, fastidiously, she put it back on the table, Nita seized it, held it close to her eyes, and gave it a hard puzzled look. 'He's stunning looking in the flesh,' she said.

'I'm sure he is,' said Juliet politely.

Nita put the photograph back into her bag. Juliet said, 'I am one of those rare creatures born without sexual feelings.'

Nita cast her a glance from big blue eyes still reddened by tears. 'I thought there was supposed to be no such thing.'

'Except me.'

Juliet leaned neatly forward in her chair, her elbows at her side, her pale, tissue-wrinkled hands folded in her black lap. Nita put her head on one side and pensively smiled as she ran a finger round and round the glass of her wrist-watch. Juliet also glanced at it. It was a good watch, black and white, a Tissot.

'I often wonder, in fact,' said Juliet, 'why I was given all the right equipment.'

'You don't feel embarrassed talking about it?'

'Why should I? Any more than you feel embarrassed to speak of your feelings. I've found the deficiency has many advantages. For example, it has made me an impartial observer, and one of my conclusions is that when men of fifty become infatuated with young persons, which my second husband *regularly* did, they don't get over it in a few weeks, or a few months.'

'But the young persons do.'

'They usually tire sooner, I admit, but when they're infatuated too, as you say this girl is, *not* in a few weeks, or a few months. She's a poet, you say?'

'Yes, I thought they were supposed to be sensitive. She was over there in one of those readings.'

'So many of the men are gay that there are never enough to go round. And then along comes Ralfe with his – very masculine looks, and his boat.'

'I know in my heart you're right.' Nita's tears started up again. She pulled a handkerchief from her pocket and wiped her eyes. 'I'm sorry to howl like this. It was the disappointment of that phone call with the STD pips started me off. Along with what Harriet said. Harriet is my best friend, Harriet Matthewson. She has a shop near us, old wares. We've had some long talks. This morning she said he has got someone in for the cooking. Not too bad, either, she said. About half as good as me. But that could be her loyalty. I don't dare think of what I owe Marco for my calls to Harriet. She suggested this morning that she takes some of my Dutch plates and sells them for me. I haven't a penny.'

'And you won't go back?'

'I just said I haven't a penny.'

'If you really wanted to go, you would get the fare. Marcus – ' said Juliet, shrugging – 'that fur jacket – your watch – '

'Listen, I would be *frightened* to go back, and see what he said I would have to see.'

'Well – I can understand that. Now that you see the situation so clearly, I expect you'll get a job.'

'I don't want to tie myself down, and make promises, when he could ring tomorrow. Well – today!'

'Aren't you rather contradicting yourself?'

'Of course I'm bloody contradicting myself. I've gone mad. Do you know what I feel like? A stray cat. And

I look the part too, as I know only too well. Oh, I think it's weird how you look so different in different places. At home, whenever I used to pass a little round mirror we have, in a little hall with bronzy wallpaper, I used to shake my head at it, like this, and I used to think, Well, kiddo, you look pretty good. And I did, too. But I come to Sydney, and I get off at the airport, and go to the ladies, and all those women are lined up looking at themselves in the mirror, peering into their eyes and yanking at their clothes, and I catch a glimpse of myself behind them, and I couldn't bear the sight. I just scuttled along behind the row of them. Cat? More like an old fat rat, scuttling along. Where's it gone, what I had? Whatever it was, and I know what it was, it's gone. Every mirror, I look away, I look away. And I keep seeing that girl, with her legs – as I told you, and him. And then I think of the others, and how I suffered because of them – '

'If you had a job, you would have less time – '

' – but how it turned out all right, and I still had my nice big bed, and a man to snuggle up to. And go shopping with. Or just to be there, standing beside you.'

'Yes?' said Juliet. 'Yes?'

'And I see Marco and Beth, how they can't keep their hands off each other, though they try, because I'm here – '

'It can't be easy for them,' Juliet quickly interposed.

' – and I don't feel jealous. Well, I do, but not jealous so much as sad. Saddened. So I get Marco to do some little thing for me, like going to buy me envelopes and stamps. Or I get him to tell me what he wants to eat, and I make it for him. For them. For them both, of course.'

'Listen, suppose you had a temporary job, that you could leave if he rang? When he rings?'

Nita did not seem to hear at first. Then she turned her head, looked through the windows, and said, 'I know I'll have to do something.'

152

'Well, you're a professional cook.'

'Who says?' said Nita dreamily to the window.

'I think it was Beth,' said Juliet. 'Or did Beth tell a friend of mine, and he told me? Yes, that was it.'

'I could be called professional. But I've only ever cooked professionally in that one place, which I laid out to suit myself.' Nita, her head still turned away, spoke as if she had forgotten Juliet. 'And I had him there, to lavish praise, and to do the buying. He turned into a good buyer. I wonder who this new cook is they've got. A man, Harriet says. The business won't stand the wages. I suppose I ought to let Harriet sell my plates. She says she can get five hundred. But it won't be tomorrow.'

'If you had a job – ' said Juliet again.

Nita turned to face her. 'You've got something in mind?'

'My aunt – '

'The one who's eighty-six. I'm not a nurse or a housemaid.'

'A nurse calls. The cleaning could be done separately if you like. It's the cooking I'm thinking of. Aunt Bob was very fond of her food.'

'What kind of food?'

'Well,' said Juliet, smiling, 'what she really craves is the beef broth they used to make in the country when she was a child.'

'Never try to cook childhood memories,' said Nita briskly. 'You always disappoint. Better to give them something new. Surprise those taste buds.'

'That's perfectly true,' said Juliet with respect.

'I suppose she has guests.'

'Very few, and none for meals. I come when I can, and a clerical couple call occasionally.'

'A parson?'

'A clergyman.'

'Whatever. Two meals a day?'

'Yes. Her breakfast coffee is left in a thermos.'

'*Café au lait*?'

'Yes. And a few crispbreads. Though she would love that almond bread, if you could manage that. And it would be nice if you could stay between lunch and dinner to chat. Or while you're preparing dinner, perhaps. She wants cheerful company.'

Nita reared back in her chair in theatrical amazement. 'So that lets me out.'

'I don't believe it does,' said Juliet, as if in surprise at her own words. 'I believe it would do you good to *pretend* to be cheerful.'

'Well,' said Nita, with the same surprise, 'I've done it before. Yes! When he was on with those others, I used to put on a great big grin and go into that restaurant. Yes, and it *did* do me good. It helped. Well,' said Nita, drawing her feet, in woollen socks, up to the seat of her chair, and clasping her knees, 'she must be rich, to afford all this.'

'She's not rich. She was. She spent most of her money where she spent most of her life. In London, Paris, and the south of France. The south of France was Aunt Bob's idea of heaven.'

'Mine too!' said Nita, rolling her eyes. 'If I could be reincarnated – yummmm. But how much will she pay? if you don't mind my asking. I might be desperate, but I won't take peanuts.'

'Quite right,' said Juliet, 'and you won't have to. I'll supplement what she pays. I can afford it, and I want Aunt Bob to be comfortable. I would see that you had enough to live in a hotel within easy travelling distance – say, at King's Cross – and something over.'

But Nita had cringed back in her chair and was holding up both hands in self defence. 'Rushcutter's Bay, then,' offered Juliet.

Nita drew her hands back and held them bunched at her lips. 'Not a hotel, not a hotel,' she babbled in panic. 'Not all those people. Not yet.'

'But again, if you had to *pretend* to be cheerful – '

'One old lady, that's different. But not all those people. Not yet, not yet.'

Juliet got up, picked up the potted geranium, and said, while wrapping it in the paper in which she had brought the fern, 'Until you are feeling better, you could come and stay with me, and send your husband my phone number and Aunt Bob's. I've plenty of room, and there's reasonable public transport to Aunt Bob's. I've had a sick friend staying with me, and now he has gone home, I confess I rather miss him.'

Nita was looking at Juliet with one eye half shut. 'Oh, yes?' she said, in a sagacious sing-song, 'and I suppose that if I run the vacuum over the carpet? and give the kitchen floor a bit of a wash? that's okay too?'

'It is not okay at all,' said Juliet. 'I have a woman who comes in every day, an arrangement I shouldn't care to risk.'

'Well – ' said Nita.

'That I shouldn't *dream* of risking.'

'Well, you see, I've been down and out before.'

'And seem determined to be so again.'

'You don't understand what I feel like.'

'Your description was extremely graphic.'

'I'll get you some string for that.'

'I'll manage, thank you.'

'I don't know why you're offering all this, that's all.'

'Then I'll tell you.' Juliet put the wrapped geranium down on the cuboid table, which made a little run on its castors. 'I am very fond of Beth. Beth is in love with Marcus. No doubt I am a sentimental old woman, but I would like to see their marriage, or relationship, or whatever they choose to have, succeed. You know about the baby. Beth told me you do.'

'I know she's pregnant.'

'Well, if they should choose to have, it, as I believe they will, I want them to have the chance to become a stable family unit. And I think your presence, your *indefinite* presence, in these cramped quarters, is not good for a pregnant girl, in this time of decision, and certainly not conducive to stability. I *want* them to be happy. And I should think you would too.'

Nita stared at Juliet for a while, then said, 'You don't believe he will ring at all, do you?'

Juliet, after an audible exhalation, picked up her handbag. 'I think he could very well ring. From what you've told me, the marriage and the good business were interdependent. Why should he throw that away? But I don't believe it will be soon.'

'It won't,' said Nita, her soft voice flattening in a note of doom. 'It won't.'

'Well, then?'

'Well,' said Nita vaguely, 'I'll just put on these shoes.'

She set her feet on the floor and loosened the laces of her running shoes. 'Well, it has done me good to talk to someone who doesn't dither. It helped. Harriet has been a help, but she's the scholarly dithery kind. And Beth and Marcus are only kids. And to be candid, I can't warm to Beth. I'm fascinated the way she manages to take Marcus away just when I need the company. She's young to be so sly.'

'She's intelligent.' Juliet was writing on the card she had taken from her handbag. 'We expect young people to have intelligence, then call it slyness when they use it on us. Are those shoes really so comfortable?'

'They're a godsend. She's a pretty girl, in that pale-all-over way.'

'It's very charming, that paleness.'

'It needs a bit of something. I got out my eyebrow pencil and went to show her. But you should have seen them. Both of them.' Nita got to her feet. 'You would have thought I was desecrating the Mona Lisa. Yes, they're comfortable, all right.'

'Look, Nita – I may call you Nita?'

'I'm not holding out for Mrs Vyner-Unwin, just at present.'

'And I'm Juliet. Look, here's my card, and here's Aunt Bob's number on the other side. I shan't mention my proposal again. Ring me when you've decided. If you do come, I'm sure Marcus will bring you, in his little, in his car.'

Looking at the card in her hand, Nita said heavily, 'Just let me give him one more day. Just one more.'

TWELVE •

Though Nita was no longer in the next room, Marcus and Beth whispered, making love in the morning, and were secretive, by conspiratorial choice. Then they kissed each other many times, and laughed aloud, and shouted, to find out how it sounded. Beth put pillows behind her bare shoulders and luxuriously stretched her arms. But Marcus, curled beside her, was suddenly subdued.

'Poor ma. Thank God we didn't do our blocks and tell her to go.'

'Thank Juliet.'

'Would it have come to that?'

'If she had refused Juliet's offer, we would have found out.'

'Ha! Just as well?'

'Mmmm.'

Beth felt among the bedclothes for her discarded shirt. These cold nights, Marcus and she went to bed in rough gaping shirts picked out of the laundromat bag. She put it on, and contentedly drew Marcus's head on to her breast. This was one of the times when she wanted to say, 'Yes, let's have the baby.' But each time, she had cautiously resisted the words, and each time, they had proved a passing impulse. She said, 'I'm going to paint a country petrol station on that wall. The blind could be a roll-up door. But there's the space between the floor and the window. I could try a *trompe l'oeil* ramp. Now from what angle would I trompe l'oeil?'

'Somebody owns that wall.'

'Mil might help.'

'Listen, why did Juliet do it?'

'I told you. She and Miles are always doing things for people.'

'I don't know about Miles.' For the first time, Beth heard hostility in his pronunciation of the name. 'But if Juliet's a fixer, she has a motive.'

Beth, reasoning from her own recently exposed jealousy, had reached a suspicion that Juliet would go to great trouble to keep Miles and herself apart. Yet last night, when they had driven Nita to Juliet's house, she had felt, emanating from Juliet towards herself, a benignity deeper than she had ever felt before. She said, 'I used to feel a sort of churlishness about accepting what Miles or Juliet did for me. But I didn't feel it last night, not at all.'

'I did, a bit. But I'll give Juliet the benefit of any doubt going. It was a big thing for her to do. And the way ma cheered up, it was great.'

'It was the house, so warm and comfortable.'

'Right, after our floor. But what happens if bow-wow never rings?'

'Something will happen. Something else. Don't worry. Now the cohort can come again.'

'You couldn't blame them for stopping away.'

'I think I could do that wall without Mil. No cornices. That's good. It could be night time. A young couple in a small car, coming for petrol at night. Attendant in pyjamas.' Beth, one hand lightly on the side of Marcus's head, started to laugh. 'No. Captain Cook. Bigger in scale than the others. Serving petrol from the pump. Cigarette behind his ear.'

'Beth – ' Marcus rolled away from her and lay flat – 'you know we've got to move. You know we can't bring a baby to a place like this. Beth, you know damned well it's showing a bit. Look for yourself.'

'It's the way I'm lying.' Beth put her head back and looked at the paper lampshade. 'We have the moon already. No, that wouldn't work.'

'Look, now ma's gone, let's start thinking.'

'I am thinking.' And Beth suddenly cried loudly, 'I am *desperately* thinking.'

'Well, while you're about it, think of this, please. Here I am, with my mind made up.'

'You have a reputation for changing it, Marcus.'

'Not this time, not when it feels so right.'

'Both of us have to feel right. I don't.'

'What do you feel? Nothing?'

'No. Now and again I want it – '

'There – '

'Because you do, so much. But mostly, incredulous. As if I had been given the wrong result. I find myself thinking they must make mistakes. And I've no symptoms. None. None of Judy's tell-tale little signs. So it's easy to feel incredulous.'

'You say you love me – '

'Can that be a symptom? That feeling? After all, I must have become pregnant in those first days. Yes, it's probably a symptom.'

'There's something cold about you, Beth Jeams.'

'There's something warm, too.'

'Not right through the grain.'

Now Beth was really offended. 'That's playing dirty, Marcus Pirie. It's not cold to want to be reasonable. We're not even twenty-one, and we want so much to go away.'

'Right, and do you know why we keep changing our minds about where to go?'

'Ho-hum, don't tell me! We really don't want to go at all.'

'Right.' He put a hand on her belly. 'Because *this* is what we want.'

She brushed his hand away. 'You would do *well* in sales, Marcus Pirie.'

'I *will* do well in sales.'

'Marcus, it's time to get up.'

'I'll get up when you do.'

'I'll get up when you do.'

In this contest, it was usually Beth who gave in. She flung both legs together into the cold air and came to a thudding stand on the Afghan rug. She marched into the bathroom, where she immediately lifted her shirt, retracted her chin, and looked down between her breasts at the mound of her belly. The thickness was slight, but undeniable. Tears of panic filled her eyes, and, uncontrollable, squeezed between her tightly shut lids and joined the water of the shower to which she presently raised her face.

'Even as a little kid,' said Nita, 'he was a sexy little customer. Put him beside me in the ute, and next thing, there he was, standing up in the seat hugging and kissing, not to say crowing and chortling. Arms tight round my neck, kissing everywhere he could reach. And that chortle. Seat belts were optional then. But I got one. A good strong one. The risk!'

'How old was he, then?' asked Juliet.

'No more than three. That was on the commune.'

It was cold and dewy in the early morning garden. Both wore rubber boots. They were putting in Juliet's spring seedlings, Juliet lowering them into the little scoop of her gloved fingers, and Nita using a bare fist which she turned over to punch down the earth with her knuckles. At short intervals, each stood to straighten her spine, but when they did this, neither looked away from the earth. Nita stood and said, 'At twelve he was well and truly into the real thing.'

'Gracious. Who with?'

'Girl about fourteen lived next door to us. Gavin and us. At Cronulla.'

'They do say it's very prevalent at the beaches.'

'It would have been the same in the Great Stony Desert. His father used to say that in certain ancient societies it would have been his profession. Sex. Marco's profession. Well, he certainly doesn't have another. This computer sales thing, I'll believe it when I see it.'

Juliet rose as Nita bent. 'His father was a professional man?'

'Pirie was a physicist with ASNC. Pirie could have commanded his own figure. That's where Marco gets his maths. According to Garth Pirie, all the others at Toomba were a lot of piffling romantics.'

'Yet he's religious.'

'Beyond me. So far as I'm concerned, he's a real cold intellectual.'

'You've done a lot of planting.'

'No.'

'You look as if you have.'

Nita rose, looking pleased, pushing her hair off her forehead with the back of a dirty hand. 'I like to get on with things.'

'So do I.'

'It doesn't suit me to hang around waiting.'

'Nor me.' Juliet knelt and said, 'The child will have good blood.'

'Oh, well,' said Nita modestly.

'And considering Beth comes from sound little business people.'

'You seem pretty sure they'll have it.'

Both were now kneeling to the row. 'Of course they will,' said Juliet.

'Well, I won't be here to see it. And I suppose I can break it to Ralfe by degrees. Granny! I can hear him. I don't feel so bad about it after what Harriet said last night. And again this morning. But when Marcus and Beth first told me, all I can say is, psychologically, they couldn't have picked a worse time.'

'I doubt if they picked – '

'Oh, I know. It was only thoughtlessness.' Nita had pushed her watch far up on her forearm. She put it to her ear for a moment, then gathered up a seedling and said, with her sweet seriousness, 'I'll never be able to thank you enough for having me here. Cheering me up. And I'll soon have the money to reimburse you for those calls. Harriet wasn't talking through her hat. If Harriet says she has a buyer for the plates, she has a buyer. And if Harriet says Karen's getting sick of it, Karen's getting sick of it. I knew it would happen. But the relief!'

'Are you still determined not to go back till he asks?'

Nita got to her feet and looked at the finished row. 'I'm not so sure of that now. Once she goes, I could just turn up.'

Juliet also rose, with difficulty, both hands pressing on one knee. 'That's the way.'

'Harriet will give me the word. I told her she can sell my art deco vases, too, if she likes. They were my mother's.'

'I don't care for art deco myself, but I believe the best of it is becoming quite famous.'

'It's not as if I had a daughter.'

They took their boots off in the laundry. 'Now,' said

Nita, 'I'll make us both a lovely breakfast.'

'No. I can't have that. I'll get it while you shower. And as soon as Mrs Ho comes, I'll take you and introduce you to Aunt Bob.'

There was a little mirror in the laundry, beside the gardening hats, and as Nita followed Juliet out, she eyed herself sideways, and tossed her curls.

Mrs Ho's mother was not sitting in the car when Juliet came home, driving sedately down the street. She put her own car into the garage and went straight upstairs. She now kept the key to the drawer on a ribbon round her neck, under her clothes. She unlocked the drawer, took out the ledger, and sat down. She had not had lunch, and was hungry, but was afraid to let any more time elapse between her recording of the dream – at 2 a.m. – and tracing, as she still believed, its origins. While she turned the pages of the ledger, she shrugged off her soft black coat and let it fall, inside out, over the back of the chair. In her haste to write the dream down, she had not numbered it. She picked up her pen and did so now, neatly, at the head of the wild scrawl.

DREAM 24 = Me and Nita stand in paddock look at rug on grass. N gushing How lovely How bright. I say It is not meant to be exposed. Shadowy figure man says angry Look at the time. Then me walking up hill behind school late. School uniform but present age. Shy. 2 men further up hill tight grey suits blowing tails show big bottoms comic bowler hats too small. Ralfe and Marcus. Hurry catch them up want to tell them problem. Think, Salesmen will know. Catch up but now not Ralfe and Marcus but

Marcus and Clem. Nita between them doing hula bowler hat too. All stand looking at rug in surround of grey concrete. I say, urgent, It is not meant to be exposed. Nita ogling Clem. Calls out What a darling. Clem holds picture frame in front of face pokes out tongue at us all. Blank then me driving daddy's Packard to ocean Angela and Beth in back. Ocean absolute silver dazzle. Angela calls out Thalassa Thalassa. Then alone diving into water not ocean river lonely. Shadowy figure woman calls out, Don't do it. Take no notice glide on lovely. Man's voice calls out I will wait. Other shore coral hills then coral moving then not coral but people in pastel clothes pale flowers or pale flowery hats all moving waving arms having party happy.

As Juliet picked up her pen again, she heard Mrs Ho in the corridor outside. She got up, went to the door, and called her name. Since Miles's stay in the house, Juliet used less mime with Mrs Ho. She did not make wings of her arms, then put her hands together to ask for a chicken sandwich, nor raise an imaginary cup to her lips to ask for tea. She spoke each word slowly, and Mrs Ho nodded after each, repeated them all in order, and went away. Juliet shut the door and returned quickly to her table.

ORIGINS DREAM 24 = Debris it goes without saying. But many messages.
Rug = When I showed Nita to her room she gushed on and on about Beluchi rug.
Time = N showing me that damn watch. Tissot still ticking etc.
Aunt Bob very amused however. Thank heaven they hit it off. Also worried about time I shall be

forced to have her here.

Men on hill = At first both same type as man fornicating on grass in 23, also as awful gross Ralfe in photograph N showed me. But when I caught up with them, gross Ralfe melted away and there were Marcus and poor Clem????

Bowler hats = When Marcus and Beth brought N here last night, Marcus told me he met Beth at a party and she was wearing a <u>bowler hat</u>. I found that very sweet and touching, I don't know why, and felt so glad I was helping them to be happy, even at such damn inconvenience to myself. It was the first time I have ever liked Beth in quite that way, though of course I have been fond of her for years.

Salesmen will know = Marcus telling me that if Beth will have the baby, he will ask his company to try him in sales. Beth started making faces, but I said I had a <u>great respect for salesmen</u>, they are so helpful, and where would we be without them.

Rug in concrete = No getting away from resemblance to grave. Aunt Bob going on about her <u>funeral</u> again. Prefer not to speculate on Clem nor put latest news on paper even though I do lock this up.

Not meant to be exposed = A warning to myself about news of C.

Picture frame = Yesterday was looking for something to put in silver <u>frame</u> Aunt Bob gave me. Exactly the kind of thing Clemmie would do in real life. Doesn't bear thinking about. Real life doesn't bear thinking about.

Angela and Beth = Sounded out Miles yesterday about seeing more of <u>Angela</u>. Careful not to hint at replacement for <u>Beth</u> but only as acceptable public partner when necessary. Miles hardly luke warm, said he saw enough of Angela at ten-nis, thank you. Yet everything about her is right. Good looks, refinement, intelligence, perfect taste remarked on by everyone. It's very mysterious. Though I must say I don't care for those crying fits I've heard about. As if she's in mourning for something and doesn't even know what. And as for Thalassa Thalassa, Liz Ballard used to drive the rest of us mad by saying that whenever we caught sight of that wee bit of ocean from the hill above the school. Then always adding, My only Greek. So it seems I must somehow associate Angela with Liz, which is not a good omen, as Miles can't endure Liz, and it would be better for him to find some other lass, which I am sure he will do one of these days. Water = I am still sure that this pleasure in water is some kind of reward or encouragement. Naturally, there is always someone who doesn't want one to be happy and will say <u>Don't do it</u>. I will wait = Told Miles yesterday that he ought to make it clear that the "waiting" he has announced so publicly is only a game or a passing mood. He smiled and said, But it is not a game or a passing mood. I asked what about the risk of Beth and Marcus parting, and Beth taking him seriously. He said, Juliet, I would welcome it. He said, I have made that declaration my stopping point. But more importantly, he said, I am relinquishing control. He said that twice. Relinquishing control. I said his reasoning if you can call it that is beyond me, and so it is. I agree that he still loves her. I agree to that, I am beginning to love her myself now that she is more herself, but I know the waiting part is one of his games, whatever he may say, or ceremonies,

perhaps would describe it better, and it is a foolish
and dangerous game or ceremony. Marcus seems
very loving, but so did Fergie with that Korean lad,
and I think of his utter ruthlessness when he
wanted another one, just a change. I couldn't
believe it at first.

Mrs Ho's knock sent Juliet to the door to take her tray.
Then, wanting to know if Mrs Ho's mother had been
enticed into the house, she pointed towards the laundry
and said, 'Moth-er?' But Mrs Ho, in a most dramatic way,
threw both arms into the air, threw back her head, and
cried, 'Sick. Sick.' Juliet said slowly that she was so sorry,
but Mrs Ho had already turned away, and was going down
the corridor, running. Juliet shut the door and returned
slowly to her table.

People having party = Last night it did flash
through my mind that if Beth and Marcus marry,
which of course they must if they have the child, I
will give a party for them. Nobody from the
erstwhile "group", but their own friends, and
Beth's family if feasible. Yes, certainly her family.
It must be made feasible. It would give weight. And
surely other things would give weight. Surely fear
of the unmentionable malady would make even a
sexy little customer inclined to monogamy. There
are those rubber things, but apart from the
aesthetics, as Fergie would say, rubber does break.
What would Fergie say now? Hard luck, we had the
good times. I can hear his laugh.
Pale clothes flowers etc. = Party would be in late
spring. Flowery hats used to be worn at weddings.
Nothing like that, of course. Too much weight.
Informal. Out of doors. One of those celebrants.

168

NOTES ON DREAM 24 = Absence of broken walls and unsound houses. In spite of news about C, I am feeling less "uncertain". Like N, I like to get on with things. Yesterday rang about lease of little house at Bronte. Up in early September. Would not look well to offer for nothing. Shall get agent to suggest old rental.

Shadowy figures = It says in that green book that those shadowy figures are ourselves. Not so in my dreams. And in this one it was certainly Miles's voice saying, as I swam out, I will wait. His voice. Yes, only his voice. How very mysterious. Miles has not appeared in one of these dreams.

I have just checked. Not one. Yet they have all concerned him. Oh, what can that mean, if any of it means anything?

I almost wish I could take this ledger to a psychologist person, but it is too private. They are supposed to keep confidences, but you can't tell me they don't talk to their wives. Think of the things Fergie used to tell me.

I would have to find an unmarried one, like that young man Lorna says was so good with Janet's Jeremy. But to be truthful, though nobody would believe it, I would be too shy.

Beth, walking to work down William Street, speculating on how to make the ramp of the petrol station deceive the eye, heard her name called out of the traffic moving slowly in the street beside her. She recognised Kyrie's car, but not the girl at her side. This girl was releasing the catch of the back door, and almost obscured Beth's view of Kyrie at the wheel.

Beth ran and got in the back. To combat her jealousy,

she put out both hands and lightly squeezed her cousin's shoulders. Touch animated affection, and indeed dominated her jealousy. Kyrie said, 'Beth. Jeannie.'

'Hello,' they both said.

The hairdresser who had cropped Jeannie's thick dark hair had left a sculptured wedge lying on the back of her neck. Beth, interested, memorised it for Marcus. Kyrie called over her shoulder, 'Still pregnant?'

'Who told you?'

'Marcus. Who else? I saw him with Mil in the Federal Hotel. He says you're having it. But I wondered.'

'So do I.'

'I got pregnant a couple of years ago,' said Jeannie. 'I sort of wanted it, but the man I was with, he said he couldn't think of anything he wanted less. So I had an abortion, because it was him I wanted most.'

'Marcus really wants Beth to have it,' said Kyrie.

'He tells everyone,' said Beth in wonder.

'Why not?' asked Jeannie, slightly aggressive.

'You won't change that, Beth,' said Kyrie. 'It's his tribal upbringing. The fire flickering in the dark night and all that. His mum still staying with you?'

'Not now. I'm going to buy paint today to do a mural on our bedroom wall. I'm going to *trompe l'oeil*. Did he tell you all his mother's business too?'

'Why not?' demanded Jeannie again.

'Beth had a feller, Jeannie,' said Kyrie, 'whose name I am not allowed to di-vulge, who was manic about privacy, and who warped her little mind.'

'Miles isn't like that any more,' said Beth.

'What changed him?'

'Various events.'

'See what I mean?' said Kyrie to Jeannie.

'Sure do,' said Jeannie, moving her shoulders in disgust.

170

'But,' said Beth, 'some people need to go apart sometimes, and be private, or they can't think.'

'Why can't their friends help them think?' shouted Jeannie.

Kyrie laughed. They had arrived at the College Street corner. 'I get out here,' said Jeannie angrily.

'It's okay, Beth,' said Kyrie. 'She always gets out here.'

Jeannie kissed Kyrie. '*Au 'voir*, lover,' she said.

'See you tonight, lover.'

Jeannie jumped out and hurried along College Street. Watching her red coat blowing, and her wedged tail of hair unmoving, Beth said, 'Kyrie, really?'

'Sure,' said Kyrie. 'Why not? I want to live. And rotten aids is going to move into the general community, nothing more sure.'

'Is that the only reason?'

'No. She was selling me some kitchen equipment, and we got that married feeling over the food processors. She's nice. Last week she moved in. We're redecorating. We like it. It's cosy. And listen, she got me to give up smoking. What's this about a wall painting? You did one on your bedroom wall when you were a kid. It was great.'

'Oh, it was not. It was terrible. I painted it over.'

'Isn't that you! "Oh, it was not, it was terrible." Well, it wasn't, it was great. A big window with little figures on a hill in the distance.'

'I copied it,' said Beth bitterly.

'So what? Come and do one for us.'

'I don't think Jeannie would let me.'

'Yes, she would. She's just a bit evangelical at present. It's her first time with a woman. It's not mine, but before it was only something on the side.'

'I know. Marcus told me about your group sex.'

'Did he?' said Kyrie, looking pleased. 'Yes, it was fun.

And now here we both are, into safety.'

'That's why he wants this baby so much.'

'So what? It's a good motive. Want me to drive you to Sussex?'

'Town Hall, thanks. You go on into George.'

'It's not his only motive, stupid. He loves you. Oh, really, yes, he does. But it's a reasonable motive. Look at it like that. I'll drop you here.' Kyrie put her head over the back of the seat and pursed her lips. 'Kiss-kiss.'

Beth burst into irritated laughter and kissed her. Kyrie drove round the corner into George Street, and Beth joined the cluster of pedestrians waiting for the green light. She could not look forward to telling Marcus of Kyrie's new union; he would already know about it. Artlessly frank though he was with others, her jealousy had frightened him into wariness. Beth did not want that kind of mastery over him; she was ashamed of having induced his fear.

Early for work, Beth sat down and did a quick sketch for her wall painting. Jack Best came and stood at her table.

'What's all this, Beth?'

She showed him. He said, 'Your Captain Cook's too big.'

'He's supposed to be. It's the ramp I'm worried about. I can't make it look convincing.'

'Here. Let me.'

She ceded him her place, and as she watched his hand move over the paper, she recalled the desire his proximity used to arouse in her. It had been like a connective tissue between them entangled by her embarrassment. It had gone, but had left them with a little intimacy. In the bodily smell that used to attract her, she now noticed a change. She said, 'Are you smoking again, Jack?'

'Yes. Fallen. Can you smell it?'

'Faintly.'

'You've not joined the new puritans, I hope?'

'Not me. Marcus and I have friends who smoke. And my cousin Kyrie never used to stop.'

She thanked him for his sketch. Though she saw it would not do, it showed her a way she could take. 'Jack,' she said then, 'are you jealous of your wife?'

'I used to be at first. A madman.'

'Did it make her reserved with you?'

'I don't know. I didn't notice. It might have.'

'Are you jealous now?'

'Nup. Why, is Marcus jealous?'

'Not much. But I am. It makes him reserved with me, and it makes me dislike myself.'

'There's a sure cure.'

What?

'Time and indifference.'

'Oooh!' sighed Beth.

'Face it.'

'I won't. Never. It's worse than the disease.'

'Then keep the disease, and try some alleviation. Take to drink, or painting walls. What paint will you use?'

'I don't know. I'm going out to buy it in the lunch hour.'

'Fired up?'

'Yes. From the moment I thought of it.'

'I can tell.'

'Especially now I think I can do the ramp.'

When Beth came back at the end of the lunch hour, carrying her heavy bag of paint, she walked into an argument. Maria was heatedly proclaiming their right to a work place free of smoke. Some were agreeing, some asking what, in a city full of pollution, did a little more matter. Jack Best, laughing and hooting, was standing his ground.

'You're the only smoker here now,' someone reminded him.

'So you need me. Too much purity is dangerous. It gives you acidie purosa. Fatal.'

During the afternoon, it was decided to settle the dispute by voting. Hearing Maria going about with her petition, Beth became resistant to her tone of righteousness, the sententiousness with which she spoke of their duty to others.

When Maria reached her, Beth said, 'There wasn't much complaint when there were three or four smokers here.' 'Why all this fuss about one?'

'Because a lot has been learned since then about the dangers of passive smoking. Why should I end up with lung cancer because of Jack Best?'

Jack Best renewed his hooting nearby.

'All right,' said Maria. 'Forget me. But say I start a baby? Barry wants another. It could happen any time. Why should Jack Best be allowed to harm my foetus?'

Jack Best caught up with Beth as she left work.

'Bloody Maria bullied you into that. You were on the verge of tears, you poor kid.'

Beth shook her head; she would not look at him.

'Hey, don't tell me they've won. That's sick. Take it back tomorrow. Don't let them win.'

Marcus was waiting for Beth. 'Hey, Marcus,' said Jack Best, 'this woman has joined the new puritans. She objects to my smoking at work.'

'She does?' Marcus gave Jack one of his droll disbelieving looks, but this look vanished when turned on Beth's face. He said to Jack Best, 'That's because she's pregnant.'

Nobody spoke for a while. Beth looked stupid and uncaring as she stared into the distance.

174

'Then,' said Jack Best softly, pointing his cigarette at the bag of paint, 'you can't use that, either. According to my daughter, the fumes can damage the foetus.'

Beth turned and walked quickly away from them both. Marcus caught up with her and took the bag of paint. She did not alter her pace, and as she spoke, looked only at the pavement.

'I detest that word. Judy kept using it when she told me the facts of life. "What is in here is a *foetus*, Beth," she kept saying. "You can feel it, Beth. Come and feel it, Beth, the *foetus*." '

'It seems a bit rough telling Andy and Kirk they can't smoke,' said Marcus gloomily.

'And all because of an accident.' She was still walking with her head bent, and spoke dazedly, without looking at him. 'So accidental. I don't mean the conception, though that was, too. I mean the accident of Maria – of all people – saying just those exact few words.'

'You didn't come to a decision. It came to you.'

'As they say.'

'As they say.'

'And, she said 'they're right.'

'Well,' he said, 'now we know where we're going.'

'Yes, into the trap you and the others are always talking about.'

'Ha! Let's hope it's nice inside. I asked today about sales. Okay. It's okay. That way I won't be a caryatid. I can move about more.'

'Among the mass of sober maniacs.'

'That's the deal.'

'At least we don't have to marry.'

'Sure, fine, no problems, that's a social choice. And look, who says you can't paint that wall? Jack Best? Ask your doctor.'

'So now I have a doctor?'

175

But their spirits were rising. They looked at each other sideways; they smiled. And when Beth began, rather recklessly, to laugh, Marcus shepherded her with the side of his body into the recess of a closed shop, put down the bag of paint, and kissed her on the mouth. When he said, 'It isn't so bad for you, is it?' she gravely replied, 'No, not now that I've said it. Said yes.'

The doctor at the clinic, a woman, advised Beth to limit any painting to about two hours a day, and to avoid sleeping in a freshly painted room. Beth regretted her bush petrol station until Mil, one night, brought photographs of street and café murals on which he had been engaged. Some were comments on the surroundings they were to be seen in, and many used the cartoon style he and Beth had chosen for the cinema entrance. But when Mil gave Beth the three on which he had been the project artist, and stood back, swallowing, Beth's disappointment fell away, and her ambition grew. Prim-faced, modest Mil was a skilled romantic realist, and capable – Beth saw at a second and third glance – of a subtle surrealism. He did not speak of *trompe l'oeil*, but of illusionist painting. Marcus, looking at the photographs with Beth, said there would be a wall in that house Juliet owned.

'Didn't she offer to let us rent it when it comes vacant?'

'Yes,' said Beth, engrossed in the photographs. 'Yes. She did.'

'I show some talent with a snap line,' said Annette, rather drily.

The doctor at the clinic made a note that Marcus and Beth had been tested for aids, but asked no questions about their sexual histories. Beth told her, all the same, rather hurriedly, about her own, and explained that she didn't know much of Marcus's, because he couldn't trace it himself for even the last three years, let alone the seven the newspapers were beginning to mention. Beth felt rather angry with Marcus as she explained this, but the doctor said, smiling, that if even marginal risks were to be avoided, very few children would be born at all. Then she stood, smiling again, and opened the door for Beth to pass through her crowded waiting room, where – Beth told Marcus when she got home – the lumps and slumps were lined up on both sides.

THIRTEEN •

'Juliet thinks there's an ocean view from the back,' said Beth.

'I suppose she bought it as a long-term investment,' said Marcus.

'Her second husband bought it.'

'The one she calls Fergie?'

'Yes.'

Beth and Marcus were looking at the house from the car, Beth sitting straight, Marcus, at the wheel, bending to peer past her. 'He bought a lot of cheap houses close to beaches,' said Beth.

'Right, its time will come, but it hasn't come yet.'

'Forget that peeling paint.'

'And remember the rent. Right.' Marcus took the agent's keys from the glove box. 'Come on.'

Beth, with her hands in the pockets of her red cotton dress, and her suede jacket over her shoulders, went first up the path. She had taken the red dress from the suitcase under the bed; Miles had never approved of tight dresses. When Marcus had praised her appearance in it, she felt he had subtly betrayed her.

Another of Miles's opinions had echoed in Beth's mind as she and Marcus drove to the house. One of his constant themes, the paltry suburbs that had been allowed to disfigure a magnificent coast, had found such a willing response in Beth's own nature that when Marcus had slowed down at the row of shops, pointing out that there was everything they needed there, she had been forced consciously to reassert the robust equanimity that had been her prevailing mood since agreeing to have the child.

'Yes. Everything.'

The house had been vacated three days before. Marcus opened the door, and Beth slipped into the narrow hall that ran from front to back. The back door was wide open. In the tunnel of wind it banged hard against the inside wall. Running to secure it, she was barely missed by glass falling from the hanging lampshade which the wind had sent crashing on to the ceiling.

'Jesus!' Marcus followed, kicking coloured glass aside, and hooked the door on to the wall.

Beth shrugged and went outside to the little concrete landing. Four steps led down to a sloping unkempt yard. Beth put her arms into the sleeves of her jacket and drew it tightly around her. 'Look, you can see a bit of ocean. Between those two roofs.'

'Great!' said Marcus angrily. 'But why was the bloody place left unlocked?'

Beth was determined to maintain the note of approval. 'Marvellous salt wind. Someone forgot.'

'Not on your life.' Marcus's voice had moved away. 'Look here.'

He was in the kitchen. Beth hugged her jacket around her and went in. He was lightly kicking a canvas pack propped against one wall. Banana peels and the foam plastic bases of food packs lay on one counter. Beth heard thudding footsteps and turned to see a boy standing tensely in the doorway.

Marcus gave him a sympathetic grin. 'Bolted without your pack.'

The boy came into the kitchen. Ignoring Beth, but

without looking away from Marcus's face, he swooped for his pack. He was a thin muscular boy, perhaps seventeen, and would have closely resembled Beth's third halfbrother except for the bleached bristles covering his cranium. Shrugging into the straps of his pack, he engaged Marcus's eyes and said, with uneasy belligerence, 'Okay, mate?'

Marcus averted his face and smoothed the air with one hand. *No worries*. 'Thanks-mate-much-obliged,' said the boy as he bounded away. From the window Beth saw him cross the yard, his casque of hair bright gold in the sunlight. His egress was hidden from her view by a fibrocement addition on her right.

Marcus was perched on a stool, his cheeks puffed out and his eyebrows raised in a parody of resignation. He had these spells of nostalgia, ironic or morose, for his lost freedom. They made Beth angry. He had been infected by the remarks of the cohort, especially those of Kirk, who had a part in a soapie, who smiled at them from the pages of newspapers, and who came to show them his new clothes. Marcus was to start tomorrow in sales, in the company of an experienced man. Beth, looking at him sideways as he perched puffing on his stool, opened a narrow cupboard and took out a dustpan and a ragged brush.

But when she went into the hall to sweep up the glass, he ran after her.

'Keep a look-out for syringes.'

'Shut up,' said Beth. She found his anxious concern as insulting as his nostalgia. It was as if, she told him one night, the whole of her, from her hair to her toenails, had turned into a child-bearing sac.

He took the dustpan and brush from her, swept up the glass, then held her in his arms. Tears came to her eyes. She brushed them away, saying, 'There they are again.'

180

'Your only symptom.'

She trembled and laughed. 'My only symptom.'

'Come and let's look at this place.'

Beth took a notebook and pen from one pocket of the red dress, and a pack of colour cards from the other. If they accepted the house, Juliet was to have it painted inside and out, though, at Marcus's insistence, ten days were to elapse, to eliminate dangerous fumes, before they moved in. Beth, on annual holidays, could cover the move. In Marcus's car, she could drive to the warehouse shops on the outskirts of Sydney to buy, with the money saved for their airfares, kits of simple and ingeniously designed furniture they could assemble themselves. She would buy paper lampshades and strong cotton for curtains. There was enticement in this for Beth, and as they went through the rooms, she became reconciled to the flimsy structure that limited the choice of colour, and casually dropped the reds and greens she had envisaged back into her pocket.

In the living room, the window opposite the door was filled with the glossy green of a cuprosma hedge, and another window overlooked the street. But the end wall was unbroken.

'Perfect for Mil and me,' said Beth.

They lingered, backing away to survey it, Beth proposing the ocean they were denied in their view. Seeing it already there, in thin repeated washes, she speculated on clouds, birds, an aeroplane, a daylight moon . . .

Then they made a second quick tour of the house. They enriched the colours and decided on red and white for the kitchen. They looked into the oven and spoke of meals that made the saliva run into their mouths. Merriment seized them. Beth held her stomach, waddled down the hall as if more pregnant than was possible, and called out in a quavering voice, 'Our first little home!'

Marcus struck a bridegroom's pose. 'Equity made our first home possible.'

She put a hand in the crook of his arm and snuggled up to him. They turned their smiles forward.

'See Equity about *your* first home!'

The routine derived from Kirk. Before his shadow could fall, Beth unlinked from Marcus. 'But where's the loo? There's no loo.'

They checked the bathroom again. 'Bloody Equity,' said Marcus.

They found the lavatory, with the laundry, in the fibro addition at the back. While Marcus checked the flush and the washing machine, Beth jiggled up the big crooked blind and saw, between the trunks of tall pines across the street, the cemetery. She opened the casement window wide. Headstones and monuments were regularly spaced in her near view, then descended a hill until they were compacted, in the valley, into a white and limestone mass, like dried coral, then straggled out of this mass and marched up the farther hill in regular but now distant rows. She leaned out of the window and saw, at the head of the valley, flat land where taller monuments were dominated by a big imploring sandstone figure of Jesus Christ. The whole confronted the sea. Beth could hear it now, its deep hypnotic note. Marcus was at her side. She said, without turning, 'Juliet said it was here. She thought we might mind.'

He said in a hushed voice, 'That's why that bloody great hedge is outside the living room window.'

'You do mind?'

'Well,' he said, 'they won't be revving up their motor bikes.'

'You *do* mind.'

'A bit.'

'You!' She jostled him with a shoulder, laughing. 'The

very first time we met, you were chatting about sarcophagi.'

'Showing off my plurals. Didn't know what they were.'

'*I* didn't. You did. Coffins, you said, and showed me the animals on them. You've regressed. And look, there's one of your fabulous creatures.'

The nearest angel stood on her pedestal between two pine trees, wings folded, one arm raised, the forefinger pointing to the sky, the others curved, relaxed. 'It can be our statuary garden,' said Beth. 'I like it. I'm glad it's there. It deserves its situation. Would you rather have a row of houses?'

'No,' said Marcus, 'I definitely wouldn't. Okay. It's okay. And another thing, I think there's rock fishing down there. I'm pretty sure that's where Gavin took me once.'

'Come for a walk and we'll see.'

'I want to take a look at the beach and the pool.'

'So do I. First this, because it's nearer, then that?'

'Right. Then we take the keys back to the agent and say yes. Any doubts?'

'None,' said Beth.

'Great for the baby.'

She did see herself, pushing a stroller past the shops. She did remember the barber standing in his door. But she gave a slow, judicious nod.

'Open space, and a sea wind to blow all the pollution away.'

Walking on the narrow cemetery paths, making towards the sea, treading on long grass freshly cut but not raked, they read names aloud. Neither had explored a cemetery before, neither had lingered, and the age of the place having made them expect the usual British predominance, they spoke with the surprise of discovery. Chicogna, they said, Ricone, Taranto, Fiaschi. And here – O'Mara, Coorigan, and all these O'Hallorans. Only two other figures, distant and slowly moving, were in sight. Mynah birds rose from the grass before them. A plane passed over, low, making them raise their voices. And look, Azur, Ayoub. And here is a Lopez, a Hong.

But presently, taking notice also of Wilsons and Tuckwells and Georges, they turned their attention from this variety, and began instead to discuss the statuary. They passed by obelisks, Celtic crosses, stone urns, and other inanimates, but lingered at the angels. Both having former Italian glory lodged in memory, they could not help trying to extract from these something of that. On the rim of the glory was the conventionally majestic, such as they had seen from the laundry window, but none was awe-inspiring, none dramatic, none stood in a chariot or crouched with great wings about to spread. Some, small girlish angels in short skirts, each with a star in her hair, carried flowers in the sling of their aprons while offering a single flower with the other hand. Some were infants, fat-legged cherubim who also offered flowers. One knelt as if in passing to pick an eroded sandstone flower from a slab. One, inclining in a maternal gesture, held in her hands, to receive her kiss, the face of a naked muscular child who stood on tip-toe before her. A few leaned pensively against sturdy crosses, and it was while they were facing one of these, and Beth, with an arm slung round Marcus's shoulders, was leaning in a similar attitude, that Marcus said, 'Now that one could be called Wendy.'

Beth yawned. 'She looks as sleepy as I feel.'

'They would have been a problem for my list of fabulous creatures.'

'Mmmm.'

Creeping into Beth's consciousness was a harmony new

to her. She felt it in the conjunction of her side and arm with Marcus's body, in the scent of the cut grass, and the boom and salty smell of the sea. It encompassed the rising field of stone, and the rows of small houses beyond. It was like the bliss of sexual love, but carried not excitement, but acceptance. Flooded with this happiness and acceptance, she disengaged herself from Marcus and said, in a gentle dazed voice, 'Well, let's go and see if there's rock fishing.'

She did remember that euphoria was also a symptom, but the knowledge was discounted by euphoria itself. Following Marcus on the narrow path downhill, she put a hand on his shoulder. The enquiry employed by Miles's group returned to mock her, the naively eager tone in which they had said, 'I suppose it is impossible to put your belief into words.' Yes, she agreed, keeping her hand on Marcus's shoulder, but whatever it is, it wants to radiate.

They reached a fragile white railing fence. Nearby, a gap and a narrow flight of concrete steps gave access to a wind-bitten outcropping of rock overhanging a turbulent sea. Spray rose to the claws of its rim, while beneath it, sea surged in to thud land invisibly; but on the south, a path led to rock platforms at sea level, and on the biggest of these, a fisherman, feet apart and tense arm extended, confronted the zesty waves.

Another low-flying plane made Beth shout. 'Is this where you went with Gavin?'

'I think so.'

The receding roar seemed to draw his *oooh* away, then, most strangely, to send it towards them again.

'Ooooh – '

Both turned their heads this way and that, confused.

'Marc-oooh.'

They turned from the railing. Nita, still distant, was

running down one of the paths, laughing and waving something white. 'A letter,' said Beth, while Marcus said at the same time, 'Heaven be praised. Bow-wow's come good.'

'She said he would. But how did she know where to find us?'

But now Marcus sounded a note of warning. 'Wait . . . hang on . . .' And Beth saw that what had appeared to be a laugh was the distortion of grief or fury. She started towards Nita, but Marcus caught her arm and said grimly, 'Wait. Take it easy.'

Nita reached them, ignored Beth's anxious questions, and slammed the letter hard and blindly against Marcus's chest. He had to clutch it to prevent the wind from taking it. Nita sat heavily on a slab, her forehead on her peaked knees, her face hidden, her sky-blue running shoes planted flatly in the green grass. To Beth, who knelt at her side, she gasped with harsh anger, 'Leave me alone.' Beth slowly raised herself and went to join Marcus.

Marcus was reading the letter, and after he whispered, 'Harriet,' neither of them spoke nor moved except when he extracted a page, or when Beth touched his hand to make him wait before doing so, or when she held this corner or that as the wind tried to puff between the flimsy pages. There were a number of pages, covered in a loose thin graceful cursive hand, and if Beth read slowly, it was not because it was illegible, but because its message of helpless treachery, of guilt and of larky happiness, left her incredulous. There was a cheque, too, and Beth was reading, on the last page: *Now let me explain this cheque* – when she saw in her side vision that Nita had risen. Marcus looked up at the same time, and immediately moved forward, stuffing the letter into a trouser pocket. Beth, beside him, saw Nita run through the gap in the white railing. Nita's mouth was wide open as if in a shout, but Beth heard nothing exept the roar and hiss of the sea. Nita ran across the big outcropping as Marcus, followed by Beth, moved through the gap in the fence. Beth heard her own and Marcus's feet pound the concrete steps, and saw, in precise detail, Nita's thick bright clothes against an explosion of aerial spray. She saw Marcus grasp Nita's nearer arm, and then noticed the firm stance of Nita's big pale shoes as she drew back her free arm before shooting it forward to expel from her fist the black and white watch.

Beth saw it, for a moment, the precise little object, waving its thin black straps as it tossed in the aerial spray. She slowly exhaled, a hand at her breast. She heard Marcus's voice as he spoke to his mother, but not his words. Nita did not respond, but turned inland, opened her mouth wide, and screamed. She continued to scream at this pitch as Beth and Marcus led her back across the rock outcrop, Marcus making with one hand a reassuring gesture for the attendant who came running and leaping down between the headstones.

When Nita stopped screaming, she began talking. She could not stop this talking, this babbling out of a tale broken by sudden wounded cries, hoots of laughter, and comments on the messages from her eyes.

She told them how she had taken the letter from the box an hour ago, on her way out of Juliet's house. She remarked that they died young in those days, and said that as soon as she held the letter in her hands, she knew, yet could not believe, and opened it in hope, at the same time understanding why she had not been able to get Harriet on the phone for three days. She said how miraculous it was that all these thoughts could occur in the time it took to open the letter. She said this cemetery was a gloomy place, and that Marcus and Beth had queer tastes, and hooted, and told how she had read the letter, standing there in the street, then had turned round and round, staring at nothing, then started back for the house, then remembered that Juliet was at the hairdresser's, then saw a taxi . . .

She asked, as they went slowly uphill, what she would do without these shoes, said that this uneven ground was hard on the feet, and that people were lucky to be born with good feet, but that she had been like Hans Andersen's little mermaid, wearing high heels for the sake of love, and that the address of the little house had been graven on her memory because she had sat staring at it on Juliet's phone pad for the last three days, while trying to get Harriet, and being told by some absolute stranger, when answered at last, that Harriet had gone to a big auction. She shouted, 'Big auction!' and laughed loudly.

Marcus laughed, too, at this more natural mirth, and said quietly, yes, and he had told her that Beth and he were looking at the house that morning. But before he could say anything else, she broke away from their hands to make kissing puss-puss noises at a grey cat on the path. She said Ralfe hated cats, that he was a dog man (Beth and Marcus refrained from exchanging glances), but that Harriet had two Siamese she worshipped, and that Ralfe had always called Harriet Miss Prim. Harriet did her hair in a French roll, wore spectacles and pleated skirts, and was the same age as Nita.

That Harriet was her own age became Nita's wondering refrain. At the gates of the cemetery, the wonder stopped her in her tracks.

'You can see the attraction of seventeen. And twenty-five. And thirty. But she's forty-seven. My age. My age.'

Beth was reminded of her own babbling to Kyrie after breaking with Miles, her weeping and repetition. But I know I have changed, she thought uneasily.

Nita was saying that when she found the little house locked and deserted, and the taxi gone, she ran to the end of the street (she pointed) and saw Beth and Marcus going through these gates.

'A taxi came along and I got in it, but at the shops I got out and came back to find you two. But first I chased after another couple I thought were you. I ought to wear specs myself, that's the truth, but the irony is, I thought it would put him off. So there I was waving that thing at those two. They thought I was mad. They were scared. Then I saw what had to be you two, so I came on down.'

She was much calmer. 'The letter seems so sincere,' said Beth.

Marcus gave her a look of reproach, but Nita said humbly, 'Yes, darling, that's the worst of it.'

As the house provided no seating, they sat outside, in the car, where Marcus took the letter from his pocket and smoothed the sheets out on his knee. Nita sat beside him, her face half-hidden from Beth by the high headrest. She had stopped talking, perhaps soothed by the enclosure of the car. Beth thought of Mrs Ho's mother, who, at eighty-six, having survived what she had survived, now lay very ill, near death. Beth recalled the smiling mask framed by the window of the Holden. Marcus was saying, 'Now listen, ma, this is all very well, what she says about you getting every cent of your share, but you ought to have something from him.'

'Oh, she'll see to that,' said Nita, with intense but quiet bitterness. 'Look at that cheque. Nine hundred for my Dutch plates. That's her guilty conscience.'

'All the same, you must get something from him.'

'Never mind that, darling.'

'Ma, we've got to mind that.'

'If you must know,' said Nita, 'I've got something.' She

took a folded sheet of paper from her bag and gave it to him, her face averted. 'I was ashamed,' she said angrily.

Marcus took the half-sheet of paper, read the message, then handed it into the back to Beth. Nita peered round the headrest as Beth read. She was quite calm now, and looked alert.

The note was typed, and headed – To Nita Vyner-Unwin.

I endorse everything written by Harriet Matthewson in her letter dated 12.9.86. Sorry, old thing, but it is for the best. I was only a worry to you, Nita. We will divorce when the year is up. Will be in touch about legal arrangements and division of property. Harriet is a stickler for doing the right thing, as you well know. Don't worry, she will take good care of me.

The signature, *Ralfe Thomas Vyner-Unwin*, was neat and childlike.

Nita's crushed little face was still tilted at Beth. She nodded her curls when she saw Beth's revulsion.

'Oh, he means it all right, darling.'

Beth handed the note back to Marcus.

'Yes, that's what they want,' said Nita, nodding again at Beth. 'A whore or a mother. Don't think Marcus will never do this to you, darling.'

Beth crushed her hands between her knees and looked through the window. She hoped the acceptance she had felt enter her could also encompass this. She looked at the living-room window of the house and envisaged the mural – the sea, and in the foreground, the outcropping of rock, its hollows containing water in shining pools, and beside one of these, two sky-blue running shoes. Marcus was speaking to his mother with warning steadiness.

'Ma, where were you going when you got this letter?'

'I don't know,' said Nita, still peering at Beth. 'I'm sorry

I said that, sweetie. I say awful things sometimes. They just come out.'

'As your former friend Harriet says,' said Marcus, '*it just happened*.'

Nita faced forward again. 'You're the one who ought to know,' she said. 'It just happened to you often enough.'

'Not any more, mum,' said Marcus. 'Not any more.'

Beth leaned forward. 'Were you going to Juliet's aunt, Nita?'

'The Charleston girl. I suppose I was. Well, sorry, *old thing*, no cheery chatter today. Won't she love it, though, when she does hear! I've been making a great joke of it, feeding her bits of it every day. Making up bits these last two days, to feed myself, yes, and never admitting it. Well, anyway, she can get to the fridge by herself – ' Nita brought her wrist forward to look at the time, then clasped it in the other hand, threw her head back, and shut her eyes.

'If you two had any sense, you would take me back to that place. I just want to lie down somewhere and die.'

Juliet, pleased to see a visitor, a young man, sitting by Barbara Philp's chair, stood with her hands clasped in front, smiling and waiting to be introduced. The young man rose, but Barbara Philp looked angrily at Juliet and said, 'You've been to the hairdresser.'

'Do you like it?'

'Ff, it has that hairdressery smell. You brought no flowers.'

'Tuesday's will still be fresh.'

'Look for yourself,' said her aunt, and added to the young man, 'Sit down.'

He sat down. Juliet said, 'They're not so bad, Aunt Bob.

I'll cull them and change the water. I thought Nita would be here by now.'

'Well, she's not.'

From the kitchen, Juliet could hear the young man's voice, speaking at some length, and her aunt's voice briefly replying. The geranium she had taken from Beth's and Marcus's window sill had put out, through a spread of green and bronze leaves, a stalk bearing a cluster of buds each slashed to show the red of petals still tightly furled. A shining glass jar full of Nita's almond bread stood on a counter. The china was clean, and the refrigerator a little treasure trove of good food. Juliet took the culled flowers back and said cheerfully to the young man, 'I am Juliet McCracken.'

He rose again. 'Roger Palmer.'

Barbara Philp said, 'Mr Palmer is just about to leave.'

Roger Palmer stood straight. 'I think that's quite a good idea. Perhaps,' he said, speaking to Juliet, 'you can tell me how the buses run.'

'I have no idea,' said Juliet, and Barbara Philp said, 'And I certainly haven't.'

'How did you come?' asked Juliet. He was rather a shabby young man, wearing a grey polo-necked pullover and cord trousers.

'Taxi.'

'Fff. Janet and Malcolm sent him. Let him ring for another taxi.'

'Only Janet, in fact,' said Roger Palmer.

'It's quite a short walk to the train,' said Juliet in dismissal.

'Now Malcolm's trying to get into parliament,' said Barbara Philp, 'Janet has taken up with the caring and counselling trades. And as she thinks I'm insane, she sends me Mr Palmer. Mr Palmer calls himself a psychiatrist.'

'A psychotherapist,' he said to Juliet. He had flushed to his dark hairline.

'I would like to know who told Janet I tore up their piffling photograph. Was it you, Juliet?'

'No, darling Aunt Bob, it was not. Mr Palmer, my car's not far away. I'll drive you to the train.'

'Then it was that wretched little Lorna. Fff.'

'But if it's only a short walk,' said Roger Palmer.

'Short, but very complicated. It's no trouble at all.'

'If you're sure. Goodbye, Mrs Philp.'

'It's no use sending me an account.'

The young man shook his head and raised his eyes as he and Juliet went through the door. 'He can't be much good,' Barbara Philp was saying loudly to herself. 'He hasn't even got a motor car.'

'I'm so sorry about that,' said Juliet, on the stairs.

'Your aunt is beyond the kind of help I am capable of offering,' said Roger Palmer. He held the front door open for Juliet. 'The crust is too thick and hardened, and there is too little time.'

They walked down Beach Road. 'I suppose you asked my aunt about her dreams,' said Juliet teasingly.

'God, no. Speaking of whom, religion would be the only therapy with the necessary speed. Betwixt the stirrup and the ground,' he said, with faint disdain, 'I mercy asked, I mercy found.'

'My second husband used to like quoting that, but when they told him he was falling off his horse, he decided not to bother.'

'What a wonderful car!'

'Thank you, Mr Palmer. Some people are so nasty about it.'

'I can see it's cherished.'

'I live in fear.'

'I'm sure you've no need. Years in it yet. Enjoy it.'

'I hope to.' In the driver's seat, she turned towards him. She frowned. 'Mr Palmer, I do wonder about dreams.'

'We all do. No radio – wonderful.'

'It would be vandalism. I write mine down, for fun, you know – well, a kind of a game – and then trace the origins. But it's so contradictory, and the books don't help.'

'Is it any use sending *you* an account?'

'You can if you like.'

He laughed. She also laughed. They drove along Beach Road and up the Yarranabbe hill. 'I did it as a favour,' he said. 'Now I see how your aunt could have taken it as an impertinence.'

'Yes indeed. This is the long way round, but it's prettier.'

'I'm deeply ashamed that I let your cousin – if Janet's your cousin?'

'My nephew's wife.'

' – that I let her talk me into it.'

'I'm wondering how you gained entry.'

'Your cousin Lorna helped.'

'No relation. Now I know who you are. You're the man who was so marvellous with Janet's Jeremy.'

'Humphrey.'

'Humphrey, was it? I thought you might be.'

'Most of my work is with children.'

'Before the – what did you say?'

'Before the crust thickens and hardens, yes.'

She laughed again, then said, 'No, but seriously, dreams. Sometimes I'm sure they're telling me important things, and at other times I'm convinced they're just a lot of rubbish.'

'Possibly both are true. If we don't look for messages, and prophecy – '

'Prophecy has never even occurred to me,' said Juliet sharply.

'Then if we forget that sort of thing, dreams can be

194

useful, I suppose, as a way into reflecting on one's problems.'

'What!' said Juliet. 'But I wrote that down once, that very thing. And here you are saying it. Isn't that uncanny?'

'We have probably both read the same book,' he said soothingly.

'Oh. Well, anyway, I just wrote it down without thinking, then forgot it and went on to something else.'

'Because you found that something else more attractive. You wanted it more. Generally speaking, I find the meanings people give to their dreams more revealing than the dreams themselves.'

'Oh?'

'Especially in the case of domineering personalities. Your aunt, for example, would certainly manipulate her dreams to make them mean what she wanted them to. But I'm sorry, I shouldn't. You're obviously fond of your aunt.'

'She was the idol of my youth.'

'Hard luck, I should say.'

'But listen, dreams.'

'How good the old church still looks.'

'Doesn't it?'

'When you consider the possible alternative.'

'What – '

'Another block of flats.'

'Oh, yes. Yes, rather. Look, do you mind if we turn in here for a minute. You are so interesting.'

'Isn't this a private driveway?'

'They can beep. Do you mean that only people as domineering as Aunt Bob do this manipulating?'

'I shouldn't have let your aunt get to me. I'm ashamed. To some extent, we're all inclined to do it. I'll give you an example. Now, you've probably noticed that dreams use incidents from the day before – '

'Oh, *yes* – '

' – so if I were to dream tonight of being rooted to the spot, unable to move, while a deadly snake was about to attack – well, say no more. I *am* ashamed. But the real origin of that dream could be something quite different, and could also be irrecoverable.'

'Or have too many meanings.'

'Multiple meaning, mmm, yes. I think this car wants to get out.'

Juliet waved impatiently to the driver of the car bearing down on hers, backed the Jaguar out, and joined the traffic. They were almost at the station. She said hurriedly, 'As if dreams wanted to defend themselves.'

'Well, that is new – '

'As if they weren't meant to be exposed.'

'Well, professionally, I hesitate to agree with that one.'

They were waiting near the corner, among stationary cars. Juliet tapped the wheel and murmured, 'Well, it's very mysterious.'

'Privately, I must certainly agree with that. Just when I was about to leave you my card.'

They both laughed.

'I'll hop out here, Mrs McCracken,' he said, 'and just dash across. Thank you so much, Mrs McCracken.'

When Juliet returned to her aunt's flat, she found her asleep in her chair. Barbara Philp was a decorous and silent sleeper. She had been taught the trick of it, she often said, on the Orient Express, but unfortunately could not pass it on because she had forgotten it; it had entered her second nature, from where she could not retrieve it.

Juliet looked into the empty kitchen, then rang her own house.

Beth replied. Juliet spoke to her for a few minutes,

murmuring in reply, 'Goodness . . . goodness gracious . . . how too damn awful . . . Yes, do . . . I shan't be long . . .'

She hurried back to her aunt. Barbara Philp was awake. She always awakened refreshed from these silent sleeps, but she had forgotten Roger Palmer. 'Miles was here,' she said. 'Miles Ligard. I didn't encourage him to stay. If he has chosen to throw himself heart and soul into working with diseased people, I can't have him using my tea cups. What does that clock say? Where is Nita? I believe I am rather hungry. Miles looked quite shabby.'

'Nita can't come today, Aunt Bob.'

'What, it's two o'clock.'

'Yes, indeed.'

'Fff, once they start that, it's time to get rid of them.'

'Aunt Bob,' said Juliet, 'no time could be worse. Her husband is divorcing her. He has another woman.'

'The girl with the legs. I know all about the girl with the legs.'

'No, not with legs – '

'What – '

'No, I mean, a serious older woman. The one with the legs departed two weeks ago. This one did the consoling.'

'Fff, I knew it would end badly. She has bad luck written all over her. I'm sick of those shoes flapping about. And I'm sick of her unending jollity, and her hectic stories. She's one of those people who uses up all the oxygen in the air. Have you noticed that, Lorna?'

'Juliet.'

'Have you noticed that, Juliet?'

'Yes, I have, in fact.'

'You've been looking fagged out.'

'But you love her cooking, Aunt Bob.'

'It's time I had a change. Lorna spoke of a girl, a student, who has been living in Mexico. That could be amusing.'

'I have to go now, darling Aunt Bob. I'll make you a sandwich.'

'Boil me an egg.' Barbara Philp shut her eyes and said, 'A two-minute egg, with six little soldiers to dip, and after that, a dish of ice cream with grated chocolate, dark chocolate, then some milky coffee.'

Juliet stood silently. Barbara Philp opened her eyes and said, '*Very weak* milky coffee.'

Juliet said, 'And after that, second thoughts about Nita, I hope.'

'Nita who?' asked her aunt. 'Who is Nita?'

Beth and Marcus stayed with Nita while the tranquilliser took effect. Marcus sat by the bed, where Nita had asked him to sit, and Beth stood at the window, her hands in the pockets of her red dress, watching for Juliet's car.

Mrs Ho's car, empty, stood in the street. Beth recalled the warm winter day when she had run past it and seen, through tears, the smiling mask, and again, not much later in the winter, when she had hurried past it saluting and laughing. She supposed a recovery like her own was possible for Nita, but could not imagine what would bring it about. The question in Beth's mind had a sardonic ring. 'Once again, love?'

She heard Marcus give an abrupt sigh. 'Well, she's fast asleep.'

Beth went to the bedside and picked up the little bottle. It was nearly full. She mouthed at Marcus, 'Would she?'

Marcus vigorously shook his head. He repelled with a hand the very idea. But Beth restored the bottle to its place reluctantly.

Nita lay curled on her side, one fist lightly clenched

beside her face. Marcus rose, put his arms round Beth, and kissed her at the junction of neck and shoulder. The white fist on the pillow was worn and gnarled. Beth knew that many of Nita's ventures, such as her most recent one, had demanded hard physical labour, and that in her first enthusiasm, Nita had never spared herself, and nor, provided she had a master, had she relaxed in the following period of settled hard work. 'She works like a maniac,' Marcus had said. Beth put her hands over Marcus's hands, which were now covering her breasts. Though it was Marcus who had told her how hard Nita had worked, it was Nita herself who had exposed, by her behaviour and her many random remarks, her need for a master.

The wrinkled pages of the letter waited on the table in the breakfast room downstairs, beneath an ashtray. 'Let Juliet read it,' Nita had said, through her sobs. 'Juliet will know what to do.'

Beth turned in Marcus's arms. 'All this is hard on Juliet,' she said. But Marcus put a finger to his lips. Nita was sighing, turning and sighing.

Beth released herself and returned to the window. Nita, while waiting to submit once more to the mastery of love, would find a substitute master. Her first headlong instinct had been to appoint Marcus, but he, with his own kind of instinct, and with Beth's scarcely less instinctive support, had rejected the role.

Marcus was standing behind her again. 'The important thing,' he said, 'is to get mum's money out, and the quicker the better.'

Beth gave a nod. 'But it's not the only important thing.'

He kissed her neck again, then raised his head to whisper, 'Do you love me?'

Juliet's car appeared at the end of the street. 'I love you more than I can say,' said Beth. Nita turned and sighed.

*

Beth and Marcus, at the table in the breakfast room, waited for Juliet to return from Nita's bedside. The pages of the letter lay face down, beneath Juliet's handbag, in the order in which she had placed each one after reading it. Beth could hear Mrs Ho moving about in the kitchen next door. Juliet, returning, stopped to speak to her, then came into the breakfast room and put the bottle of pills on the table.

'Just in the meantime,' she said.

'Ma would never – ' began Marcus, but Juliet said, 'It's that moment when you wake up, you see.'

Beth, made wise by her lesser griefs, nodded. 'Yeah-yeah,' Marcus softly agreed.

'I'll give her one when she needs it.'

'Right,' said Marcus sadly, and Beth said, almost as sadly, 'She won't resent it at all.'

'Now, this Harriet,' said Juliet, touching the letter, 'this poor woman – '

'She's no poor woman,' said Marcus with vigour. 'She's a weak woman. Or she would have rung – ' He gave the letter a thump – 'instead of that.'

'If it had to be done,' said Juliet, 'don't you think a letter was the better choice? Shock can prevent one from quite understanding spoken words.'

'There's no good way to do a thing like that,' said Beth.

'Then a letter was the least bad way,' said Juliet. 'Here we have her written words, and his. I'm thinking of her money, of course. Marcus, did Nita actually sign her rights away? Is there a legal document?'

'I couldn't get her to say. She would just go off about love and loyalty and the Tissot still ticking.'

'I had the same experience,' said Juliet. 'So let's hope this Harriet is not weak, or she'll be in danger of being per-suaded by this damn man, whose name I refuse to say – '

200

'Bow-wow,' said Marcus, barking.

Beth and Marcus burst simultaneously into giggles, which at once became helpless laughter. Marcus leaned back in his chair, roaring. Beth stifled her laughter by lowering her head into her folded arms. And even as she shook with laughter, she was shocked that they could do this to Juliet, who presented today, groomed and controlled though she was, the perfect mask of exhaustion. She raised her head and said, gasping, 'Nita called him her sea-dog, you see.'

'I see,' said Juliet coldly.

'I'm sorry,' said Beth, wiping her eyes.

'So am I,' said Marcus. 'I don't know what got into us.'

Beth turned to him and said accusingly, '*It just happened*.'

'Please,' said Juliet. 'We must continue this no-doubt boring discussion. Someone must soon go upstairs, to be there when Nita wakes.'

'Right,' said Marcus. 'Beth and I have been sitting here like schoolkids. There must be something we can do ourselves about ma.'

'What? Take her to sleep on your floor? Give her your bed and let her have the discomfort of having ousted you? Send her alone to a hotel, in the state she's in?'

They were shaking their heads. 'But,' said Beth, 'we could move into the house earlier.'

'*No*,' said Marcus, while Juliet said, 'Then you looked at the house?'

'Sure, before ma arrived.'

'We told the agent we wanted to take it,' said Beth. 'We love the salt air.'

'I have never seen it, myself,' said Juliet, sounding pleased. 'I don't care for the salt air. Only the coarsest things grow, and it rusts your car. But Fergie used to say it was a marvellous situation, and that one day, terraces of houses would be modelled to the contours of those slopes and cliffs, all in pale colours.'

'It sounds wonderful,' said Beth.

'All radiating from the cemetery,' said Marcus, laughing, 'like massive headstones.'

'No,' said Beth. 'Like a beautiful big coral reef.'

'Coral,' said Juliet. She took off her spectacles and said slowly, 'I think he saw it as something like Tangier.'

'May I do a mural in the living room?' said Beth.

Juliet put on her spectacles and said briskly, 'Do all the murals you like. It's a relief to get good tenants.'

'Perhaps a sea view,' said Beth, 'but I still regret my bush petrol station. Listen . . .'

Juliet listened politely, then said, 'It sounds very amusing. I can't quite see why Captain Cook should be on a bigger scale, but I'm sure you have your reasons. Give me your list of colours for the rooms, and I'll ring the agent as soon as we've settled our present problem. Now, Nita must stay here in the meantime. There's no alternative. She may want to go to the West and confront those ridiculous lovers, but I don't think it likely, and if she does, we must discourage her. At present she needs three things. Money, a lawyer, and rest.'

'We have money,' said Marcus, 'and credit, too. But mum's very strong and resilient physically. She doesn't like too much rest. You'll see – in a day or two she'll want to go back to your aunt.'

'Oh, my aunt,' said Juliet. She touched her hair lightly, here and there. 'My aunt is a very capricious woman. When she was younger, and so beautiful, it seemed like an added charm in many doting eyes, including my own. I see it differently now. Nita had better not go back there. We'll keep her occupied in some other way. The first thing is to find her a lawyer. I'll ask Miles to recommend someone.'

'Of course,' said Marcus, 'he couldn't do it himself, being such a big shot.'

Beth sat up straight. 'What's the matter with *you*?'

'Marcus,' said Juliet, 'someone really had better go up and see if Nita's all right.'

Marcus went at once, shrugging, looking sullen.

'Retrospective jealousy?' enquired Juliet, smiling at Beth.

'Only since he became ambitious,' said Beth.

'What a good thing it's retrospective. You could explain to him that Miles is not such a big shot now. He's still with the firm, but they've confined him, or he has confined himself, to what he calls the more abstract matters. And much of his time goes on voluntary work connected with aids. It's become quite a crusade, as the right to privacy used to be. Unfortunately, Clem's disease has very quickly progressed. I tell you in case you want to write to him.'

'Oh, I do,' said Beth. 'I shall.'

'Since you won't visit him?'

'No.'

'No,' agreed Juliet.

Marcus came back. 'Still asleep,' he said. He stood by the window, his arms folded. 'Juliet,' he said, with an edge of hostility, 'about having ma here – you and she aren't naturally compatible, it's no use pretending you are. Ma can get people down, and Beth and I have both noticed how tired you look.'

'Thank you,' said Juliet, 'it's always nice to be told.'

'Yes, Marcus, shut up,' said Beth. She put a hand on Juliet's arm. 'But it's true, Juliet. We're worried about all the trouble you've had in this business. And are still having.'

There was a question in her voice. Juliet laughed, shrugged, then put an elbow on the table, and a hand on a cheek. 'You mean, Why me? Well, no doubt I had some dark and sinister motive at the start, but it does seem to have simply melted away into the particulars of the case. I wonder if the best explanation I can give is that it just happened. Perhaps we are all more like this poor damn Harriet than we care to believe.'

She took Beth's hand from her arm and laid it against her other cheek. 'And I do sincerely want your happiness, child. Trust me in that.'

Beth's readiness to trust Juliet in that gave her the measure, for the first time, of the reservation with which she had trusted her before. 'I do,' she said, 'I do trust you.'

Marcus came forward. He sat down and folded his arms on the table. 'We could come at night and take ma out to dinner.'

Juliet put Beth's hand down, patted it, and said, 'When she is well enough, she would love that.'

'When I go to choose the furniture,' said Beth, 'I'll ask her if she would like to come.'

'And when we go out in the weekend to buy it,' said Marcus.

'Oh, no doubt we'll manage. When do you two intend to marry?'

They said together, 'We don't.'

Juliet drew back her head and smiled in comic disbelief. 'What? Never?'

'We don't say never,' said Marcus.

'Some time – ' Beth shrugged – 'maybe.'

'But if some time, why not now?'

'Because that's a social matter,' said Marcus, 'a free choice. And we don't have too many of those left.'

'But surely, surely,' said Juliet, laughing and spreading her hands, 'you will have many, many free choices.'

'You would be surprised,' said Marcus sombrely. 'I am surprised.'

'It *took* me by surprise,' said Beth. 'It *took* me.'

'And if there are some areas where we can exert our free will,' said Marcus, 'right, we want to keep them.'

'And if that's an illusion,' said Beth swiftly, 'we want to keep that.'

'Well . . .' Juliet looked alertly from one to the other, 'I am disappointed. I was planning to give you a wedding party. I didn't intend to frighten you with anything ecclesiastical. I thought I would get you one of those nice celebrants, perhaps in ethnic clothes, who would say something modern. Or a poem or some such evasive thing. It would still be a ceremony. And I wanted to ask all your friends, and have tables in the garden, or indoors if it rained. And some really splendid food, and champagne for the toast.'

'It sounds like a great idea,' said Marcus, 'without the celebrant.'

'We're sorry, Juliet,' said Beth.

'So am I. You know how I do love giving parties.' Juliet picked up the letter and looked thoughtfully through its pages. Then she set it down suddenly and said, 'Well, since it was going to be in early October, we could make it a party for Beth's birthday. What do you say, Beth? Would you mind if I asked your family?'

Beth first looked shocked, then drew her eyebrows together and was silent.

'Listen,' said Marcus, putting an arm along the back of her chair and leaning close, 'why not? They've got to know about me sooner or later. And about the baby.'

Beth said, 'We were just talking of exerting our free will.'

'Short of being bloody offensive to each other. You know what? You're making me the invisible father in this act.'

Beth looked at Juliet. '*All* my family?'

'Judy, Bill, and six boys,' said Juliet. 'That's only eight.' She took a notebook and biro out of her handbag and wrote: <u>Family</u> = <u>8</u>. 'Now, how many friends?'

'Say, ten,' said Marcus.

'Kirk won't come,' protested Beth.

'He'll come. Yeah, ten. Or eleven with Kut.'

'Kut?' said Juliet, her pen poised.

'Kutei. Staying with Kirk's family. Japanese. Here to learn English.'

'I expect he is,' said Juliet grimly, as she carefully made the two little strokes of the eleven. 'That's nineteen. And with us three and Nita, twenty-three. Quite a nice number. Now all we need is Beth's consent. Then you two must go up and sit with Nita. Beth, I love making parties, as you know. I believe it's what I miss most. And think what it will do for Nita. Nita will be needed. This isn't my usual affair. I'll need her help and experience. And she will have her legal affairs to keep her busy, too.' Juliet shut her eyes for a moment, then opened them and said, 'She and I both feel better when we're getting on with things. Beth, do say yes.'

'Well, as the football season will be over,' said Beth, 'what else can I say? Thank you, Juliet.'

'If family is coming,' said Marcus, 'what about Kyrie?'

'Yes,' said Beth, 'and Jeannie.'

'Jeannie?' asked Juliet.

'Her companion and lover.'

'Goodness.'

'Is that still on?' said Marcus incredulously.

'Twenty-five,' said Juliet, crossing out and substituting, 'is the *perfect* number.'

After Juliet rang the agent, she went to her bedroom, raised the key from its hiding place in her clothes, opened the second drawer in the desk, and took out a brown paper parcel fastened with adhesive tape. She cut the tape, spread out the paper, and picked up the photograph in its heavy silver frame.

They had warned her about the obscurity that would result from isolating and blowing up one small section of a small photograph. Beth had worn her hair cut with a fringe then, and her face, seen against a background of pale blue (which was, in fact, Miles's shirt) was like one of those ghostly faces, of unidentifiable gender, not yet faded out of an ancient fresco. It seemed a suitable device for a knight-in-waiting, so intent on his crusade. Juliet sat down and wrote the note she would send with it.

FOURTEEN •

After many trials, Beth wrote in plain words to Clem. She told him about the irresistible protectiveness that had developed for the child, and again used the words, *So little is known about that malady yet*. She wrote of her sorrow that they could not meet – but not of her sorrow for the stiff embarrassment with which she was writing – and said that she would always think of him with affection.

To avoid provoking another of Marcus's foetus-defending outbreaks, she wrote the letter at work, and posted it in her lunch hour. At her drafting table that afternoon, she found herself reflecting on the essential conservatism of motherhood, and wondered if to exempt oneself – as Nita had done – was to reject the role. She felt suddenly, with dread, that it was a hardened and dark old shell that she had got herself into. Later, she asked herself why she had not said *that* to Clem. He would have understood that. She thought, Plain words are too plain. If he answers, I'll write again and say that.

But by the time he replied, that moment of dread had been submerged by the renewal and deepening of the sexual flow between herself and Marcus, by the domestic pleasures of furnishing the house, and by her sympathy with Marcus's initial uncertainty in his new job.

Clem wrote: *Thank you for your lovely letter. Have you*

seen Miles lately. Doesn't he look awful. Well it goes to show it's impossible to be stylish and virtuous. All the best – Clem.

She knew him too well to feel this as anything but scornful. Humiliated, she thrust the letter deep into the big shopping bag she now always carried. Later that day, she tore it up and dropped it into the waste basket beside her drafting table. But it had affected her, and was like a stiffening in a small joint – say, a joint in the little finger, no longer quite flexible.

It was Beth alone who called for Nita in the evenings and took her to dinner. Marcus, after his first day in sales, had come back to the flat and solemnly announced that he did not know his product.

'But you said you did,' said Beth.

'Bloody ignorance. Bloody *depth* of ignorance. I don't. And I've got to. I've got to know everything about it.'

'He is learning his product,' Beth explained to Nita at their first dinner, 'and everyone else's product, too. He hasn't a spare moment. He runs instead of walking. He says he's worried stiff, but his eyes are shining. And it isn't as if he has lost interest in my product. I mean,' she added, as Nita looked at her blankly, 'the baby.'

'Oh, the baby. I'll give you my china canisters for your kitchen. If she'll give them up, that is.'

'But Harriet hasn't made any difficulties yet. Quite the contrary.'

'That's her guilty conscience, darling. It'll be different with those canisters, wait and see. They're real antiques. And those dooners. She hasn't answered yet about those quilts. They're mine, those quilts. So this is how they do Fritto Misto in Sydney? I knew it would be no good, this place, there's too much variety in the menu. And the prices, darling. We wouldn't have dared. The new

209

man had better be good. She hasn't an inkling. She would live on Vegemite toast.'

Beth, finding herself either numbly listening, or talking into Nita's abstracted or angry silences, persisted in the dinners, for Juliet's sake, until Nita herself said she couldn't be bothered, and would rather stay home. The journey to choose the furniture was more successful. Beth let Nita drive. She was a much better driver than Beth, and the exercise of this skill brought her relief.

'Tell me about Marcus's father,' said Beth, on the outward journey.

'Garth Pirie,' said Nita, 'had a wonderful intellect, and would be the first to say so. But it made him contemptuous of others. Then he started despising possessions too. He gave me all the money, what he didn't lose on Toomba. He wasn't mean, not with money. Marco can have all his letters and photographs, from his parents, his grandparents, and everything. He despised them, too. He dumped them all on to me. And Marco didn't want them either, darling. They're all over there in a sandalwood box inlaid with ivory. Unless she decides to keep it. That box is mine.'

'Marcus will want them now, and if he doesn't, I do. We'll look at them all, his and mine, then put them away carefully.'

'You ought to write and ask your father and stepmother to bring yours up when they come up for the party.'

'I have. I've made a list.'

Since the evening of Nita's arrival, Beth had attempted many times to ask her if she remembered the cloister, and Marcus's list of animals, but each attempt had foundered in Nita's preoccupation with Ralfe. And now, when she tried again, and said, 'And speaking of lists – ' Nita broke in to say, 'Juliet wrote to your father and confirmed all the arrangements made on the phone.

Juliet's a first-rate organiser. She ought to have been in business. I'm going to rig up one of my magic circles over the tables in the garden. They keep the flies away, and it'll look pretty in the trees. It looks like tinsel, but it's not. It's some long name. Strictly speaking, that equipment is mine and mine alone, but I can't make that young Angela attend to the fine legal detail. She gets that injured look.'

But while examining the furniture, Nita became interested. Measuring while Beth took notes, she let the tape snap back loudly into its coil.

'Those stools are just the thing for lunch counters. Juliet says I ought to go into lunches when the money comes through. In Brisbane or Adelaide, she suggests. The Sydney rents are killing. I get keen as mustard at times, and then, wham, I'm as scared as a little kid.'

Nita thrust the tape measure at Beth and turned her face into the wall of kitchen modules to weep. Beth now knew better than to offer physical comfort. She waited until Nita said, with scarcely smothered anger, 'Well, better get on with it.'

On the homeward journey, with Nita triumphant behind the wheel, Beth said, 'Do you remember when Marcus was seven, in Rome, getting him to make a list of animals?'

'I'll say I do. He waved it under our noses often enough. He was smart as a tack, Marco. It was only application he lacked.'

'Not with that list. Do you remember going out to see Burt Lancaster acting in a film?'

'Will I ever forget it! That was through my friend Erica. She's a big wheel in movies here now. Juliet says that film crews need catering, and that I ought to get in touch. But I couldn't keep up, darling, not the way I am now. I've lost my go. Me of all people, with all the go I had in me.'

'When you went to see Burt Lancaster, do you remember leaving Marcus with his list of animals in the cloister of a museum?'

'It did him no harm!' Nita was instantly defiant. 'He was old enough to know not to talk to strangers.'

'I only wanted to say that was where Marcus and I first met. I was there with Bill and Judy.'

'Well, that's a coincidence. Not that life's not full of them, coincidences. That was the place with the old dry fountain in the centre and the animal heads around it. Before we settled him down there with his clipboard, we all went and looked at those heads. I was never a neglectful mother. There was a horse and a bull and a camel, and I don't know what else except a rhinocerus. I remember the rhino because the ivy on his pediment had grown right up through his head and was spilling out of his mouth, and Gavin got Marco to write that down. Gavin was good fun over there, but as soon as we got back home, all he was interested in was the financial pages.'

'I'm glad you remember the rhino. That's the one Marcus and I remember best.'

'Then you ought to put him in this famous mural you're going to do.'

'No-no-no.'

'No need to bite my head off, darling. It was only a suggestion.'

But Beth, having tried one day to draw the rhinocerus, and failed completely, had come to suspect that she had never seen it at all, but had constructed it from the words that had leapt into her mind from Marcus's page. She said, 'I do think we had better leave him where he is. Then he will always be perfect.'

'You know best, darling.'

'Everything else will change. But he never will.'

'Change is right. Gavin was fifteen years older than

me. Juliet suggested I look him up, but it turned out he married some old duck and has gone to live on the north coast. Where I can just imagine him, with his fish and his financial pages.'

'Now the house is painted, would you like to come out and see it?'

'No, thank you. I couldn't go out there. It would bring that day back.' Tears fell from Nita's eyes as she skilfully changed lanes. 'Juliet says I'm the sort whose motto is Onward Ever Onward. And I say yes, that's true, but it's my go that's gone. I've got to get my go back first.'

It was midnight. The dream had occurred during Juliet's first sleep. She got up at once. In no danger of forgetting, she wrote deliberately and neatly.

DREAM 25 = I am walking on rough dry paddock grass towards my cedar table and chairs. Two people shadowy sit there. A voice says clearly, Now that she has gone. I look up. I see an angel beside the table. Bigger than human. Carrying a tray with 3 glasses of wine. Angel puts wine glasses down one by one. I look at its feet and see them stretched downwards toes inches above the rough grass. Pink feet with beautiful skin. I look into my wine glass and see an interior shining red as if a ruby were suspended in the fluid. Don't look at angel but know it is growing bigger and bigger and then is gone. Don't look at other two but feel them there. Indescribably peaceful. Wake up with same feeling.

Without pause, Juliet continued.

The peaceful feeling is still there. I know better now than to try to trace origins or to manipulate the voice saying, Now that she has gone, so that it will mean how peaceful it will be when Nita has gone. Besides, it could mean – – But there I am, doing it, and straight away the peace starts to run out. Well, I allow myself this last indulgence = I walk on rough paddock grass because yesterday I decided again on a house in the country, though not so far away this time. Clem wants to come, for as long as he can. And Conrad will come. And Miles, perhaps, occasionally. That's all. Let 25 be the perfect number, as with the guests for Beth's party. <u>Pure</u> coincidence. Stop. No more.

Except to say = <u>Colour definite</u>.

In a succession of still, clear, shining days, Beth assembled furniture alone. Few cars passed the little house; no wind disturbed the stiff cuprosma hedge sheltering the side window of the living room. Beth, unused to being alone, hearing across the quietness the sigh and gulp of the ocean, came gradually to a realisation that the child she was bearing would be a being from whom she would never be capable of detaching herself. She was not enthusiastic about this decree, but it did not make falter the gentle hammer taps with which she was settling a dowel into place. She liked this work, so precise, useful, and sure of success. When Marcus came that night, he seemed a noisy stranger until they embraced.

She had not expected him to become suddenly so whole-heartedly absorbed in selling. She did not know how she could get used to it.

He said, 'You've no idea of the ton of money there is out there.'

'But who wants a ton?'

'It's always useful. This is the real stuff. I've never even had a sniff of it before.'

She began almost to take comfort in Nita's examples of his lack of persistence.

'Like the time I left him in first year science at Sydney Uni, and next thing I know, there he is galloping past me in Singapore airport, with two minutes to make his connection.'

There were Marcus's shining eyes, however, when he spoke of money, and his excitement, as if in love.

On Sunday, Mil, Andy, and Stathos came; Andy and Stathos to help Marcus with the larger pieces, and Mil to consult with Beth on the mural. Annette came with Mil, but after leaning against the wall, with her arms folded, saying that she felt totally useless, she went out for a walk. Beth admired Mil's big delicate square-palmed hand assessing the wall as he spoke.

'Your Captain Cook scheme would only be a wall-painting, Beth. I like it. I really like your louche-looking pair in evening dress, and the man lolling back smoking. You've got a great imagination. But it's not an illusionist painting. It's a waste of a good wall. And it's no good just sticking a window round it. That's feeble. And anyway, there wouldn't be a house with a window, out there in the bush.'

'No,' admitted Beth. 'Isolation was part of the point.'

'Right. Then forget it. With a wall like this you can extend the room. Nothing incongruous. No classical columns or marble halls. But the possibilities are terrific. Only, listen, Beth, are you up to it?'

'Mil, I'm pregnant, but my health is perfect.'

'I didn't mean that, Beth. I mean, are your skills up

to it? We did the cinema attendant. Right. But that was very simple stuff. Are they up to this?'

Beth descended her spiral of enthusiasm and admitted that they were not. As Mil went on speaking, offering himself, with sympathy, as artist-in-chief, she fiercely determined that one day, she would have such skills, and by their power, would concentrate her petty romanticism into something quite unlike itself. She went to the window, and through the gap in the cuprosma hedge made by the painters' ladders, saw Annette, with her arms folded, trudging uphill through the cemetery.

'If you like,' Mil was saying, 'we could both do some sketches, and pick out something Marco and you and I all like, and that will do justice to this wall.'

'All right,' said Beth, as Annette disappeared into the mass of thick rounded glossy leaves. 'That's what we'll do.'

FIFTEEN •

The boys came in a group across the grass. The twins, Mark and Peter (who were nineteen), walked with a dogged firmness, slightly ahead. The others, Andrew, Warren, Gerard and James (who was fourteen) looked bashful, and slightly jostled each other. All were tall slender light-limbed boys, and Nita said indignantly to Beth, 'They're not football thugs at all.'

'They play Rules, ma,' Marcus said patiently.

In the confused huddle they made around Beth and Marcus, some kissed Beth, and some shook Marcus's hand. All said, Happy Birthday, and spoke of the drive, and the mad truckies on the Hume Highway. Then there was an abrupt silence into which Warren said, 'What's that silver stuff up in the trees, anyway?'

'I'm glad you asked that,' said Nita, coming forward, taking charge. 'That's my magic circle. It keeps the flies away from the food. And speaking of food, you young men will be hungry. And I need some help with the drinks.'

Only James lingered with Beth and Marcus. 'Hey,' he said, 'Beth, do you remember the bedtime stories you used to tell me?'

'Some of them,' said Beth. James wore his thick curling hair long, in the old-fashioned sixties' style. Beth picked a fleck of silver from it.

'Do you remember the one about the beautiful princess imprisoned by the six ugly giants?'

'Ha!' said Marcus. Beth pulled a lock of James's hair and said, 'Ding-dong, who won?'

'Hawthorn,' said James with disgust.

'Where are dad and Judy?'

'Still in there. Dad's talking to Mrs McCracken, and mum's doing her hair and all that. Hey – ' James began to move away – 'will you look at that tucker!'

'Not too much,' Nita was saying. 'Only a pre-luncheon snack.'

'Don't come with me,' said Beth to Marcus, when he started towards the house at her side. 'I want to speak to dad alone first.'

As she reached the porch, she saw Kyrie and Jeannie come round the corner of the house, and heard a shout of welcome from the twins. The twins had always been infatuated with Kyrie. Mil and Annette and Stathos were following close behind.

Bill Jeams was sitting alone in the hall, looking at his watch. He jumped up when he saw Beth, and stretched his arms quickly to ease his sleeves before embracing her. They managed their kiss without bungling and drew apart, smiling.

'Happy birthday, daughter.'

'Thank you, dad.'

'Twenty-one, eh?'

'Twenty-one.'

'Judy and I were just telling Mrs McCracken how disappointed we were that you didn't manage to get down home for this one, for the party Jude planned.' He lowered his voice. 'That's a good friend you've got there, Beth, and this is a fine home.'

'Where *is* Juliet?'

'She's with Jude. Jude's feeling a bit mussed up. That's a journey, Beth, I won't undertake again.'

'The killer truckies.'

'You wouldn't be smiling, Beth, if you had been in one of our cars.'

'Oh, I know,' said Beth, in quick apology, 'I know it's bad.'

'So bad that we're breaking at Nowra on the way home. Which means we stay for your luncheon, then we're off.'

'That's a pity. But listen, dad, I want you to meet Marcus Pirie. He's out in the garden.' Smiling, she nodded in the direction of the babble of voices. 'Listen to them. Marcus is the man I live with, dad.'

'Well, Beth, in the absence of information, we've done our share of speculating, Jude and I, and we thought there must be something doing in that direction. Do you mind if I take this chance to ask what went wrong between you and Miles?'

'It would take too long to explain, dad.'

'I won't pretend we aren't disappointed.'

'Yes, dad, but I love Marcus.'

'What does he do?'

'Sells computers.'

Her father gave a slight shrug. 'Why not get married?'

'Maybe we will, one day.'

Bill looked beyond Beth for a moment, then gave another slight shrug. 'Well, this thing has happened to so many of our friends, Beth, and in spite of all the fuss and bother in some cases, they've all survived it very nicely. Very nicely indeed.' He took a step backwards and ran a hand over his head. 'Did you notice I'm thinner on top?'

'You look just the same.'

And indeed he did. His thin, high-shouldered figure, his long slightly knock-kneed legs, his mildly handsome face, his inoffensively expensive clothes, his possibly kind eyes . . . Beth always suspected that her own vision was at fault, and at each meeting hoped to see something more than this. Stroking his head, he asked confidentially, 'And what did you think of the boys?'

'Wonderful!' In her relief, Beth almost shouted. 'They look *wonderful*.'

'We think so,' he said quietly.

'I love James's luxuriant curls.'

'James is our Bohemian. I had better leave it to Jude to tell you our news. Well, here she is.'

Judy was preceded by Juliet. On seeing Beth, Judy halted, covered her eyes with one hand, and said, through smiling lips, 'I am so ashamed.'

Beth, educated by the lumps and slumps at the clinic, estimated that Judy was about six months pregnant. Judy peeked through her fingers and said, 'At my age.'

'Why not?' But Beth did wish she had made her own news known before Judy's entrance. 'Congratulations, both of you.'

'Wait, that's not the whole joke,' said her father. 'Go on, Jude.'

'Well,' said Judy, 'if I only had the decency to have a girl this time. But – no – '

'Another boy, Beth!' said Bill.

Judy dropped her sheltering hand and came forward to kiss Beth. 'I had the Ultrasound, of course,' she said briskly, 'and the Down's, naturally.'

'I shan't ask what these mysterious words mean,' murmured Juliet, while Bill said, 'Not that we were worried.'

'Judy,' said Beth, 'I live with a man named Marcus Pirie. You and dad are just about to meet him. Marcus and I are having a baby next March.'

'I tipped that,' said Bill quickly.

Judy put an arm round Beth's shoulders, and, being taller, twisted her neck to look into Beth's face. 'That's too early for the Ultrasound.'

'Oh, much. The only test I've had was for aids.'

Bill said, 'Nobody suggested that one to Jude.' But Judy tightened her grip on Beth's shoulders and said in a low voice, 'And it was okay?'

Beth burst into laughter. 'I wouldn't still be pregnant if it hadn't been.'

'Really, dear? We happen to believe that nothing gives us that right.'

But now, above the noises from the garden, came a triumphant note from a clarinet, then a little run on a drum. 'Andy and Kirk,' said Beth joyously, walking out of Judy's arm. 'Nobody mentioned music. Juliet, do you mind?'

'No, no, no.' Juliet, herself looking joyous, vaguely ushered Judy and Bill with one arm as they all moved towards the garden.

'What is it, exactly?' asked Kyrie. 'It's not tinsel.'

'Some space age stuff,' said Jeannie. 'Some long name. I've forgotten.'

Kyrie tenderly removed a speck from Marcus's hair. 'Sure to be radio active.'

'I always knew ma would do for me,' said Marcus.

'Where's Beth, anyway?' asked Kyrie.

'In there breaking the bad news to her dad. Listen – ' He spoke to Kyrie, though his glance included Jeannie. ' – I've got news too.'

'What?' they asked together.

Now he spoke only to Kyrie. 'I'm going to make serious bikkies.'

'Not news. I said you could. Right from the time you

sold those fingernails.'

'Fin – ger – nails?' said Jeannie softly.

'At first it had me stunned. I thought it couldn't be that easy. Then all of a sudden, I knew I could do it. I wanted to jump over the moon.'

'Yaaah,' said Kyrie, mocking but sympathetic.

'Oh, *false* fin – ger – nails.'

'There's Beth coming now. Will you *look* at Aunty Jude! Go on, Marco. Go and front up.'

'Yes, go on,' said Jeannie, giving him a little push.

As Judy was still not feeling herself, she and Bill were standing aside. Beth and Marcus confronted them. Nita tentatively lingered.

'It was in Rome,' said Marcus.

'In that cloister designed by Michelangelo,' said Beth.

'The one with the heads of the animals in the centre, Bill,' said Judy. 'You remember, Bill.'

'Vaguely,' said Bill.

'Well, I do,' said Judy gallantly. 'And I remember a boy, too, and the list, and the photo Beth told us I took.'

'He was mad about making that list,' said Nita. 'Are you enjoying those, Bill?'

'Enjoying them! Darling, have you had any of these?'

'I have indeed.'

'What are they, Nita, exactly?' asked Bill.

'Only tiny pasties of spiced beef.'

'Only, she says!'

'They are very, very yummy, Nita,' said Judy. 'Now listen, that time in the cloister, Nita, wasn't Marcus waiting for you?'

'Sure was,' said Marcus.

'We used to leave him there for twenty minutes or so,' said Nita comfortably.

'It's really very extraordinary,' said Judy. 'Here we all stand!'

'Except Gerard,' said Beth. 'Marcus, Andy isn't enjoying Gerard playing his drum. Look.'

Marcus looked, then rolled his eyes. 'Suffering.'

'I'll run and get Gerard to stop,' said Beth.

'Do remember to be tactful, dear,' Judy called after her.

'Give me your plates, you two,' said Nita. 'And let me get you another helping. And some vegies. Any no-nos?'

'No,' said Bill and Judy, 'no no-nos.'

Alone with Marcus, Judy and Bill showed a coolness. Judy picked a strand of silver from Bill's forehead and said reproachfully, 'Do remember to *duck* when you go under it, darling. What is it, exactly?'

Marcus said, 'I love Beth.'

'Nita says it's not tinsel. But what?'

Marcus said, 'I love Beth, and whether we marry or not, I intend to stay faithful to her for the rest of my life. I've never said that aloud before. I know it sounds impossible – '

'We happen to believe it's quite possible,' said Bill.

'We happen to believe it's normal,' said Judy.

'Not for me,' said Marcus. 'Look at Kyrie over there. I could go over right now and race her off into the bushes. And her mate Jeannie too, if it comes to that. I'm made that way. It's my nature. Right? But you don't always have to say yes to your nature. And I'm going to keep on saying no to mine. It's me for Beth, and Beth for me.'

'Aids has frightened a lot of people, I suppose,' said Judy.

'Frightened the hell out of me,' said Marcus. 'Aids was a big factor, that's for sure. It might even have been the original one. It's hard to tell now. But once I made up my mind, the great feeling, that was the most influential thing. You might think it was only the novelty, but listen,

I'll tell you. One day, one peak hour, I was waiting to cross the street. There was a crowd on my side, and a crowd on the other. So there I was, looking at all the girls on the other side, picking out the one I would like most, the way you do. Right? And I kept coming back to one, and all of a sudden I saw it was Beth. I was amazed. I hadn't noticed her before because I was too busy looking at the whole lot. But as soon as I saw it was her, I thought, That's the one. That one's mine. And I felt so bloody good. Right?'

'When you didn't even notice her at first?' said Judy.

'Yes,' said Marcus emphatically. 'She wasn't the most noticeable one. She didn't stand out.'

'I hope you and Beth will be very happy,' said Judy with formality.

'I suppose,' said Bill, smiling at Marcus, 'you didn't have the temerity to relate that little incident to Beth?'

'Sure did. She understood totally. We don't always agree. We have fights. But that was one time we were in total agreement.'

'Do you hope for a boy or a girl?' asked Judy, still formal.

'I don't care. Either will do me. Names. We've decided those. Garth if it's a boy, Cynthia if it's a girl. And this – I've decided this. As soon as the kid is old enough to hold a pencil, he or she starts to learn to read and write.'

Beth, approaching in time to hear this, knew that Marcus's father, though they may never see him, nor hear from him, would nevertheless enter their lives. She took hold of Marcus's nearer arm with both hands. 'Andy said that if you come, and say you want to play, Gerard will stop.'

'Can Gerard *harm* the drum?' Judy asked with bewilderment.

'Ha!' said Marcus, as he went off with Beth. 'That's a two-man drum.'

'Did he mean,' said Judy slowly to Bill, 'that Beth understood, because, while he was looking over the girls, she was doing the same to the men?'

'Well, darling, happily, Doctor Gelthartz's fears for her haven't been realised.'

'No, she seems quite able to relate to men, thank you very much. First Miles, now this one. And right now, she and Mil, or Mal, have their heads very close together.'

'Only looking at some papers together, Jude. Judy, I am thinking this. When their baby comes, we'll send them a whopping big cheque.'

'The size of the cheque must depend on this,' said Judy, giving her belly one of those circular little rubs commented on by Beth.

'Oh, certainly. Cynthia. Cynthia. That's a queer old-fashioned name to pick.' Then, meeting Judy's wide-eyed look, he said, 'What – what – ' He flicked his fingers all over his forehead – 'more of that damned stuff?'

But when Judy continued to look, he said, whispering with shock, 'Oh. Oh. Oh, my God.'

She put a hand on his arm. 'Darling, don't. Don't blame yourself.'

'Oh, my God. It could have been Beth that I said that to.'

'Stop it, now. None of us can remember everything.'

He said with anguish, 'It was such a long time ago.'

'Billy, pull yourself together. Here is Mrs McCracken.'

Juliet was carrying two plates. Bill pressed back his head, pinched the knot of his tie, and said, 'Dear lady, please don't think us stand-offish. Judy's still not quite up to par, and we're just staying here quietly for a while.'

'Is it the music?'

'There have been studies done on the effects of vibration,' murmured Judy.

'I've suggested they stop at the end of this . . . piece,

or whatever they call it. It's damn awful, I agree. Nita asked me to bring you these. You can see how busy she is with the ravenous young.'

'Those boys of ours have hollow legs,' said Bill.

'I didn't imagine we would need such quantities. But Nita knew. That's professional experience for you. I have my wonderful Mrs Ho, but her mother died and she had to take a few days off. What I would have done, at such short notice, if Nita hadn't been staying with me, I do not care to think. She did all the ordering, all the cooking.'

'All of it?' asked Bill, holding up the morsel on his fork. 'This, too?'

Juliet shut her eyes and said, '*Everything*.'

Bill shook his head. Judy said, 'Certainly scrumptious.'

'Not only did I lose Mrs Ho, but my aunt Bob needed me at the very last minute. Of course, no good caterer will come at such short notice. But Nita simply took over. That is the kind of person Nita is. She takes over.'

'I wish I had someone like that,' said Judy.

'There are good prospects in the offing, Jude,' said Bill.

Juliet folded her hands at her waist and leaned forward slightly. It gave her a neat, respectful look as she said to Judy, 'How *do* you manage?'

'No trouble when mother was there, but then the usual happened.'

'Time,' intoned Bill.

'And now it's a nursing home.'

'Oh dear, oh dear, I do sympathise. I had to get my darling Aunt Bob into one last week.'

'Where no doubt she will be much happier,' said Bill.

'She's certainly giving them something to talk about.'

'Jude's mother is as happy as Larry,' said Bill.

'So now you've nobody?' asked Juliet.

'We're not sure. Just as we were leaving, ours gave us a few dark hints.'

'They come and go, you see,' said Bill. 'The boys can be a bit rambunctious.'

'The boys have their studies,' said Judy indignantly, 'and their football practice. We make that clear.'

'Is that little fellow carrying the ladder Chinese?' asked Bill.

'Japanese, they say. His name's Kut, would you believe? I've never seen anyone eat so much in my life. I thought they ate only a little fish, and a cube or two of that odious bean curd, and of course rice. But no, he simply *demolished* that roast beef.'

'Our boys did their bit, I bet,' said Bill.

'Beef for boys, Nita says. Nita intends to open a little lunch counter. It will be a huge success. She has the capital, and she certainly has the energy.'

'And the good humour,' said Bill.

'Yes, indeed. You never see Nita depressed. She cheered poor Aunt Bob up enormously.'

'Look here, Mrs McCracken, should she be getting up that ladder herself? Surely one of the boys – '

'No, they're moving the ladder for her. She says she's the one who put it up, so she knows how to take it down. She says the tinselly stuff must have deteriorated. And even though in a wide circle like that, it can't fall *directly* on the food, most of us do seem to have a speck of it somewhere.'

The music had stopped, but Marcus, still at the drum, looking up, open-mouthed, at his mother on the ladder, gave a gentle tattoo.

'What's her position, exactly?' asked Bill.

'A mistaken marriage to an unspeakable tomcat of a man. She had the patience of an angel, but it got too much at last, and now they're divorcing.'

'Two failed marriages,' remarked Judy.

'Goodness, I believe I've even got some of it down here.'

Juliet moved aside the neck of her dress, revealing for a moment the thin red ribbon supporting the key, and drew specks of silver up with her fingers. 'Not one of Nita's better ideas,' she said indulgently.

'She's certainly causing some amusement,' said Bill.

Arms were raised to receive the silvery ropes. There were laughs, soft cheers, and Marcus's little tattoo.

Juliet, laughing herself, said, 'Unfortunately, her capital's too small for Sydney's evil rents. We were thinking of Brisbane for her lunch counter, but she and I and your twins were chatting just now, and we came up with the idea of Ballarat.'

'Ballarat is a good town,' said Bill respectfully.

'Ballarat *is* a good town,' said Judy.

'Goodness, they had better tie that bag up very tight if they're going to put it in the garage with my Jaggy. Do excuse me. You will join us for the toast, of course, and cutting the cake.'

'Of course,' said Bill and Judy together.

They watched Juliet hurry away.

'Jude,' said Bill, 'we could put Nita up while she's sussing out Ballarat.'

'Well, she seems to get on with the boys,' said Juliet cheerfully,

'Doesn't she! And she has a ton of go.'

'It would commit us to nothing.'

'Nothing. And if it turns out well, we'll make it worth her while to stay. And you could come back to the city shop, and be my right hand man again.'

'Speed the day!'

'You ask her. It will look better coming from you.'

'The relationship bothers me a bit.'

'She said herself that she and Marcus aren't close these days. One thing, though. Is she a bit odd in the hoof?'

'Is she?'

'Just you watch for a while.'

Nita and the twins had compressed the glittering ropes into a big green plastic bag and tied the top, and now Nita gripped it in both arms and ran with this big ball towards the door of the garage, which was held open by Juliet. Nita ran fast and prancingly, raising her knees high, her curls jumping, her profile broken by her big grin. There were cries of *Wrong game!* and *Kick it!* But when she set it in the doorway, with a neat little bow, cheers went up, and laughter, and shouts of *Goal anyway!* and a loud tattoo from Marcus's drum. On raising her body she did press the toe of one foot to the ground, as if to ease the heel, but it was the merest moment before she had made fists of her hands and was trotting back veering and grinning across the grass.

'I see,' said Judy, laughing and clapping as they went forward, 'but as long as she wears that kind of shoe – '

'Besides, as you say – ' said Bill, clapping beside her.

'Quite. We would not be committed.'

Beth and Marcus walked up Juliet's path towards the gate. Mil and Annette had already crossed the street and were waiting beside Marcus's car. Mrs Ho's car was drawing up near the gate.

Beth said, 'Dad whispered to me that they were going to send us a whopping big cheque for the baby.'

'Why did he have to whisper it?'

'Don't ask me.'

'Probably about as much as I'll make in a week.'

Mrs Ho got out of her car as they came out of the gate. Beth had never spoken directly to Mrs Ho, and nor had she offered sympathy to a bereaved person before. Repressing a vague fear that Mrs Ho would break down, she stood like a good schoolgirl, and spoke very slowly.

'Mrs Ho, I am so sorry about your mother.'

Mrs Ho gave her familiar babbling laugh, reached out a hand that looked as weightless as a leaf, and patted Beth's hair with the same condescension and encouragement that she had once bestowed on Miles. It was Beth whose eyes filled with her ready tears. She turned abruptly and put her face on Marcus's shoulder.

Juliet and Nita came out of the gate. 'Oh, Mrs Ho,' said Juliet. 'I am so glad.'

'I come. I promise.'

'We could have manged,' said Nita. 'But you go on in and start. These two are the last to leave.'

'What is wrong with Beth?' asked Juliet, very softly.

'Nothing,' said Marcus fondly into Beth's hair.

'I get like this,' said Beth, raising her face and laughing, 'or I get mad euphoria.'

'There's always something,' said Nita.

'Goodbye, ma. We'll see you before you head south.'

'It's a week yet, Marco. Give me a tinkle.'

'Nita,' said Beth, 'listen, are you sure about working for dad and Judy?'

'You listen, Beth. I don't have to be sure or not sure. It's only temporary. But actually, to be quite truthful, I think I'll be as happy as Larry.'

'What is this Larry's other name, do you suppose?' murmured Juliet. 'Oh, I am so tired.'

'Right. Let's go. Mum, make time to come and look at the house.'

'I could avert my eyes from the other, I suppose.'

'You might see the start of the mural,' said Beth. 'Mil and Marcus actually picked my design. Arise, Sir Beth.'

'Not till Mil has fixed the perspective,' said Marcus.

'Please don't think I'm not interested,' said Juliet, yawning.

After the kisses, Beth and Marcus, crossing the street, had suddenly to run to avoid a Porsche that came speeding through the street with open throttle.

'He'll buy one of those,' said Nita. 'Marco will.'

'Never!' said Juliet, opening her eyes and slowly taking her hands from her ears.

In the car opposite, some dispute was in progress about who was to drive. 'It had better be Annette,' remarked Nita. 'The boys are over point-o-five, and Beth's no driver. What did Beth think she was doing, warning me like that?'

'I can see you being very happy, Nita, in a houseful of men.'

'Well, that's it! No offense, but I'm a man's woman. Always have been, always will be.'

Marcus had ceded the driver's seat to Annette and was pushing forward the front seat so that Mil and Beth could get in the back.

'I suppose I could warm to Beth in time,' said Nita. 'She won't hold him, though. Not if he makes those serious bikkies.'

'What are these damn serious bikkies?'

'It means big money. I'll give them the true-love-usual.'

'Whatever that may be,' said Juliet crossly.

'Three years. You know the owner of the flat kept their deposit? He said that cinema painting was defacement. You ought to think again about that mural.'

The car moved forward. Beth put an arm out and waved. Nita returned the wave, and so, absent-mindedly, did Juliet as she sighed, 'What, Captain Cook?'

'No, there's this wide verandah, and at the end of that

a garden with this more than life-sized angel serving wine to a beat-up looking young couple.'

On Juliet's distractedly waving arm, the gooseflesh rose, and the hairs so nearly invisible she usually forgot they grew there.

'Plus some other stuff,' said Nita, 'that I've forgotten.'

When the car was near the corner, Marcus reached over and gave two little toots on the horn, as country people do.

FOR THE BEST IN PAPERBACKS, LOOK FOR THE

In every corner of the world, on every subject under the sun, Penguin represents quality and variety—the very best in publishing today.

For complete information about books available from Penguin—including Pelicans, Puffins, Peregrines, and Penguin Classics—and how to order them, write to us at the appropriate address below. Please note that for copyright reasons the selection of books varies from country to country.

In the United Kingdom: For a complete list of books available from Penguin in the U.K., please write to *Dept E.P., Penguin Books Ltd, Harmondsworth, Middlesex, UB7 0DA.*

In the United States: For a complete list of books available from Penguin in the U.S., please write to *Dept BA, Penguin*, Box 120, Bergenfield, New Jersey 07621-0120.

In Canada: For a complete list of books available from Penguin in Canada, please write to *Penguin Books Ltd, 2801 John Street, Markham, Ontario L3R 1B4.*

In Australia: For a complete list of books available from Penguin in Australia, please write to the *Marketing Department, Penguin Books Ltd, P.O. Box 257, Ringwood, Victoria 3134.*

In New Zealand: For a complete list of books available from Penguin in New Zealand, please write to the *Marketing Department, Penguin Books (NZ) Ltd, Private Bag, Takapuna, Auckland 9.*

In India: For a complete list of books available from Penguin, please write to *Penguin Overseas Ltd, 706 Eros Apartments, 56 Nehru Place, New Delhi, 110019.*

In Holland: For a complete list of books available from Penguin in Holland, please write to *Penguin Books Nederland B.V., Postbus 195, NL-1380AD Weesp, Netherlands.*

In Germany: For a complete list of books available from Penguin, please write to *Penguin Books Ltd, Friedrichstrasse 10-12, D-6000 Frankfurt Main I, Federal Republic of Germany.*

In Spain: For a complete list of books available from Penguin in Spain, please write to *Longman, Penguin España, Calle San Nicolas 15, E-28013 Madrid, Spain.*

In Japan: For a complete list of books available from Penguin in Japan, please write to *Longman Penguin Japan Co Ltd, Yamaguchi Building, 2-12-9 Kanda Jimbocho, Chiyoda-Ku, Tokyo 101, Japan.*

Gen 1/10/15 TD